FOUND LOST

a puzzlingly different disappearance

by

N N Wood

Copyright © N N Wood 2019
This book is sold subject to the condition that it shall not, by way of trade or otherwise, be lent, resold, hired out, or otherwise circulated without the publisher's prior consent in any form of binding or cover other than that in which it is published and without a similar condition including this condition being imposed on the subsequent publisher.
The moral right of N N Wood has been asserted.
ISBN-13: 9781097450121

This is a work of fiction. Names, characters, businesses, organizations, places, events and incidents either are the product of the author's imagination or are used fictitiously. Any resemblance to actual persons, living or dead, events, or locales is entirely coincidental.

to Alice and Laura

ACKNOWLEDGMENTS

Many friends have been supportive in ways that they may not have realised. Tony from way back set me on the path of thinking of writing a novel and Stephen set a fine example by actually writing his own novel, which was the final spur to my getting started. A few close friends were each invaluably helpful in setting the right direction and tone. Any and all of the errors and inconsistencies are of course all down to me.

ONE

This was fun. They had left their B&B after a hearty breakfast and had hitched a local lift to get to the start of a South Downs path for a bracing walk in the weak morning sunshine of the early autumn. They planned to reach a secluded country pub for some real ale and some classic pub grub for lunch. Then all downhill back to Mrs Brown's in the village. A leisurely Sunday tomorrow and then a train back to town Monday morning just in time for work.

James and Molly had known each other for over a year at work and had struck up a close friendship outside work almost at once. They didn't need a car in town and every so often liked to get away early on a Friday afternoon and take a train to any village with real ale pubs and good walking country. It was a change from the grind and long hours of the week.

A 4x4 had picked them up almost immediately outside the village and the two men in the front seemed normal and were probably on their way to some odd-job Saturday morning work. James and Molly were put in the back and the two men didn't seem to want to talk much apart from asking where to drop them and that it was the way they were going. James and Molly whispered and gestured to each other in the back for what was only going to be a few minutes at the most.

The car took a hard right up a farm track and came to an abrupt halt. The two men got out each side.

'You,' one said, pointing to Molly, 'stay where you are.' The other taller man pulled James out of the car, hit him hard and put a cloth over his mouth and nose. James fell to the ground, senseless from the blow and the drugs. The tall man dragged him to the hedge on the inside edge of the field away from the road, took his phone and wallet, and left him under a blanket.

Molly meanwhile was locked in the back of the 4x4 and screamed to no effect. She too was then rendered limp with an impregnated cloth pressed to her face. They put a blanket over her in the back of the car and drove off at speed.

It was hours before James came round. The light was going and the sun well over what he could make out as the shape of the Downs on the skyline. He blearily shook off the blanket and looked around. He was in a field; the sharp stubble of the recent harvest matched the stubble on his unshaven chin. There was no car, no Molly, no evidence of what he dimly remembered happening, nobody around and no houses or cottages to be seen. He even wondered if he was or had been in a bad dream. He wearily picked himself up and started the hour's walk back to Mrs Brown's. He had not the faintest idea what to do next.

TWO

James and Molly had started work at a medium-sized service company within a week of each other. It had been set up a few years previously by two former colleagues of a well-known bank which had decided their services were no longer required. With good severance packages they were able to start their own company on the fringes of the City.

The company offered any services it could think of to other companies, business-to-business style, and had found itself doing piecemeal virtually everything except the core, confidential work central to a client company's function; things like data capture and entry, low-level HR work, payroll stuff, janitorial functions, holiday and maternity/paternity cover. The owners had kept in touch with previous colleagues and friends, partly because they wanted to but mainly because of their good connections. Expansion had been steady but the work did fluctuate. Their connections meant access to funds for working capital and, as their good reputation spread, they had even picked up a little government work which certain Whitehall departments wanted to offload. Staff were expected to be versatile, IT literate, fit, personable and friendly. The employment contract was loosely worded on the type, location and hours of work but it seemed to attract a certain type of person.

James and Molly both fitted that. Each had a degree and they had followed that up with some professional training. But the worlds of their work were changing fast and each of them had separately come to the conclusion that they wanted a change and some variety. Parents and siblings were miles away and neither had any particular liabilities or dependencies. They lived in flats not that far apart with two other girls in Molly's case and three other guys in James's case. They were put together as fresh new recruits on the same client project to supervise the installation of unisex lavatories for a client company, who wanted this facility to meet any transgender or cross-dressing dilemmas. James and Molly took to this with energy and enthusiasm and were able to confront the issues with male and female humour.

They had worked on many separate assignments subsequently, but that initial bonding had cemented their growing friendship. They always knew where the other was working and occasionally they were seconded to the same project, which they put down to good sense and tact on the part of their employer. They met regularly for drinks after work and theatre/cinema/restaurants were always to hand. The weekends away started as an effort to get out of their respective flats and away from flatmates, to get into the country for some air and to be alone together. There was no problem jumping into bed. Their parents might have expected them to be thinking of 'settling down' at their age but with no house or sharing a flat in prospect, they were content with their lot, had a happy life, incomes that slightly exceeded expenditure, and were happy to continue as they were. They had come to love each other and neither was thinking of looking for anyone else.

THREE

James reached Mrs Brown's just as the evening light was fading. He had not seen anyone on the roads and paths and there was not much sign of life in the few cottages he had passed. His pockets had been completely emptied. No money, bank cards, mobile. He felt his whole identity had vanished or been stolen and that there was another James Longton wandering around being him.

Mrs Brown was looking out for them both and she could scarcely believe his story. After being pulled from the car, he remembered nothing until he had come round. He had a few bits and pieces in the bedroom and luckily some money. Mrs Brown let him use her phone while she prepared a simple supper. He phoned his parents and also Steve, the senior of his flatmates. His father wanted to drive down straightaway and take him to the police station but it was too long a journey and James said he would phone the police that evening. He aimed to be back at work on Monday and find a way back to Molly. Her mobile did not answer; he did not know either her parents or flatmates. It would have to be done through work on Monday.

He phoned the police and reported what had happened. The police said they would ask around and make it known locally and asked if James would come along in the morning to make a statement. Suddenly Molly had gone and he had no way of finding her or contacting her. He missed her practicality and fun. Sleep didn't happen.

FOUR

James had grown up in the country with his brother and sister under dutiful parenting by his parents, Reginald and Margaret. They were of safe, sensible stock; they liked to talk through problems and took great exception to rows and to childish or teenage tantrums. Reginald, always Reggie to Margaret, was a serious mentor to his three children all of whom depended on this aspect of his character. With Margaret, always Maggie to Reggie, as a homemaker, it was a settled and happy marriage and family. Reginald was a respected and reliable employee and eventually rose to middle management in middle age at a light industrial company in the East Midlands. He would not have thought of moving job to better himself and he would not countenance his wife working other than raising their family. So private education for the family was not available and all three of them went to local schools. James scraped into university and equally scraped a degree. He was the social one and had wide contacts during and after college. In his last term, he pursued many interviews with companies, entrepreneurs and government departments; but none of them grabbed his attention and equally none of them showed much interest in him. So a period of drift, even aimlessness, followed college. Finally, Dad stepped in and said James could do a lot worse than get a profession. It would show commitment, sincerity and some gravitas – these were his dad's words – so with a little application to that, James again scraped through to get some more letters after his name.

James persevered in a local medium-sized firm which his father had helped to arrange; but he wanted more out of life. With his brother and sister, they made their own social life with, for him, limited success on the girlfriend front. James's social sense and ability meant that getting to know girls was never a problem but most of them seemed a little too obvious, or not with his sense of humour, or were too high maintenance. His initial fumblings with sex had led him to believe that there should be more to sex than sex and though he might smile at the thought of being experienced, he put his limited experience down to learning and was looking forward to some really good practice with a future girl.

So one day James announced to the whole family out of the blue that, as he was nearly thirty, he was off to London to share a flat somewhere and try his hand at something different. He invited his siblings to come with him but they didn't.

He found a flat-share with guys similar to himself and did a bit of temporary work to pay his way. He responded to an advertisement for a versatile project manager with energy and experience and found the interview was a meeting of the minds. They liked his personality and what he had done and he was offered the post there and then, starting as soon as he could. That was no problem and among the other new recruits was a certain Molly Otsworth.

FIVE

It was dark. Molly slowly became aware that she was alive and in a dark place. She could make out no shapes but she could tell from her own smell that she had been asleep or unconscious for a long time. She groped around to find she was lying on a mattress on the floor in a bare room. She felt her way to an edge of the room and then felt her way around it. There was a small window but it was dark outside with no discernible shapes or light. There were two doors, both locked. She shouted for help but there was no response. Whoever they were had realised she might need to pee. She found a bucket in a corner. There seemed no alternative but to wait for dawn and see where she was. She tried to sleep.

The morning light came gradually. It did not help much as the window looked out onto fields, some woods, and cows and sheep grazing in the fields. There was no sign of people, vehicles or buildings. Where was she? She was thirsty and starting to get hungry.

Someone unlocked the door. It was not one of the men in the car. He grunted at her and shoved a tray with cereal, bread, butter, milk and a mug of coffee. She wolfed all of it down.

SIX

Molly Otsworth had had a comfortable upbringing. Daddy was well-to-do and was and is a successful businessman. Henry had originally inherited the moderately successful business from his father, Robert, at a time when the business was starting to falter after a long stable period following its initial success. Part of Henry's skill and insight was realising this earlier than his father and he was able to hold on to some strengths and features the existing business still had before they withered. Henry had taken the business into new lines, recognising the internet, connections, deals, and latterly even exports to the East.

Molly and her younger sister Ellie were clear beneficiaries. They went to a weekly boarding school for girls not that far away in the upper Thames valley. This groomed both of them for a fashionable university from which they surprised themselves by getting good degrees. They had met all manner of girls and boys in their extended education. Their dear mother Annabel had tried many times to tell them about girls and their wilful ways and more recently about boys and their wicked ways and some of it had even sunk in. They were boisterous sisters and although they would argue most of the time, if anyone dared come between them they would round on them ruthlessly. They were not alike, either in looks or personality. Molly was attractive, energetic, warm, positive, game for anything, practical. Ellie had more classic features and was reflective, thought ahead, kind to a fault, and took time to make friendships. But they had one big thing in common – loyalty to each other and their family. Henry and Annabel might despair over their daughters' boyfriends, their impish schemes and plans; but they could take legitimate pride in the two very real people they had created and the values they had.

The social standing of the family in the immediate neighbourhood was high and the Otsworths were well-known for their generosity, their support of local good causes, their wide range of friendships, parties, Christmas gatherings. If ever there were problems, they were solved and all moved on.

After college, Molly did some travelling with girl groups and sometimes just with her sister. Boys came and went, usually dismissed by her. In her twenties she had some longer dalliances; but never serious as neither sister ever wanted for a partner to social functions. They were popular and their love life was well concealed and not a matter of social gossip.

Molly took up some local jobs that were stereotypical given her background. Some secretarial work, then an uplift to that badge of arrival – the PA. It was all so easy, so dull and so routine that one fine day she announced to the family that she was off to London to do the same sort of work at a higher pay and with more going on. Ellie was envious but supportive; Mum and Dad were accepting. She left for Paddington having secured a flat-share with some other girls she vaguely knew from a few temp jobs. After yet more temporary jobs, she applied for a senior administrator role 'for someone who can do anything' at a service company on the edge of the City. The interview was almost a formality and she started there the following Monday. Among the other recruits was a certain James Longton.

SEVEN

James reported to the police station early Sunday morning to make a statement. He recounted all that he had said on the phone the evening before.

'Could you describe the two men? How old, what were they wearing?'

'They were about my age and wearing dull beige working clothes as though they were going to do a light manual job. Beanies on their head, black and navy blue I think. They were just two ordinary guys, one average height, the other taller. Honestly, we were so pleased to get a lift straightaway that we hardly took any notice of them.'

'What about the vehicle, did you get the registration?'

'Sorry, no. It was an SUV, a 4x4, it must have been a few years old as it had plenty of wear and tear and had not been looked after. The seats were grey and, yes, it was black.'

'Had you seen the vehicle or these two lads earlier or the previous evening? Did you recognise them? Did you sense this was planned or just random?'

'No to the first two; we were just so glad to be out of town and enjoying time together going up on the Downs. I can't imagine it was planned, it all happened so quickly. Why us? We're just a couple from London spending the weekend here.'

'Who is "we"? Can you think why they may have targeted you?' The officer wanted more. James described himself and what he did and also the same for Molly. He realised he didn't know too much about her background having never met or spoken to her parents or sister or even flatmates.

'It seems the two men were more interested in your companion than you. They whisked her off and left you behind, knowing that you would report the incident to the police. What do you say?'

James demurred. He had no idea why she would be of interest. Molly was an attractive girl but at twenty-nine hardly suited to what he had read about children and girls being abducted for unsavoury practices. And she wasn't royalty or an heiress. He wondered about the past and the Otsworths.

'I hardly know her family; only what Molly has told me. They seem to be a normal and comfortably off family. I can't imagine it would be for a ransom; that's too far-fetched.'

'Let's not get ahead of ourselves on idle speculation. All the same, we will need to talk to her parents and her flatmates and work colleagues. Would you give us all the details you know, sir?'

James did that, realising how sketchy it was. The officer said they would alert the neighbouring police stations of the abduction and the vehicle and record Molly as a missing person. The police would contact her parents for permission to put out a missing person bulletin, her description and photograph. James told the police what Molly was last wearing. Jeans, T-shirt, anorak, brown walking boots. The police would accompany him to the site last seen for any forensic evidence. He handed in the blanket and cloth he had been drugged with.

'Don't worry too much, sir. If it's a joyride or a false sense of fun, she'll probably be dumped somewhere in a day or two. What possible use is she to them?' James couldn't see what the officer was driving at. Where was Molly? He always knew where she was or what she was up to. He hoped for a simple, silly reason for this caper and that it would all be over later today. But what if it wasn't? Bad thoughts entered his mind; thoughts that he had never had about anyone he had ever known. Like what you read in the papers; it never happened to you; it happened to other people. He realised with a jolt that he really did miss her and if anything happened to her, it would have been his fault and he would never forgive himself.

EIGHT

Molly was still in the same room. She had tried to force open the small window but, even if she had broken through, she would not have been able to crawl out. She banged on the door till someone came.

The same man re-appeared shortly. He didn't speak; grunting was his speciality.

'I need to wash, to shower, to use the lavatory, to phone my family, to eat, to get back to my flat and work and boyfriend. Don't you understand? Why am I here?'

He didn't respond but appeared to get the gist of some of what she said. He unlocked the other door in the room which led, surprisingly, to a small internal kitchen and a tiny bathroom with one bar of soap and a hand towel. No windows, just an extractor fan in the ceiling. He put some food in the small fridge and left.

Molly sank to the floor. She was a prisoner with an indefinite sentence. She could survive with supplies of food, tap water, washing the clothes she stood up in, and cope with the daily and monthly bodily functions. Unless she fell ill, or she was moved, she was here for the foreseeable future.

'I need a plan,' she said out loud. No-one was listening.

NINE

James and Clive Drewett, the policeman assigned to him, drove back to the farm track where it had all happened. There were tyre marks. There were signs of disturbed grass where a scuffle and dragging could have been. Clive searched for anything left behind but there was nothing. He cordoned off the area and said he would contact the farmer and that the forensic people would come soon to take the tyre marks and search for the slightest scraps of any hair or clothing.

'We're really good at this stuff these days,' he said, 'just like those crime series on the telly.'

Then they went back to Mrs Brown's and Clive looked over their room. They bagged up Molly's few bits and pieces.

'Recent photo, sir?' James took out a photo of the two of them taken in a booth some weeks ago.

'It's not much; but her mum and dad will have plenty.'

'Thanks, will do. Can I drive you to the station? That's the rail one, not ours?'

James promised Mrs Brown that a cheque would be in the post for her for the two nights and some cash she had lent. Clive added enough for the fare.

'Add that to the cheque and Mrs Brown here can let me have it back later.' James thanked them both enormously and after a short drive back to the station took a train back to London, requesting the police contact him as soon as they heard anything.

It was Sunday evening as the train drew into Victoria. On the journey back he reflected on the last forty-eight hours. He had lost his girlfriend, had no means of contacting her, had no money, no mobile, no explanation – not even a guess. He walked the few miles to his flat. His flatmates were in jovial mood and ready to pull his leg about his 'dirty weekend' wanting full reports on his Molly; but his face killed the mood.

'So she's dumped you, yes?' chipped in Steve, his closest mate.

'Well yes and no, you could say,' said James all despondent. He told them what had happened and that he and the police were clueless. It all happened so quickly and then nothing. By then, they were sympathetic and sensed his genuine feelings.

'What can any of us do?' This from Brian, the thinker of the group. 'We can hardly send out a search party. Shall we all go round to her flat and find out her secrets from her flatmates?'

James thought this would be counterproductive as the police would want to question them first. Also her work colleagues and family back in the Cotswolds. He was tired and left them chatting as he collapsed in his room. He hoped it was all a dream and he would wake up to a new world tomorrow and Molly would be back at work. It wasn't.

TEN

Clive Drewett was a good and thorough policeman. He had seen the young and old Morse on TV and was attracted to him as a role model. Not that they had a murder each week in the South Downs but this case interested him. For a start it was different; the usual stuff was traffic, theft, bicycles, pub brawls and the rest was paperwork and screens. He had never had an abduction before and he let his mind wander extravagantly. Why would someone do this? Money? A prank or a bet? It had been carried out with apparent ruthless efficiency and no evidence left. There were no reports of stolen or abandoned vehicles. His boss, Inspector Knutsford, called him in first thing Monday morning.

'Any progress? Put all the info out?' He was formal in spitting it out but not aggressively so. The two had a fair working relationship which did not extend to socialising.

'Yes, sir, all done and I've arranged to visit Miss Otsworth's flat, her workplace and then on to see the parents. The forensics are visiting the crime scene as we speak. And they have the blanket and cloth used to drug Mr Longton.'

'I suppose he's telling the truth. He's not making this up about a fictitious girlfriend. Seeking attention.'

'Fair point, sir, but the girlfriend I believe is real. It was pretty obvious that a woman had stayed at the B&B with James and he did seem to be genuinely upset. I don't think he's the type to show much emotion but he did seem affected. Whether for any strange unfathomable reason, he's involved in the abduction behind the scenes or not, I agree we should keep an open mind. It's happened before. I'll know more after seeing her family and work.'

'Good, Drewett. It might equally just be a silly joyride by some locals. Keep the local police where you go involved and informed, don't need any turf wars. I'll put you on this full-time until we know where it's going. Report back in a day or two.'

Drewett left the station and went back to his modest flat to take some overnight things. It would be a round trip and he chose to go by train in plain clothes. He could think and read and write on the train and this case needed it. He put in a call to James's work on the way and got the next train to London, then a taxi up to where James worked. He was shown into a meeting room and offered coffee and biscuits. Paul Williams, one of the two owners, joined him moments later.

'Sorry to keep you waiting; how may I help?' Paul was urbanity itself.

'As I said on the phone it's about Miss Molly Otsworth. Can I ask if she has reported for work today?'

'No she hasn't. And we haven't had word from any friend or family. It is our requirement of course but sometimes the explanation comes later.'

'Well let me know immediately if she turns up but as things stand at the moment, she is classed as a missing person. Please keep that to yourself at the moment until we are further along with this case.' Drewett gave a very brief outline of the weekend's events, without any mention of the abduction. In his open-mindfulness, it could even be work-related. He continued, 'Is there anything in Miss Otsworth's work or contacts that would indicate a disappearance?'

'Far from it. She is a highly personable young lady; clients like her straightforward, practical approach. She should continue to do well here and her not reporting late for work is right out of character.'

'And Mr James Longton?' Drewett left the question dangling.

'I believe they are good friends; I've seen them eat lunch at a desk together; they started here on the same client project and both have done separate projects since then. Our people are generally out on client sites but when they are in the office, it is observable that they hang around together.'

Drewett thanked Paul Williams and asked to see her desk and her staff file. Paul used a phone and his PA came in immediately.

'Rosemary will show you round. I'm here if you need me.'

Drewett thanked him and stressed that absolutely any information that came through regarding Molly or James was to be directed to him without delay. Paul nodded and inclined his head, meaning of course. Clive followed Rosemary to Molly's desk which contained no personal information or notes at all. In HR, he took note of her address and her parents as next of kin from the staff file. He thanked Rosemary and took his leave and headed straight to Molly's flat.

Paul returned to his office, deep in thought. It could be a coincidence, of course. He recalled two outside phone calls about Molly, one recently and the other many months ago shortly after she had started. He had dismissed the second recent one as a fishing expedition by a recruitment company or a competitor. He remembered giving managerial-type answers which said nothing. It was the first call that was different and had stayed in his memory. The caller affected to know Paul from some conference they had both been on. He had said he couldn't say too much because he was linked to the MoD but 'they' were following the career of Molly with interest and might have to call her up for a short training programme at short notice. 'We'll pay you for her time, obviously, and this is strictly confidential.' Paul thought the caller had said he was Julian. Nothing ever came of it, even though the company did some low-level work for one or two government departments. Paul did not mention either of these calls to Drewett and there wasn't much to say anyway; but he wondered if there was a connection. He would check if Molly had been on any government work and what it entailed.

ELEVEN

The flat was up three flights of stairs in a traditional terraced street in West London and just a short walk from the nearest tube. Drewett pressed the street level bell for Flat 4 and a female voice agreed it was Flat 4 and, after Drewett explained who he was, invited him up.

'Hello, I'm Bee. I'm sorry Molly or Dee aren't in at the moment. How can I help? Would you like some tea or a glass of wine?'

'No thanks, nothing for me. I'm here to ask a few questions about Molly. When did you last hear from her?'

'Gracious, is she in trouble? She's such a practical person, she'd never get into scrapes. Let me think, yes, she left on Friday morning normal time with stuff for a weekend away and haven't heard from her since.'

'We are trying to trace her whereabouts as she has not reported for work this morning. We are not treating this as serious, just a little mystifying. Do you have her family details or friends she was close to?'

'Yes, Mum and Dad are out in Gloucestershire somewhere and a sister, Ellie. No special friends in town, apart from James of course. We socialise quite separately so I've never met him or her family.'

The door opened and Dee, all six foot of her, waltzed in.

'Hello, I'm Deidre, call me Dee, everybody does. What's all this about?'

Bee and Drewett recounted all that had been said.

'Well I can't add anything to that except to say she was really looking forward to the Downs trip this weekend and how much she loved being with James. She's a good catch for him.'

Drewett thanked them, made a cursory inspection of Molly's room without finding anything, and took his leave, stressing that if and when there was any word from Molly, they were to get in touch immediately. He walked to Paddington, booked in at a pub near Molly's parents and caught a train to get there.

TWELVE

Molly was determined not to get annoyed or frustrated or irritated. It was traumatic, what had happened, and if she dwelt on it she would get upset, start getting weepy and pathetic. So she didn't.

'I am where I am and I have to deal with it. I haven't been harmed

– so far – and James and co. will be coming for me.' She said all this out loud. It helped, speaking, so she carried on discussing her situation out loud. There wasn't much she could do as she was securely locked up. She realised that although she had a problem, her captors, if that is what they were, had a bigger problem because eventually they would have to do something; and that would mean venturing onto unknown ground for them. She presumed the police, James and parents would all be following this up. There was no means of escape from her two rooms and bathroom. Food was supplied and she maintained a routine of washing and cleaning and exercising. So her means of escape had to be through interactions with her captors. Conversation, amiability, requests until there was a gap and a glimmer of a way out.

She had tried opening up a conversation with her food supplier.

'Hello again, thank you. I enjoyed the fruit. May I know your name? I'm Molly by the way.' Grunt, grunt. This was repeated with variations every morning but whichever of them it was, the response was always the same. Grunt. She kept a record of the days like she thought she had seen in films – four verticals and one horizontal through – to indicate every five days for Monday to Friday and a cross for the weekend. It was already two weeks gone.

THIRTEEN

Drewett called the Otsworths from the train and said he would be with them first thing in the morning. They had asked what for and he had said that it was best left till the morning. The train journey was fine, he wrote up his notes on the way and took a taxi to The Three Horseshoes, as recommended by a good pub guide. He didn't want to chat with the locals so he sat separately over supper and a beer, ordered a taxi for the morning and went to bed.

The large period property was signed 'The Manor House' and he walked up the immaculate and crunchy gravel drive to be met by a smartly dressed man, medium height, a business manner, with country shirt and tie and expensive shoes.

'Good morning, Officer. I'm Henry Otsworth, pleased to meet you. I hope this is not serious.' Henry spoke with a natural authority.

They went inside to a spacious hall and through to a large drawing room. Drewett was introduced to Annabel Otsworth, who appeared friendly and welcoming. He recognised her likeness from the photos of Molly. He accepted coffee.

'Please call me Clive. This is an exploratory matter at the moment and of course it could lead to nothing. But as of now, we do not know the whereabouts of Molly. When was the last time you spoke to her or were in touch through texts or whatever?'

Annabel immediately looked distressed while Henry was factual and to the point.

'We spoke on the phone the middle of last week. She was well, excited about work and the upcoming weekend with James. We haven't met James by the way but Molly seems struck with him. Doesn't he know where she is? Might they be off together somewhere?'

Drewett gave an account of what had happened based on what James had told him. They were visibly shocked. Annabel took out a tissue and wiped her eyes. Nothing like this had ever happened to them or to Molly or to Ellie. They discussed possibilities and who might know something but, apart from James and flatmates and work, it was all speculative.

'Would Molly or any member of your family have had disagreements in the past or just lately?' Drewett knew he was clutching at straws but he had to cover the ground for reporting back to that pain called Knutsford tomorrow. Ellie breezed in.

'Hello all. What's all this about? An inquisition?' Annabel made the introductions and between her and her husband gave the gist of the discussion.

'That's not like Mols. She's outgoing and friendly and practical. Wouldn't upset a fly. Who could do such a thing and why?'

'I was rather hoping you might as you're probably the closest to her in the whole wide world.' This from Drewett.

'Sorry, no. She's so practical and aware. I would have thought she would have seen it coming if it were a real matter. I'm supposed to be the analytical one and I can neither think nor imagine anyone wanting to do anything like this.'

'Maybe a prank to rock the James boat? Boyfriends, etcetera.'

'That's just silly, no, and sorry for my rudeness.'

'No, no. I do need a picture of her, her past, her character and personality, thank you. If she has been, well er, kept somewhere, how would she cope?'

'Absolutely no problem whatsoever. Just another situation for Mols to resolve and move on. Her brain and judgment are very sound.' Henry and Annabel nodded agreement with their younger daughter's sentiments and assessment. Drewett asked to see her room and any family photos or videos, anything. They all moved upstairs and Henry took Drewett to one side.

'Are we talking about an appeal on TV and press involvement?' His tone betrayed unwillingness.

'No, not at this stage. It's all so unclear and unlikely. It may come to that but we are hopeful that something will turn up from some quarter. Maybe a bad joke or similar silliness. Despite the ordeal of driving off and leaving James, there is absolutely nothing yet to suggest anything sinister. Let's be optimistic and patient; and, no, no need to involve the press at this stage.' Drewett kept his own thoughts to himself as so many of these cases arose from family difficulties. He thought Henry had seemed cool at the possible loss of his elder daughter. Shouldn't he be more upset? He wanted these family reactions to come to the surface to give any clue of possible family involvement.

They went through her room and Drewett took some photos and diaries, promising faithfully to return them. The comfort of this home and the normality of the family gave nothing away. All was what it seemed. Henry gave him a lift to the station. They didn't talk much apart from pleasantries on the way. As he left, Drewett stressed that he should be informed immediately if anything, literally anything, came from Molly. They were probably who she would contact first by mobile, phone, text. And Drewett promised equally to keep them informed of any leads. He made a mental note to phone the local police on his return, apologising for not dropping in on them.

Train to Paddington, tube to Victoria, train back to home ground. Inevitably Knutsford crossed his path. Drewett debriefed him about the workplace, the flatmates, the parents.

'So no evidence then. Forensics may have something tomorrow. Keep looking and keep at it.'

'Thank you, sir.' His own debriefing had confirmed that there was nothing to go on. Even if it were a sinister plot, we still have nothing and a single girl has vanished. He called the Gloucestershire local station and said his report would follow. His initial excitement of something different to tackle was fading as he felt he was merely collecting dead ends.

FOURTEEN

Barry and Jonny had been mates for a long time. During primary school, they were pals or chums and were inseparable. At the local grammar school, their friendship grew and became close, loyal and trusting. One was better at numbers and science; the other better at words and writing. Games meant healthy rivalry and it often appeared they alternated at coming first or in the first few places of any field athletics and on the rugby field, whatever position they played in, they had a knack for knowing where the other was and doing one of those magical passes to get the winning try. In cricket, their game-saving partnerships were well-known – even relied on.

Adolescence, exams, girls – none of these divided them and they had mixed academic success and were popular with the girls from the neighbouring high school. Their mutual trust meant that although they had some ups and downs with girls, they never shared girlfriends or passed a girl on to the other. It was fun.

They both got good A-levels and then on to separate well-established universities. It didn't matter too much because they were home for the vacs and had lots of new stuff to share. By the late 70s, the colleges had nearly all gone co-ed so learning and living and playing next to the girls was a wonderful time. They each had a succession of girlfriends and were gently discovering that girls in some ways thought the same and in other ways not quite what they seemed at first. They each settled into their group of friends at college and girls were just part of life.

After university, Jonny went off to London to get professionally qualified and Barry stayed locally as a management trainee at the large nationwide outfit in the local town. Both did well. Jonny got qualified and started practising in a medium-sized firm in London and Barry went up the management ranks to be in charge of his own department, still at a young age. They kept in touch; and family or other reunions, locally or up in town, were regular enough to maintain their friendship.

The 80s were exciting times for the firms and enterprises that were unaffected by the closure of old industries. Privatisation was then an attractive word and commerce and deals by the new apparent openings were there for anyone to grasp. Barry and Jonny did well in their own areas and it was not long before they each acquired the respectable trappings of a wife, a house and a mortgage and an executive car. Children followed; one had two boys, the other two girls. The two families grew up together with limited contact at a distance until chance brought Jonny and his family back to home territory.

Jonny brought his City skills to bear on the stagnating fortunes of an apparently stalling business. It needed new blood, new lines, new ways of doing things and all of these against an unpromising commercial background. He called Barry who was only too glad to come round a few days later.

'Thing is, Barry, the firm's going nowhere. Flatlining would be generous. We can pay bills at the moment but projections are not good and that's assuming no customers go elsewhere. The whole thing needs an overhaul, probably a cash injection and, frankly, bringing into the internet age.'

'Got accounts and spreadsheets and all that internal stuff?' Barry added. 'I can see through things with the numbers and come back to you. Why don't we walk round the shop and kick the tyres? Then a beer or two.'

'I was so hoping you'd say that, all of it by the way. This new email thing means I can email you everything I've got. That's if you can open them. Let's drive over now, meet the general manager, have a walk round and discuss over some ale. The Red Lion OK?'

It was ten minutes away and Jonny phoned general manager Len on the way. Len was at the entrance to meet them, tie at half-mast with a tweed jacket from yesteryear.

'Good morning sirs, the chairman is away with the auditors playing at figures and won't be back till later, if you wanted to catch him.'

'Hi Len, this is old friend Barry. No, don't worry, I just wanted to show Barry round what we do before lunch. Would you mind walking us round and tell us how it all fits together?'

The three of them walked round the premises. If it were being built now, it would be a modern crinkly shed with modern fittings. As it was, it was brick-built, metal windows, concrete floor for the production side and wooden floor with bits of carpet for the services side. The firm made and sold 'widgets' with backup services of installations, servicing and consultancy in its area. About forty staff which Len enlarged on.

'We've got a great team here, used to be nearly a hundred a few years ago but sales have drifted a bit. There are thirty on the production side, a few in accounts and personnel, and the rest in servicing and sales. At any one time about a dozen are out on client sites or representing the company for sales and trade meetings. It's all first names and many of them have been with us since school. As I did and have.'

They said their goodbyes and sped off to the pub, speedily ordering drinks and lunch. Jonny offered Barry an open question.

'That's what it is at the moment. What are your first impressions?'

Barry paused, wondering how diplomatic to be. Jonny guessed such.

'Spit it out, man. We go back to short trousers so don't go all polite on me.'

'I wasn't going to, you know me. Jonny it's awful, chronic and worse. It's just a hobby going through the motions, one day following another, drift. No plan, no big picture, it's just held together with the loyalty of existing customers and probably some old-time friendships. Fine for the past; not fine for the future. I will be positive though.' He paused for a drink and caught a smile from Jonny. Emboldened, he pressed on. 'The products do form a connected group in a niche area which won't disappear but which will ultimately be overtaken with better design, software and functionality. Sorry to be boringly technical.'

'Well done, Barry. I think you've got straight to the heart of it in minutes. Before we move on to pleasanter subjects, can I please ask you to look over the spreadsheets and reports I'm sending you tonight and come back to me with suggestions and, please, don't hold back. As a thank-you, we'll take you and Sylvia out to dinner, the full works, when it's convenient for you both.'

'No problem, will do; and, yes, I am on email now by the way. It's going to be big. Yes, we'd love to do dinner out with you and catch up properly.'

They moved on to other subjects – family, holidays, money, schools. It was like old times.

Barry got back to Sylvia and the boys and told them about the day. Sure enough, Jonny's stuff all came through in emails and as he had time and the inclination, Barry got down to it straight away.

'Sylvia love, I'll be in my study for an hour or two. Call me if you need me and keep the mugs of tea coming. Wine later.'

He pored over the reports and figures; loved it; straight out of everything he'd done over the last few years. The company was dying on its feet. All the trends were in the wrong direction and worst of all the cash flow was getting tighter each month. The crunch was only a few months away. The product area was good, desperately in need of development and innovation and a realistic chat with customers. He thought he would ram home these main points to Jonny and follow them up with giving him the lethal stuff face to face. He slept on it and called Jonny next morning.

'I got so interested in it I spent all evening on it. When can we meet?' They arranged for two days' time at Jonny's house with dinner for the four of them afterwards. Jonny chose a recommended place and even Sylvia was impressed.

The two of them met in Jonny's study in his house. Jonny started.

'Yes, I do want the drains up on this. If it's no good, I think I could still get a trade buyer to take it off our hands. But if there is a profitable future, let's do it and hope to cash out later.'

'Jonny, it's dire but not without hope because the product area is good. With development and IT, there is a future with sales and ongoing servicing. Both in the UK and abroad. Abroad's a big place and there's the same need for it there as well as here.'

He went on to outline his misgivings of the organisation, the technical backup, the worsening financial position. Feeling stronger, Barry went on with his recommendations for staffing, technical development, realigning costs, and not least shoving a whole load of excitement into the company. Jonny slurped his coffee, peering into his mug thoughtfully before answering.

'I'm totally with you on this. I think there's a future out there but I'd struggle with the what and the how. I've had a close look at what you've got up to over the last few years. Everything you've done and everything you've said convinces me that, dear Barry, I'd like you on board. Literally. Shut up for the moment and hear me out.'

Jonny outlined an offer: Managing Director, seat on the Board, a small shareholding straight off increasing with company outperformance, an increase in his existing salary and all the other usual perks.

'And before you ask, a development budget for the products and some technical staff. How you rearrange or get rid of the existing staff, including Len, is up to you. A letter will follow. I very much hope you will come over but don't say anything now. Talk it over with Sylvia. Now let's go and pick up the girls and have a good night out.'

They did. By the time the sweet trolley came round with Black Forest gateau and the rest, Sylvia was happy and Barry shook Jonny's hand, whispering that if the contract letter confirmed all he had said, then yes, he would love to join. Brandy flowed and later on Barry and Sylvia made a more than usually successful physical merger.

FIFTEEN

Molly was bored. Her chart on the wall showed nearly a month had passed. Her resourcefulness with her exercises meant she wasn't stagnating but life was dull. Food varied only slightly and she could tell that if she ate less of something it kept coming back for longer. There was a limit to how much she could flush away. Her attempts at dialogue with her jailers, now changing between the three of them, got nowhere. Grunt. She wondered if they were foreign and tried a few languages. No response. So Plan A, to get alongside her captors, wasn't working. If she broke a window, which was too small to climb through anyway, they would have to repair it and maybe that would be different people. She didn't want to break any of the 'facilities' because she was totally dependent on them.

She elbowed a metal plate to break through the window glass. And screamed. One of the jailers came. He tied her up and left her alone. Then he came back with some wooden slats, a hammer and nails. He boarded up the window and then untied her, grimacing at her with a grunt, and left.

The next day, two came in. One was a jailer, the other a glazier with some small panes of glass. The panes were industrial, with wire netting embedded in the glass. They tied her up during the window replacement but she was more intrigued by the glazier's work bag. A label with words on. Everybody knew what 'fenetre' was, with or without a circumflex. *Oh.* Her second thought was, *At least I can brush up my French. Ho ho.* They finished their work and left but not before she had pleasantly said merci and au revoir. Grunt.

So they had drugged her, stuffed her in the back and done the shuttle or ferry over to France and driven on into la France profonde. Now she looked at the vast countryside through new eyes. Yes, it did look like the French countryside and the cattle were Charollais or something. *This is not going to help James or Mum and Dad or the police; nor detection of my mobile as they would have thrown that away in Sussex.* Plans C-Z were badly needed. At least she had something new to think about.

No-one in Britain knew where she was, apart from her captors. She was in a foreign country with absolutely no ID, just the clothes she stood up in. She had conversational French. So if, a big if, she could escape, then she could make her way somehow and her captors would also not have any idea where she was. They would be on the same footing as those looking for her. Well, she hoped they still were. And it would only take one phone call to have the advantage. Conclusion: she had to escape. She had a new plan.

SIXTEEN

Drewett went into Knutsford's office. He was dreading this.

'There's nothing, sir. No forensics, no CCTV, no evidence, nothing from the families or work or flatmates. Solid disappearance. Even the press coverage, the TV appeal, posters in nearby towns have all drawn nothing. When there's nothing, the public lose interest however much a total disappearance is fascinating to some.'

There had been a 'Missing'-type documentary on national TV and, while it was indeed fascinating, if there is nil response there's nothing more to say. Knutsford wasn't being helpful.

'I can't believe there's nothing. There never is. Show me a previous case with nothing. The Yard always gets his man – eventually. This is time for policework, Drewett. Good old-fashioned policework with all the modern tools of the internet and our records at your disposal. Chew your pencil and think outside the box. Talk to Mavis.' Briefing over.

Mavis was Mavis Smith, a bright new graduate recruit at the station almost straight from police college, eager to help and please and, Clive noticed unprofessionally, shapely with it. She had joined this Sussex station only a few weeks ago and Clive had barely noticed her.

'What do you think, Mavis? When all else fails, what do you do next?'

'Well sir, in my limited experience, anything like this is a boyfriend, or these days girlfriend, problem. Or money. Or family differences.'

'Please call me Clive; we'll be working on this together for God's sake. We've looked at her past boyfriends and James's girlfriends. There's nowt. I agree that the family needs consideration. Dad was super cool and James could be making all of this up. Anything better?'

'Well, er, Clive. Maybe that was a superficial look, you know, nothing stands out, nothing unremarkable. Maybe we have to look a little deeper, with respect, sir. We can test James by strong interviewing whether he is a suspect or not – surely he would give something away. If the family is involved, that should emerge from looking into the past. If she's dead and buried, that's the end of it for her but if she's alive, then someone somewhere knows something or is holding her. She strikes me as the sort of girl who would attempt to escape or try to do something at least, not just go off on her own to make a fresh beginning somewhere. Anyone would try to phone home or the police. So as she hasn't, that means no access to a phone. Ergo, she is dead or is being held captive or James or the family is involved.'

Drewett wasn't sure about Ergo but got her drift.

'Let's assume she's alive and, on your principal thesis, she is being held captive. One – why would anyone want to hold her captive? Two – where would you hold her?'

'As I said earlier, the reason has to be boyfriend or money or both, if we dismiss the family or fresh start scenario. Which I do because she does not appear to be that sort of girl. Am I allowed time to look back at her previous relationships? Fresh pair of eyes, etcetera… and Knutsford wants you do something.'

'Some time, at least, and fitted in with your other jobs. If you do the research, I'll do the follow-up in the field. And maybe a drink after work.' Mavis smiled at him. Men, she thought, are always the problem.

SEVENTEEN

James was a lost soul. He did his work duties perfunctorily but without much enthusiasm. Molly's absence had been advertised at all the client sites and back at the ranch but again without any response. No-one knew what to say to him; he and Molly were well-liked but there wasn't much to say and when you've said it once, repetition is trite. James had been over to Molly's flat a few times and talked everything through with Bee and Dee but even that was getting repetitive. He had also been down to Sussex a couple of times to see Mrs Brown and Drewett and revisit the scene where it had happened. There was nothing new to say and it all brought back sad memories. He and Drewett needed a breakthrough.

'We need a breakthrough,' he said to Drewett.

'Indeedy. We are looking further into Miss Otsworth's previous friends and relationships, not because of any new line of enquiry but just that if she has been taken by someone it seems more likely that there is or was a connection rather than merely a random plucking off the street, as it were.' James didn't take too kindly to the plucking reference but followed his train of thought.

'I've already told you what little I know. She was, I mean is, always close to her sister Ellie and she passed over very quickly about Molly's previous boyfriends. Nothing evil about them; just conventional relationships that went nowhere. If you get a lead it might trigger something Molly said, because we have talked and talked a lot over these last few months. Where are you lot on the forensics, vehicle, mobile and local knowledge?'

'That's where this case is really puzzling, you know. So far there is absolutely nothing. You normally get a strand of something or a whisper or even vulgar gossip – but nothing. This leads me, I mean us, to think it was probably better planned than it appeared at first sight. Hence our digging deeper.'

They chatted some more before James took the train back to London. Next stop, Molly's family.

EIGHTEEN

Henry and Annabel Otsworth were stoic. They had both been brought up not to show their feelings and often had to face criticism or comment that they did not have feelings. In the privacy of their home and their marriage, they were totally distraught. Molly was their first born after several years of trying. She could not be more dear to them. And they had brought her up with as much of their own characteristics as her own personality could absorb. As a result, they had faith in their daughter to be sensible and practical. Obviously she would phone them as soon as she was able. So far nothing. Life continued much as before because Molly had been in London anyway. They kept their sadness and their hope to themselves; the village now knew as much as they did and quietly had offered their sympathies. The vicar gave prayers for Molly every Sunday but all was subdued. Ellie was more articulate.

'Surely we can do something. Silence does nothing. The TV appeal and that ghastly documentary produced bugger all. What's the next best step? If Mols is alive, she must be being kept by people and TV is everywhere. Locals usually gossip if there are strange 'goings on' nearby. She could be anywhere in the country, indeed the world. That means the internet. We should do a prominent piece on the internet and social media.' They had already done much of this. The TV appeal had been like all the others; people sigh, express sadness and switch over to something else. The TV documentary was more journalistic and they all felt that this was more for the benefit of the journalist, the producers and the TV company's ratings than yielding fresh evidence. Social media was, well, social media. All responses and comments were well-meant, predictable and useless.

James came up and they were all delighted to see him. It was the first time they had all met and Annabel hugged him tightly. James, for his part, was equally pleased to meet them, though the circumstances could have been happier. He mentioned about the police looking into Molly's past, which sounded more lurid than he intended. Ellie responded.

'Well at least that's something though for the life of me I can't see anything coming up. Mols was and is the sensible, practical girl we know. I've lived through all her friendships and we obviously confided in everything. She and I have had fun times with each other and our friends but nothing ever sinister or threatening.'

'The police have asked us to list the names of all Molly's friends, boys, men, girls whatever.' This was Henry speaking to all of them. 'Please may we all look at my list so far and you youngsters add all your known names to the list? Annie darling, can we knock up an early supper?'

They sat round the large kitchen table with Henry supervising additions to 'the list'. A selection of cold meats, cheeses and crusty bread appeared and James was relieved to see some bottles of beer. Conversation did not flow easily and he made his departure shortly afterwards with the excuse of catching the last train. They offered him a bed for the night but he declined saying he had work in the morning. He promised to keep in touch and said to Ellie that they should talk.

NINETEEN

Another two weeks had gone while Molly firmed up her plan. How do you outwit the opposition? She recalled hockey team talks at school and college: those formations, feints, endless practice and code words. Here, she was on her own and there was no team, no buddies to link up with. Brains and brawn. She had the brains and she had tried to keep herself fit inside with exercises and jogging-on-the-spot. The food had been variable; there had been fruit and veg – not just bread and mash. She imagined that the boys downstairs would want to eat well and then give her the leftovers. Well, at least one of them was French. When, not if, she escaped she would have to disappear completely to avoid any chance of recapture. All she could see were fields with some woods on the brow of the hill. So the road to and from this farmhouse must be on the other side that she couldn't see. The fields had good hedges but there were gaps with fencing and gates. If she could make the first field in the dark, there was every chance she could make the woods a few fields away. She had memorised the route to the woods through the gaps and felt confident that she could navigate that route in the dark. The boys had not touched any of her clothing as she had been dumped in this room. Thankfully she retained her walking boots and weatherproof jacket. That was good. Her upbringing meant clean clothes and a toothbrush. Astonishingly, they had given her a toothbrush and she had a routine of washing and drying her few clothes regularly so she would be entering the French unknown in good shape. All it needed now was the escape plan. It needed some interaction with the boys to get them away for the night to let her have at least a head start.

She had worked out their rota and was pretty sure that they overlapped about an hour for food and fags and chat. Then one of them would be left alone for about seven hours. Three eight-hour shifts – how boring if they have nothing else to do. There had been no conversation as yet. She had tried 'bonjour' and 'comment ca va?' to each of them with no response. She guessed that the first one to chat would be the most malleable. It wasn't a guess really; it would be all that she had to go on. She tried names Jean, Jacques, Pierre, Francois, which led her to film stars and presidents. Finally success! The oldest one said, 'Moi, Alain.'

To which she obviously replied, 'Moi, Molly. Bonjour. Comment ca va?' But that was all. Perhaps Alain had realised he had broken his boss's rules. Still, Molly thought this an enormous breakthrough. It turned out to be their little secret. When it was his turn to change trays, it was bonjour Alain and bonjour Molly. He said it like the French say jolie. Molly was happy to be the jolie Molly. *Must tell James*, was her first thought.

She worked out from the rota when Alain would be on the next night shift. It would be tomorrow night. Like the creative Baldrick, she had a cunning plan. She practiced and waited. Not long now.

TWENTY

Drewett and Mavis were spending a good hour together each day going through Henry's list. Some names had come through straightaway followed by dribs and drabs as they were supplied from Ellie, James, Bee and Dee. It was policework at its most humdrum. There were local friends, school, college, work and social. Mavis started:

'Shall we start with the boys and men during and after college?'

'It could be a girl whose boyfriend Molly had pinched.'

'But men are more likely to perpetrate this elaborate game, if she has been killed or captured.'

'But girls are more spiteful. Chaps go with the flow a bit more.'

'This won't get us anywhere. You do A-M and I'll do N-Z, by surname.' Mavis wearied of these dominant men wanting their own way. But Clive was equally agreeable to her suggestion – practical and a way of getting on with her. Their 'drinks after work' turned out to be a brief one. Each of them got calls on their mobiles calling them away. Clive reckoned, *Next time we'll switch the damn things off.*

The task confronting them was first to make sure they had identified the right person and then check police records, national insurance records, employers, family connections. Eventually Clive despaired, 'So what? We build up a picture of the said connection but how do we take it further? A connection is just a connection. A disagreement or a dispute isn't necessarily going to show up, is it?'

Mavis agreed. 'Given the lengths they have gone to, to spirit Molly away somewhere, it can't be trivial. This might be deep at the personal level but not register officially. You choose your friends but you're stuck with your family however much you love them, or not. What do you think about looking into the families, James's as well?'

Clive admitted there was plausible logic to this. He smiled at her.

'Yep, I know what you mean. Take my cousin Geoff, on second thoughts don't take my cousin Geoff.' So they rebooted themselves onto the families without knowing what they were looking for but maybe an elephant would walk into the room.

TWENTY-ONE

Molly was all prepared. Alain had brought in the evening supper. Macaroni with some gloop poured over it and possibly one or two specks of parmesan. She wolfed it down and listened carefully for the other one or two to go. She heard goodbyes and a vehicle driving off, then all went quiet, Alain probably watching TV. She prepared all the materials for her plan and stuffed everything she would be taking into her jacket pockets. If she was to send Alain off on a desperate errand, it would have to be both credible and possible for him to go to get help. It was dark and mid-evening and she had assessed between nine and ten as about right. It was time to start the Plan.

She banged on the door and wailed at the top of her voice. Agony in both English and French. Eventually, it must have been five minutes or more, Alain came up the stairs.

'Que?'

'Je suis malade, tres, tres malade.' She upped the wailing to higher pitch. Alain opened the door and came in with his torch on. Molly was clutching her stomach and rolling around on the floor. Her French deserted her but she came out with:

'Pain, it hurts, appendix, medecin, doctor, fetch doctor, urgent, vite, vite, je suis mort.'

Alain reached for his mobile. Not the right solution, Molly realised.

'Non. Non. Vous allez à la pharmacie or fetch doctor. Vite.' She needed him to get confused and not phone for help. He said the van had gone till morning.

'Allez a bicyclette ou courir, mais allez vite, vite.' As luck would have it, Alain got no reply, evidently his mates were enjoying their evening or had switched their mobiles off or both.

'OK, OK, je vais. J'ai une moto a conduire. Vous restez ici, moi demi heure.'

He took the torch and mobile, locked the door and rushed downstairs. Molly kept wailing as long as she could and shortly heard the motorbike start up and then fade into the distance. Quick, she had to be quick. Turned on both taps; threw the towel in the basin; felt round to where she had concealed a small cigarette lighter in her jacket lining and put all the paper and scraps and everything combustible together at the foot of the door and set fire to it. It seemed an age to get going; then it took hold as everything was so dry. While the door was starting to get charred and burning, Molly gathered up her stuff, put on boots and jacket and, with water starting to spread across the floor, she gathered up the wet towel and started beating the door down with her boots. It was slow work and she feared Alain and others coming back at any moment. First, she got a hole through and she need more wet towel wrapped round her right leg. Then a whole panel went; this was it. With a wet towel wrapped round her and anything wet she could lay her hands on, she crouched down and crawled through the bottom half of the door. The door frame was well alight by now and the door collapsing but this was not a time for a critical appraisal. She felt her way down the stairs, the fire giving a bit of light, went to a ground-floor window, threw a chair at it, climbed through and ran off towards her pre-planned route.

She was through the first field when she heard the motorbike and a car returning. There was a lot of shouting. She hoped it would be a few more minutes before they realised she had escaped. Through the second field; only two more to go. They would not know which direction to go looking for her so they would have to fan out in the dark. Her fitness regime was working and though it was only a slight incline up to the woods, she was still getting out of breath. *Adrenaline kicks in,* she told herself, and she was glad her sleeps during the day also meant she could keep going through the night. *Keep going.* She could see torches wandering about but not threatening in her direction or making progress towards her. They would also be focusing on the fire which from three fields away she could make out that it was taking hold of part of the roof.

Then she was safe, well, relatively safe, she thought. *I'm in a foreign country with no ID or money or mobile, just what I stand up in, and I have very little idea of what to do next. And I've set fire to a French farmhouse.* Getting rational, she reckoned that with first light they would work out her route and follow her tracks. They could encircle the entire wood, not good. The chance of a search party in the night was small, she thought. They would know she could not go far, she would not be able to hitch a lift and they knew the surrounding territory like the back of their French hands. She skirted round, looking for a route away from the wood. It was still only eleven o'clock and she was prepared to walk all night. It was not easy; there were hedges; sometimes she had to go into the wood to go further round; but after two hours she thought she must have done about three miles around the wood. Time to look for a path going away from it. She struck out at right angles to the wood across open fields. She needed a safe place to hole up where they would not think of looking. And where is that at two o'clock in the morning?

TWENTY-TWO

Ellie was restless. Nothing was happening and she herself wasn't doing much to help. She phoned James.

'Hi James. How are you holding up? I want to do something but don't know what.'

'Good to hear from you Ellie and yes, it would be really good to hear something from the police or Molly herself. I'm sure she's trying to get to a phone by all means possible.' He didn't want to add 'if she's still alive'.

'Those names. Any mean anything to you? The ones I know are either folk we know or from the distant past. I can't imagine any of them being involved with anything as brutal as this. Why would they?'

'Dunno either. I've been down to where it happened a couple of times. It's just a plain field and any locals I spoke to in shops or in pubs just shrug and say, sagely, it's all very odd. Not helpful.'

'But what can we do?'

'You want to be practical but there's no point in doing things aimlessly. Either they are cranks, who must surely be bored with their silly prank by now, or there has to be a connection. If there was or is a connection then how did they know where we were? We only decided the Monday or Tuesday before and we didn't tell anybody other than Mrs Brown when we made the booking and it's stretching it a bit to think she had accomplices.'

'Then, logically, perhaps this is more deep-seated. If it was premeditated then Mols or you have been stalked. Is that being paranoid?'

'Well, er, yes. That's hardly likely and to what end? There's no ransom note and what's the point of taking her?' He again didn't want to add 'maybe just to torture or abuse or kill her for fun'. This thought was always with him and he was grateful that the family didn't speak of it. He imagined that it was in their darkest thoughts too.

Ellie ended the call and went into Molly's room, kept by Annabel as 'Molly's room' ever since she had left for London. She looked for something different that the police might not have thought of. Nothing. Even the old diaries were full of trivia – parties, homework, holidays – each merely recorded without any hint of grievances or agonising or innermost thinking. The few files were no different; just collections of memorabilia like tickets and theatre programmes. She flicked through a few books, light romances, college text books, even a prim tome called Elementary Physics and then a floppy disk fell out. It was an old-style floppy disk with a sticky label with 'Hell' and a date long since gone in Molly's handwriting. Nothing in the Otsworth's household would be able to read this disk but she knew a man who could.

'James, it's Ellie again, can I come and see you at work sometime? I've got something that might interest you.'

TWENTY-THREE

Clive and Mavis were having a similar discussion to Ellie and James's late that afternoon. Drewett had to report to Knutsford in the morning and he imagined the response if there was not much to say. They were reviewing progress on the names and the nature of the attack. Clive could not identify with a random opportunistic grab. Mavis had said the same as Ellie: that if it was planned then one or other or both must have been stalked. Otherwise how would they know where they were?

'And as the attack was first thing Saturday morning, the two men must have been at least in the area the previous evening if only to confirm their target had arrived and checked in.' Mavis had warmed to this case and was finding it more cerebral than at first sight. Clive was happy with her imaginative leap.

'Ye-es; but stalking is a big word. This is sleepy Sussex and James's description of the two men hardly makes them sound like criminals. And why Molly? Hardly one to make the headlines. You'll be suggesting there's a Mr Big behind all this next.'

'Well, there might be. If there is a sinister reason behind it, you wouldn't want to get your hands dirty doing the grubby physical work, would you?'

'No, that's logical.' Clive wondered if young Mavis had been reading too many crime novels or seeing too many TV dramas, spiced up by those desperate TV producers.

'Go on then. Thrill me with who this Mr Big might be.' It was nearly time to go and Clive wondered if another attempt at 'a drink after work' might succeed this time as she was more involved.

'Someone who can call the shots, got a bit of clout, knows or knows of James or Molly and,' she paused, warming to her theme, 'in the absence of any ransom, someone who is prepared to play the long game.'

'And who might that be? And why?'

'Someone older, a man obviously, maybe someone who goes back a bit, maybe knows James's or Molly's family. You know my views on families.'

'That's the second time we've come back to that. OK, let's do a bit more on the Longtons and the Otsworths. You OK for another hour and then a drink at The Swan?'

'Work first, Clive.'

TWENTY-FOUR

It was nearly first light when Molly stumbled into some outbuildings and a barn. Straw bales were piled high but not so systematically that she couldn't crawl into a gap that went in at least two bales' depth. She crawled in and pulled the bales back behind her. When dawn was fully up, she could see through a tiny gap between the bales where she would be able to make out anyone in the barn – friend or foe. These bales were here for the winter and it would be a while before Farmer Jacques would be hauling them off for bedding for the cattle. It was a dusty rather than mucky place and, sparing her hunger pangs, would be safe enough for a few days. Food and water would be a problem and she was hardly a Rogue Female. She would try the outbuildings the following night for water and fodder. She snuggled down and dozed off, worn out by the overnight hike.

It was a light sleep and she was woken with the sound of a vehicle and voices. Their French was rural and incomprehensible to her but the gist was clear. They were looking for a girl, a young woman, who might be around here. They doubted she would have got this far but one never knew. They walked round the outbuildings and into the barn, turned and left. She couldn't make out whether her captors were talking to each other or to the local farm worker, who might still be there. She strained her eyes and ears for further action and sounds but there was nothing. She was hungry and thirsty now but dare not make a move till nightfall. She dozed and listened like a watchdog with one eye or ear permanently on guard.

After dusk, she crept out quietly and surveyed the outbuildings and barn. There was no house and no lights on anywhere. She had, fortunately, found a deserted outcrop of farm buildings. There must be a water trough, there always is near cattle. Sure enough there was. As it was dark she couldn't tell how filthy the water might be but it was golden ale and she quaffed deeply. On one of the shelves were old bread crusts discarded by a worker. Soaked in the trough water it was almost delicious. She took them all and crept back into her hideout.

The next stage of the plan had to be to move on and find a safe phone. She reckoned that if there was no repeat visit the following day, then she could set out the next night.

There were voices the next day but not her captors. Two or three farm workers were getting the outbuildings ready for the cattle coming in over winter. They didn't move straw that day but Molly feared they would very soon. She strained to make out their French. It seemed to be just chat and banter, boys talking about girls, cars, football, booze. Nothing apparently about the visit yesterday. Either they weren't there or the visit had not made any impact. Either way, Molly decided tonight she would have to move.

As soon as the daylight was fading, she crept out. The boys had gone ages ago; but she was fearful of someone watching. She crept silently, one area at a time around all the buildings till she was convinced there was nobody. If there had been, they would have yelled out by now. She took the direction away from where she had come from, increasing the distance and hence the ground area from where she had been held captive. The moon was up and a farm track was easy to follow. Gaining in confidence, she kept to fundamentals and in no particular order they were coffee, bread, phone.

TWENTY-FIVE

Ellie met James a few days later. It was over lunch in a wine bar near his work. They chatted and then Ellie got down to business.

'I found this; it slipped out of an old text book in Molly's room back home; see what she's written on it.'

'Haven't seen one of those for years. Might be just discarded from her first days on a desktop. Mmm. There's a weirdo geek at work called Fraser who we all know has a collection of old computer junk at home. I do him an injustice; he's actually a decent bloke and I think he can be trusted if there's anything lethal on this disk. I don't think Molly's a spy or a blackmailer. Are you prepared to let him borrow it?'

'Or should we give it to the police?'

'It might just be a list of Christmas presents. That's some people's idea of hell. If it is we can give it to them later.' Ellie thought that sounded practical.

'But call me as soon as you've read it. I fear it might be something ghastly. Will you be with this Fraser and not let him have it without you around?'

'OK but he might copy it onto a stick anyway. No, I won't let him have it. If he's at work now I could go back and suggest after work today and you could be with us. I think he would salivate over something like this.'

'Sorry no, I'm on a day return and I want to see Bee and Dee before getting back to Paddington. Phone me, please.'

He promised and they agreed it would be better to keep this totally to themselves for the moment as this disk might be trivial or dynamite. They finished their wine and Ellie wandered off to Molly's flatmates, expecting them back after their work. In truth, as she had a key, she wanted to search Molly's flat room again.

James got back to his workplace and dropped in on Fraser.

'Still got that heap of computer crap at home?'

'Och, Jimbo, do you mean my valuable goldmine?'

'Glad to hear it. Does this excite you?' He brandished the floppy disk in the air.

'An antique! Wow, let me look.'

'Not here. Any chance of coming round to yours this evening? We'll go to that Italian next door if you can open this.'

'Can we do tomorrow? I've got a new generation presentation of some gizmo that does personal ID in a whole new different way. Can't miss it. Yes, tomorrow, Seven at mine and then you treat me to something even Montalbano would drool over.' James got the reference and laughed.

'Only if you can open this.'

'Guaranteed.'

TWENTY-SIX

Jonny's offer letter to Barry confirmed all that he had said and more. A bigger salary had helped to seal it and Barry had phoned that day both to accept and thank his old friend. He started a few weeks later and with his straightforward energy set about reorganising the whole plant around the current range of products. He absorbed Len's role and was relieved to discover that Len was equally relieved to step down to what he had done before his promotion; and with no drop in salary. The reorganisation had freed up some staff but instead of laying them off he put them into customer-facing roles, either phone backup or able to go out to customer sites. Everyone had a better idea of what they were supposed to do; Barry's natural good humour had rubbed off on the place and, with none of the feared redundancies, there was a healthier atmosphere. There was positive feedback from the regular customers too; the phones were busy. In more ways than one there was a buzz about the outfit. By Barry's second board meeting, he was able to report that the haemorrhaging of business had stopped, customers were more positive about the firm and the revenue and surplus figures were sloping up slightly to the right.

Jonny introduced Barry to two new members of the board, Edward and Neville, who were full of congratulations to Barry about this turnaround. Barry went on.

'Thank you, that's fine so far but it's just the start. I've got some ideas for new products we can tack on to existing ones and beef up support services that tie us closer to the customers and equally ties them closer to us. IT needs some refreshing as we are just holding the existing spreadsheets together with sealing wax and string at the moment. I'm looking at some packages that can do the whole accounting and order processing in one, with a few terminals about the place.'

They were encouraged by these noises and looked forward to the next proper board meeting in three months' time. By then Barry would have done nearly a year and was hopeful of a healthy bonus, after the year-end accounts were drawn up. Jonny took Barry aside after.

'That went well. Well done. I know I leave you alone most of the time but you're a self-runner if there ever was one. Keep calling me now and again as you have been. Happy to be rolled out to meet customers. And let's do a dinner with the girls this weekend or next.' They agreed a Saturday and Jonny said he would book that Michelin starred place in the country.

'Taxis there and back. Why not?'

Sylvia was overjoyed, Even Barry had mentioned she was due a new dress. Sylvia thought so too.

TWENTY-SEVEN

That night Molly made good progress. If she had already covered four miles then the next mile would increase the area to search by at least twenty-eight square miles. That felt safe. There was still no sign of villages or main roads. Her captors had clearly chosen a part of France that was wholly agricultural and equally empty of people. France is a big country, far bigger than the UK, and, outside the main towns and cities, much of it is empty and the villages deserted during the daytime. She could not expect to find a gendarmerie in a remote village. There could be a public phone in a bar or restaurant but she was not ready to go there at the moment. She was in a foreign country and was now a common criminal burning down a farmhouse a few nights ago – hardly someone to sympathise with. Her immediate needs were starting to get urgent. Yes, a phone but lack of food and drink were making her low and she could tell she and her clothes were not as fresh as she was used to. Could she trust a cottage outside a village? Her absence may have been broadcast to the farmers to look out for a stray woman – a worker, a loony, a relation, an arsonist, whatever? She had to dismiss these thoughts partly because they did her no good and partly because they could help her captors if the police got involved. But what risks could she take, when she came to a deserted dwelling or a village? She decided she had to, providing they looked like decent people and who were happy to accept she was lost and had been left to find her own way back by a bad boyfriend.

She also wondered about turning herself in to the local police but convinced herself that could be counterproductive. Villages did not have a police presence and precious time would be wasted. She had not been harmed in any way – other than loss of freedom – and now she had definitely committed the crime of arson. She had set fire to a farmhouse in a foreign country; she was on the run from this crime; and her defence of being held captive would not work. The evidence of her prison was burned down; it would be all of their words against just hers that she had been staying as a guest with board and lodging in a farmhouse in the French countryside. Her own image of foreign police, even in a country as friendly as France, was a native bias for their own and against the foreigner. No, she would have to carve out her own route to justice and to home via a phone call to James or family or both to get numbers on her side and corroboration.

Her chance came sooner than expected. In the first light, she could see a small hamlet ahead, a few houses at the end of a minor road. She thought she would lay up until those working had left for the day and she would try her luck on the housewife or grandparents for her sob story. She hid behind the hedges adjoining the cottages until the time appeared right.

By ten o'clock she could wait no more. Bold as brass she walked straight down the road with her peripheral vision highly active. The third house along, the front door was open with the sounds of kitchen noises. She went up to the outside back door.

'Bonjour? Bonjour?'

A woman of uncertain years emerged.

'Eh? Bonjour? Que?'

'Je suis tres, tres fatiguée, madame. S'il vous plait, avez vous du pain, café?'

The woman motioned her to sit down. This itinerant didn't seem like a tramp to her. Foreign, yes; but they didn't get any foreigners round these parts. She gave Molly a glass of water which disappeared in seconds.

'Merci, merci madame. Je m'appelle Molly.'

The woman's name was Helene and Molly worked out she was asking her what she was doing here. In her halting French, Molly started on her sob story. Dumped by a man; left to walk to the nearest place; have been walking all night; this was the first place I came to; and yours seems such a lovely cottage. She needn't have gone on. Dumped by a man was enough.

'Les hommes. Merde.' And she spat into the fireplace.

The next hour was heaven. Bread and butter, coffee, hot water and even an old blouse that was as welcome as a new top from her favourite shop in town. And a few outsize knickers. She couldn't thank Helene enough and then asked for a phone, a mobile. But no, her man took his mobile with him and would not be back till late. The village was deserted during the day and there were no landlines in this little hamlet. Molly had to balance staying for her man to come back with mobile with the risk of a car turning up asking about strangers. She assessed that as too risky as news of the house fire would spread like, well, wildfire. She profusely thanked Helene, got her to write down her address, thanked her again and set off. Helene, bless her, gave her a water bottle and bread and butter and suggested which way to go.

Which she didn't. *Don't leave tracks,* she told herself, starting in that direction, then turning through ninety degrees as soon as the hamlet was out of sight.

By now it was midday and she was in full view of any vehicle. The lurid blouse was more likely to be noticed than serve as a disguise; but it was clean. 'Time for a new plan,' she said out loud and went and hid away from the road. Her safest bet was to remove herself from the area as far as possible. This meant hitching, not her favourite, or train or bus. People talk on buses but not on trains. With no ticket, the worst a ticket inspector could do would be to throw her off. She had no ID and hardly any French. So train it was, if she could find one. She could hardly go back to Helene and ask where the nearest train station was. Therefore she had to head to a town and get round the ticket barriers. She listened; there was no sound of a train. *Walk until you hear one.*

TWENTY-EIGHT

James arrived at Fraser's dead on seven. It was a semi with a garden and a garden shed and James knew from office chat that the shed was full of old computer stuff. Fraser welcomed him in and had already set up an old desktop with some slits for floppies.

'Here's a beer. Let's be looking at this then.'

He inserted the disk and some output white letters on a black background showed up on the screen.

'Ho ho, it's one of those.' Fraser chuckled. He found an index file that listed the files. There was MOLLY1, MOLLY2, HELL, BOGNOR, HOME1, HOME2 and HELL2.

'Can you print out all the content?'

'Not as easy as that. It's encrypted in some way. Like someone has turned a text file into code. Given its vintage and probably only personal use, I'm going to guess it's one of the low-level ones available at the time. I've got one in the shed.'

James drank his beer, wondering what on earth Molly was doing turning personal stuff into code. Perhaps someone else had done it for her. Fraser came back with another disk and inserted it into one of the other slits. He played around with the keyboard, tried opening MOLLY1 and the screen filled with text. There was no formatting, no paragraphs. It all flowed on and on; but at least it was intelligible.

'Looks like this one is names and addresses.'

'Can you print them all out?'

'Ye-es. I would need to set up a linked printer, find paper that fitted it and let it run for a few hours. I can tell that from the size of the files.'

'Can you put it all on a memory stick so I can print it out at home?'

'Sorry mate, we're talking incompatibility here and that's nothing personal.' Fraser thought he might have these peripherals in the shed. 'Then we can set up the printing, go to Giovanni's and it might be half done by the time we're back.'

James could see no choice so they did that.

Giovanni's turned out to be the success of the evening. A singer turned up and with a round karaoke baritone voice sang the opera arias we all know and love. Montalbano himself would have been satisfied.

They got back and the printer was still whirring.

'Yes, thought so, about halfway through. Can I leave it on and bring it all to work in the morning?'

James felt uncomfortable about this, remembering the strict instructions from Ellie and actually fearing what was in the files.

'Any chance of me bedding down here and sleeping through it? I'm sworn to not let the disk out of my sight. Or site.'

'OK, OK, you don't trust me, but thanks for dinner. Really good. That sofa folds out and I'll find a blanket for you.'

They drank half a bottle of whisky, went through some office gossip and before Fraser went to his own bedroom, re-fed the printer with more of the continuous paper.

James didn't sleep at first. The noise of the printer was eventually soporific and he dozed off. When Fraser woke him, it was with his cheery voice and a cup of coffee.

'All done. Here's the output, here's the disk, it looks a bit meaty but I've not remembered a word of it.'

With that, he was gone. James checked the output covered all the files, put it all in his bag, left two large notes on the kitchen table and scrawled, 'Buy yourself some decent whisky. Thanks a lot. I owe you. James'. He left for the office and texted Ellie on the way – 'All printed out. Will call tonight. J'.

TWENTY-NINE

Clive and Mavis had worked hard at the background of the Longtons and the Otsworths. They made sure that they had identified the right people first and then gone into detail. There were no police records of past crimes, as expected. There were some parking and speeding fines of no consequence and some commercial stuff of corporate activity in the companies they had worked for. There was no information about Annabel Otsworth or Margaret Longton apart from their marriage and the birth of their children. The children were the same as the people that Clive had met or been told about. All very straightforward and boring. There was an old civil case in one of the companies Henry had been a director of. Some dispute between two directors that lasted a couple of days and was thrown out by the judge who was reported to have said in dismissing the case that 'matters such as these should not be brought to court just to satisfy hurt feelings and waste valuable court time that could be better spent on bringing justice to the wider public'. Clive recognised a legal ticking off and moved on to the next speeding fine.

He and Mavis had gone to the pub after this and they did agree to switch their mobiles off. All Mavis wanted to talk about was how best to pursue her career.

'Should I transfer if there's a vacancy?'

'Do you want to? Aren't you happy working here?'

'Yes, of course, but I don't want to get stuck in a rut and be stereotyped as an assistant for the next five years.'

'You're not that. We're on this case together and you can come in with me tomorrow to report to Knutsford if you want.'

'That would not be right and it would not make you look good. I want to get credit for my own work.'

'I'll tell him what part you've played and by the way this is by far the most puzzling case we've had here for months, if not years. I want to crack this one. With you, of course.' He tried to shift the talk on to a life outside work but apart from finding out that Mavis lived in a flat in the next village and went to the supermarket in the next town, he learnt nothing further.

'What do you get up to in your spare time?'

'I don't have spare time. I do some studying and reading and go to the gym and very occasionally go out with friends. That's all. What about you anyway?'

Clive admitted his life was much the same although he was learning golf. He saw himself as a loner which suited his golf though it was fun to go round with some of the others at the club.

'That's so boring. Golf's for fuddy-duddies. What a waste of time. Birdies, bunkers and bogies. Who said it spoiled a good walk? Well said.'

'There's more to it than that.'

Clive thanked her for a nice time and saw her to her car.

Next morning he went in to Knutsford's office.

'Well, any progress?'

'Nothing specific but we've done a lot of background work on the families. Mavis and I think that if there is anyone involved in a so-called kidnapping then it may be rooted in the past. It's not a ransom situation as there has been no contact with friends, family or work.'

'Mmm. Not good. She might be dead and gone of course, weeks ago.'

'Yes but Mavis and I . . . '

'Never mind what young Mavis thinks. I want to hear it from you. We can't have two of you tied up on this case forever. We've got those car thefts down the high street and could do with some more manpower on those. You can have another week, Mavis when she's available and not dragged from other work; report back then and we'll see whether to move it from active to dormant. Good luck.' That last bit was added as he thought he might have been a trifle hard on Clive. He was a good copper and would not want to lose him.

Clive gave the gist of this to Mavis without mentioning the probability of the case transferring to dormant.

Mavis sensed some of his gloom.

THIRTY

James didn't call Ellie till well past nine the next evening. These files were strange. First of all:

> they read like this without any stops or paragraphs going on and on with this tiny point size and a typeface that read as though it had come straight off a mainframe when computers were the size of buses and you had to order your printouts through a computer department and you did not receive it for a few days and so on and so on and so on and no upper and lower case and strange spacing.

which made it a strain to read and digest at the same time. MOLLY1 and MOLLY2 were relatively straightforward, being names and addresses and some dates like a haphazard diary with brief comments after. You could say it was a file of the 'significant events' of a young girl or teenager. A typical entry would be a date then 'Amelia and Woolworths Blue Medium for bonfire party. Never again.' After reading a few dozen of those, he got fed up and moved on to HELL. This was a long diatribe, not making much sense but consistently mentioning Ken and Dad and that she was highly worked up and indignant about it, whatever 'it' was. There were no dates or places and no other names. James thought that Molly would not need any reminding of the background or situation as it had had such an effect on her. The tone wasn't traumatic, it was outrage. He could imagine her going to her room and pouring out her anger and annoyance into this file and then putting it away. Like writing that angry letter, feeling a lot better in the morning and never posting it.

James went on to HELL2. This was the Molly he knew better. It was an apology to herself, to not be such an idiot, to grow up, girl, and move on. Significantly it ended by adding that she would keep these two files safe just to remind herself how stupid they and she had been and how she got over it.

BOGNOR was an account of a weekend there with a girlfriend and two boys. James didn't want to recall losing his virginity but evidently Molly did. Like his, this did not seem to be one of life's great moments and James dwelled on the much better moments that he and Molly had enjoyed. And would in the future.

HOME1 and HOME2 were merely a few words on family tribal events – births, weddings, funerals, Christmases – from that time.

Then he phoned Ellie and gave his version of the seven files, concentrating on HELL and HELL2.

'If Dad is your father, who, excuse me, the hell is Ken?'

'Could be anyone. No-one springs to mind. She is eighteen months older than me so although we had friends in common, we also had our own friends. There were Kens at both the schools we went to and there would have been at uni too.'

'It may be earlier than that; more like the first years at boarding school.'

'Yes, there were Kens. I'll run through them; I won't mention this to Dad yet because it could all be girly fantasy; but Mols is not remotely one to indulge in that. It could just be a junior moment, if you see what I mean. Over and done with. She has never mentioned getting all het up about something not involving me.'

'Shall we tell Drewett? By the way, I think we should but it could get out of hand.'

'Not yet, do you mind? Let me think about it and I might drop a 'Ken' in family chats back here.'

'Sounds OK. I'll call in a few days.'

Molly does not react like that to anything, James recalled. Was there more to this?

THIRTY-ONE

'Guv, she's gone.'

'What do you mean?'

'She set fire to the place and ran off in the middle of the night. We've combed the neighbourhood but not to be found and nobody knows nothing.'

'Wankers. What's so difficult to keep a girl locked up in a deserted farm building until I say what do next?'

'Sorry, Guv. She pretended to be ill and while Alain got on his bike to fetch the doc, she burned the door down.'

'Oh, by rubbing two sticks together I suppose. Wasn't she strip searched? Or should I say why wasn't she strip searched?'

'We did obviously but we think a fag lighter might have been hidden in one of those inner pockets of an anorak or her bra.'

'Widen the search; talk to the local villages; the bus stations; train stations. You've got the photos. She could have hitched a lift but my betting is she wouldn't trust that again.'

'OK, Guv. We've done that but we'll do it again. What's plan B?'

'Plan B is bloody well find her. There's no comeback from her because she won't recognise anybody or know what all this is about. Use your wits and find her. I'm staying in the UK; you fix France.' End of conversation. Pete did not enjoy that and had been fed up with this caper right from the start. First, hiding the drugged girl in the back of the 4x4 on the ferry over and then the long drive to this neck of the woods. Right at the beginning from tracking this girl for a few weeks, then the transfer and now this. There didn't seem to be any point to it. And the lads agreed with him. He got his map out and drew big circles round the farmhouse at distances he assessed for each day's slow walking, allowing for hiding and sleep. There were one or two bus and train stations inside these circles. Best target those.

THIRTY-TWO

Molly had kept to farm tracks and crossing fields, avoiding roads and the traffic. She had less luck than with Helene at the next two cottages where she had tried the same yarn. The third was better. An older man who took sympathy on her. The coffee and bread and dry cake were not up to Helene's standard, *But who am I to quibble?* she pondered.

'Ou est le train?' It was the best she could do.

'La, cinq kilometres.' And he pointed vaguely down the road. Molly got the direction in her mind given the time of day and set off down the road, quickly diverting to a field track as soon as she could. Five kilometres is just over three miles so two hours should easily do it. If there was an evening train anywhere, she would try to board the train somehow and then be miles away by nightfall.

She made the tiny village and its station by late afternoon. There was a local train early evening. This gave her time to scout the station and see if she could gain access to the train without any ticket barrier or ticket inspector. The other side of the line looked more accessible but the doors might not open that side. They may be operated electronically by the guard, not good old-fashioned manual. The French are proud of their trains. She thought that when the light faded she would be able to get into the station from the wrong side and then cross the tracks to the right side without being seen. Risky but doable.

She redoubled her steps back to where she had come into the village and looked around. This would be one place they could be watching. There were no waiting cars with a driver. There was no-one loitering around. She didn't recognise her captors among the few villagers wandering around. This was not a commuter village, there were no housing estates, merely the usual few cottages and farm buildings and agricultural support services as in thousands of French villages. Nor were there any cafés or bistros and those hunger pangs were coming again. She decided to risk an outlying cottage on the edge of the village. The same yarn and this time to a young mum and baby.

'Mais oui. Help yourself, du pain, café.'

'Merci, merci.'

'Un homme est venu pour vous ce matin.'

'Merci, merci, c'est mon frère, au revoir.'

Molly fled. They were on to her here. The station was now the key. She reckoned they would be back around the time of the train. How could she get on the train without them seeing her and what if they got on the train? She had to out-think them. She reckoned there would only be one of them because they needed to cover all possible directions from the farmhouse. *So one man, it would be a man, cannot cover both sides of the track. So I need to see him before he sees me and then I can respond to whatever he does.* It was at least a plan. She found a place to hide and waited, munching the hunk of baguette she had taken while madame was tending baby. With a quarter of an hour till the train, a car drew up and a young man in blue overalls got out and walked up and down the platforms and around the station. He could have been one of her captors and his suspicious behaviour in the poor light convinced Molly he was. There was no-one else around; sadly no throng of commuters or partygoers filling up the platforms. It was darker now and she was able to move to one end of the station where the tracks were exposed. She went to the other side of the tracks from where her captor was hanging around and hoped that she could either clamber on the train on the wrong side or slip round to the right side and get in without him noticing. She could make out where he was as the train drew in. When it stopped, Molly went round the back of the train to the platform side, keeping him in view. A lady alighted and her supposed captor enveloped her with hugs and kisses and she was sure she heard, 'Maman cherie.' She opened the nearest door and got in, smiling to herself and the whole world. Some passengers returned her smile.

There was no ticket inspection, the train stopped at every station and she stayed on all the way. There were a few other passengers and two in particular caught her eye. A boy and a girl, late teens, sitting close to each other and gawping at a screen on his mobile. A phone. It was nearly nine now, that's eight mid-evening in the UK. If she could make just a short call should she call James or Ellie. She chose James as he was the more likely to be on his own or to detach himself from a group and, endearingly, she hoped he was hanging on to his phone for dear life for a call from his Molly. She sidled up to the couple.

'Bonjour. Je suis Anglaise. Puis je utiliser votre mobile?' Her French was faltering and she suspected the French didn't call their mobiles 'mobiles'.

'Eh? Pourquoi?' He was more irritated than surly.

'J'ai perdu mon mobile et je suis tres loin de chez moi. Tres, tres bref?'

'OK. Vous voila. Vite.'

She stabbed out James's mobile number complete with the +44. He answered on the second ring.

'James, it's Molly. I'm OK. Find out where this call is in France and get here. I'll try again soon.'

'Darling, are you OK? So relieved to hear your lovely voice. Where...?'

But the French boy had worked out this was a call to the UK and he wasn't going to waste his mobile package on silly calls to England, especially after that football defeat last month.

'C'est fini. Angleterre trop cher.' And he grabbed the phone back off her.

'Merci, merci.' And she went back to her seat. At least James knew (a) she was alive and sounded OK, (b) had a French mobile number and (c) with police assistance might be able to track very roughly where she was. These were all positive but not in themselves a solution. By now it was nearly nine-thirty, when the train reached its terminus. A town she had heard of! She was probably safe, with no money or plastic, hungry and tired and nowhere to go for the night. She stepped down off the train and a recognisable figure stood abruptly in front of her.

'Nice to see you again, dahlin', you've been givin' us the run around, haven't you? But you're back with us now.'

It was the tall man from the 4x4 in Sussex, one of her captors at the farmhouse.

THIRTY-THREE

Clive had just steered Mavis into a corner seat at a local gastropub when his mobile played that familiar riff.

'Clive, may I call you Clive? It's James. James Longton, you know, the Molly Otsworth case.' He sounded breathless.

'Yes, James, how can I help?'

'I've just had a five-second phone call from a French number. She's sounded OK and asked us to trace the whereabouts of the number. Can I give it to you now?'

'Well, it's late and I'm a bit tied up at the moment. I suppose I could phone the number through to the office that traces calls and they could be working on it. Let me have it.' He wasn't best pleased to be disturbed at an important time like this but this did sound like a really significant breakthrough.

'Yes, yes, got a pen?' Mavis handed him hers and James read out the number. At least it had the right number of digits and a 33 upfront.

'Yes, got that. What else did she say?'

'Nothing more. Just for us to trace the call and get here. She must have had access to a phone but then cut short. Maybe to escape. She sounded in control and making a call she wanted to make, not because someone was telling her to make it. That's reassuring. I'm guessing it means she's on the run on her own.'

Clive thought that was a leap of the imagination but plausible.

'OK, leave it with me and we'll talk in the morning.'

He filled Mavis in on the substance of James's call.

'How long does it take to trace a call? Will we get cooperation?' Mavis didn't know either but she did have an idea of who to call as she had had a case like this in training.

'I know where to call; but it's getting the authorisation. British and French.'

Clive placed the call and logged the French number with them. He urged them to do what they could and he would speak to his superior officer in the morning. Knutsford would like this, he thought. Mavis got her phone out of her handbag and called the French number. It rang in her ears and then stopped.

'Well whoever it is, doesn't appear to want to speak to the UK.'

'It's later there than here. Now back to more important matters. Are you having the prawn starter?'

THIRTY-FOUR

Knutsford didn't show displeasure so Drewett knew that this progress had been well-received. First, it meant Molly was alive; and second they had a number to go on. Clive had called the number again first thing and had exchanged bonjours with some French lad. He hadn't meant to sound threatening, indeed he thought he was being friendly. He didn't think the French lad was part of any conspiracy so that mildly supported James's theory that Molly was on the run. The evening with Mavis had gone well, he reflected. Didn't somebody once sing a kiss is just a kiss? Clive thought it was a giant step forward, thinking back on some, only the few, of his previous amorous trials. Mavis had volunteered that her French might be more recent than his and she had followed up his call. They actually spoke for a couple of minutes. Her debrief to Clive was that he was a student in a French province, had been getting back home with his girlfriend and some British woman had borrowed his phone and, the cheek of it, had phoned back home without asking. They never saw her again but he did say which town they and the train was heading towards.

Clive reported all this to Knutsford who said the mobile phone number check would still be useful to verify the boy's account and someone should interview him to get as much about Molly as possible. When they knew the area and which local prefecture, they would contact them to do this. Clive saw a trip to France vanish in a trice.

'Would you like me to go there, sir?'

'No, that's a waste of everyone's time. The local police are quite capable of interviewing this student and report back to us. It doesn't sound like he's involved. Useful corroboration. Set out a brief and a list of questions for their interview and I'll look into how we liaise with our cross-Channel friends. You should bring Longton and the Otsworths up to date and see if there is a French connection in the family.'

Drewett couldn't disagree with Knutsford's approach. When he got back to his desk, there were already two missed calls from James Longton. He phoned back and James picked up on the first ring.

'Well, where is she? I'm ready to go. Eurostar, ferry, Heathrow, whatever.'

'James, it's OK. We've got the lead and following it. The mobile is a French student's and the call was from a railway carriage that clearly Molly was in too. We don't think she phoned under duress and the boy has nothing to do with it. Our French liaison people are briefing the local police there and they will report back.'

'No matter, I'm going today.'

'That's admirable but to do what exactly?'

'Molly phoned me and when she is able to she'll phone me again and I'll be there. You can't stop me and I'm no good here. Work has given me time off because I'm pretty useless at the moment.'

'No, sir, I can't stop you but I would like you, please, to call me every day to say where you are and what you are doing or have done and not getting in the way of proper police work. I don't want this getting complicated. Mavis, er, Miss Smith and I are on the case and our earnest wish is to recover Miss Otsworth back to the safety of her family and to you of course. And not to have to rescue you as well.'

'I'm fine. I can look after myself. Yes, agreed of course. And if I can be useful in France, just say so.'

They wished each other luck and finished. Clive turned to Mavis.

'He's off to la France to cherchez la femme.'

'That's lovely, so romantic. They must mean a lot to each other.

She rang him, not little sister or M and D.' This time it was Clive who grunted that he would phone the Otsworths. He also recognised that this meant Molly had been kidnapped and that neither James nor the family were involved in the physical kidnapping – that is apart from any other family connection with the kidnappers.

THIRTY-FIVE

'Guv, we've got her back. We guessed which station she would make a run for and that she would stay on the train to the end of the line. Met her off the train and, with a bit of assistance from yours truly, got her into the van. Can't go to the farmhouse, it's half burnt down. Where now?'

'OK, that half makes up for letting her go. Better be the other house the other side of the country. She may have said something to someone and got a message back home. We have to assume the police know about her little adventure and will be searching the area. Drive through the night, keeping to minor roads, and blindfold her or drug her or both and you should be nearly there by first light. Take side roads and take Alain with you for any French lingo. Keep her in the room in the loft, total strip search if you know what I mean, and no torches or matches, no nothing. Phone when you're there and I'll think what to do next.'

Pete said cheers and dawdled to the van. This was turning into a right bore; how long would it last? He was now clearly implicated as an accomplice and if any charges were brought, he could imagine most of the capture would be down to him. It was a long time since his spell inside and he was not going down again. His bonus when this was all over was the only thing keeping him on mission. Well, and working for the Boss in the future, of course.

He and Alain went to the back of the van and opened the doors.

'We've got to blindfold you and if there's any trouble we'll drug you as well like the last time. What do you say?'

'It's OK, I won't resist, blindfold is fine. Can you make it a little more comfortable if we're going for a trip?'

Pete threw two blankets at her and he and Alain blindfolded her and tied her hands together with six inches of play between the hands. Similarly with her ankles.

'Do you need to pee, young lady? We're not checking into the Ritz.'

'Yes.'

'We'll drive into the country and stop in a few miles.' They locked the doors and went to the front.

Molly was so annoyed with herself for getting caught again that her only modus operandi at the minute was to go with the flow. No resistance and wait until circumstances changed or James or the police got on track.

She assessed that James would be much relieved to hear her voice and probably he would know that she had not made the call under forced circumstances or as instructed. He would now be thinking that she was free and wandering around some French town trying to find her way back to the UK. Ditto the police. *Neither would know I've been captured again, dammit, and these boys are going to drive as far as they can. The couple on the train know nothing of my intentions. But with James having the number and the police able to track its location, they will be there. Maybe someone will have seen me bundled into this van. Not much hope of that.*

All she could do at the moment was to make a rough calculation of the length of this journey.

The van stopped and they shoved her through a gate into a field.

'Is this private?'

'Yes, luv, we're the only ones here and we're not looking.'

Then back in the van and locked in. It was a long drive through the night.

THIRTY-SIX

The firm's progress continued. Barry was now a fixture and he had fashioned the climate that new products and services were to be expected. He discussed possibilities with his team and also with Jonny over coffee or even a beer. Jonny asked him to put his detailed conclusions for the proposed new products and services, and any to be withdrawn, with approximate costs, in a paper a week before the next board.

'Ballpark is fine, Barry, spare us the decimals. It's the big picture we want to see with rough estimates of sales, income, development costs, expenses and that lovely word profits.' They laughed.

Barry worked hard at it. He did not believe in making the figures look better than they would be just to get board approval. Costs were costs. Development costs were always understated and IT even more so. He put in his best judgment and added a margin for good measure. Equally, there was no point in glamorising sales. Selling was hard work and selling into both existing customers and new sceptical customers would take time, effort and money. After a few late nights, after the children were in bed, he was eventually pleased with the result. It was sound expansion coupled with progress on existing and new fronts and with development costs that he considered both achievable and income-producing within an acceptable period.

He found Jonny the next morning having a quiet smoke with some of the sales guys before they left for the day.

'Hi, I've done the projections and draft figures for the board. Do you want to look over them before I send them out? They do add up.'

'Course not, Barry, send them out to me at home, my desk, Edward and Neville. Any questions, we'll give you a bell. Nice timing by the way for the meeting next week. It'll be good.' They chatted over family and the cricket and got back to work.

Barry heard nothing from any of the three of them over the next week. This was mildly surprising as he had expected some comment, however gratuitous. Normally Jonny would make a small point about something just to show he had read the whole thing in his capacity as

Executive Chairman. The evening before the board meeting, he casually mentioned it to Sylvia.

'It's the future strategy and new projects meeting in the morning. Don't you think it's strange I've had no comments, not even bad ones?'

'Don't be silly, love, you would have covered everything just like you always do. Thorough and professional as ever. Let's get the neighbour's daughter in tomorrow and go down to The Bloated Drake to celebrate.' This was just about walking distance, even with heels.

'You're right. Let's. Give Polly a bell in the morning.' Their two boys didn't like the word 'babysitter' but Polly was good company and, even at their age, they were starting to notice girl differences, particularly this curvy eighteen-year-old.

Barry was at his desk early and had already walked the shop. The work atmosphere felt good. Jonny, Edward and Neville were late for the meeting and they all arrived together in Jonny's car, he having met them at the station.

All had coffee and Jonny opened the meeting.

'We've got Barry's big paper to concentrate on this morning so let's get the usual stuff out of the way, taking by exception, so we can get on to the future.'

They waded through sales figures, key customers, accounts, and passed over health and safety and compliance matters. After forty-five minutes, this all done, Jonny pushed his chair back.

'Good, that's that, let's get on to the meat. Neville, would you like to kick off?'

This was also unusual but Neville's other directorships were at bigger companies. He launched into what Barry soon recognised as a prepared statement.

'Barry, this is excellent and flows on naturally from the sterling work you've done in turning the company round. And you are right to set out a future, building on where we are. My comment at this point is that it is incremental whereas we are looking for a quantum leap. The emerging income streams are safe, unexciting and not representing the sort of yield we are looking for.'

'Can I comment on that?'

'Not just yet, Barry, let me carry on for the moment. We see the expansion of business with the existing customer base plus the new products and services into new markets, not just in the UK but in the East, as our big chance to make that leap. This opportunity may not come again and we can't let others who are on the fringes of what we do come in and steal our business or merely replicate what we do. Our plans are to re-capitalise the business, bring forward all this development outlined in this plan and do it on a much larger scale. If it's right for a thousand widgets it's right for a million widgets.'

Barry had to butt in here. He didn't like the sound of 'we' and 'our plans' and 'widgets', nor 're-capitalise'.

'Well, I suppose that is a vote of confidence in what and how we are doing but expansion beyond our ability to manage it, cope with it, afford it plus the usual problems with upscaling any existing operation means high risk. Over-reach is dangerous. Don't get me wrong, moving to a bigger operation is right where I am but saying it and wanting it are not the same as managing it and it happening.'

It was time for Jonny to come in.

'Look Barry, everything's fine. In a way it's an endorsement of all that you are doing but with the added dimensions of a shortening in the timescale and input of capital. Edward, could you chip in about our meeting last week?'

'Thanks, Jonny.' Edward was smooth urbanity in spades. 'And may I be the first, well third, to congratulate Barry on what you have done. I, we, feel that the right path has been properly set out for products, services and markets; only we want to advance the route from a mere path to a motorway. We met with some funders last week in the City and they are happy to re-capitalise this business, with an expanded and accelerated business plan, take up some shares and utilise other spare capacity elsewhere.' He went on to mention many millions of new shares, two sites in neighbouring towns already functioning in an overlapping business and with some spare capacity, a new structure to the company, including new board members and a holding company.

'Jonny, what does this mean for us, for you, for me?' Barry's antennae were stretching far into unknown territory; he didn't like it and it showed.

'Barry, relax. The outfit here will continue as is, in fact bigger and at a faster development; you will continue as the boss here and be part of a much bigger group, working alongside the two other sites. I'll continue as chairman of the holding company and you'll probably see more of me than you have been accustomed to. You'll report to the holding company board, just like the other two sites.'

'So we've sold out to these two jokers and become just an income-producing subsidiary? What about my share holding?'

'Barry, please don't be like that. Neville and Edward are helping us through to bigger and better times. We've thought of your shareholding. You can retain the shareholding in the company here or swap it for a shareholding in the holding company. With the re-capitalisation, it would be a smaller number but potentially worth a whole lot more because the group is so much bigger.'

Barry recognised the game. He had been played and not seen it coming. He had effectively been nearly an equal partner with Jonny, now he was a function head, an employee, with a small shareholding. That's why Jonny had been away so much, that's why they wanted his projections in advance and in rough detail. He felt a fool but couldn't see what he could have done differently. He went on, 'Jonny, you've sold us out to others from under our feet, you've concealed this from me without thought for others, you've protected your own skin. Badly done, Jonny, I'm off now to consider this whole proposal, not expecting anything I say to make bugger-all any difference and I'll call you tomorrow.' He gathered up papers and without a further word or gesture, strode out. Got in his car and drove home at speed. Sylvia was in having coffee with her group of ladies.

'Sorry ladies, very sorry, but could you leave us? I've important matters to talk over with Sylvia.' Sylvia could see Barry meant business and would not be swayed. She apologised to them all and said she would call later and rearrange coffee in the next few days.

Barry outlined the meeting to her. She wasn't normally much of a help in his work, apart from appearing at work social functions and joking with the staff. But she was the only person he could talk to.

'Darling, it's not the end of the world. You keep your existing job and car and other benefits; you keep working at the site and with your people; everyone speaks so highly of all you've done to turn it round. Didn't Winston say something like keep calm and bugger on? It might look clearer in a day or two. Talk it over with Jonny.'

'It's a step change, it's not our company, it's their company; it's not our strategy and decisions, it's their strategy and decisions. Within weeks, I'll be told what to do and when, all at a distance with shortfalls criticised and any outperformance all down to their hand on the tiller. I'm not a socialist but the main dosh will go to them and the new shareholders. I'll be paid nicely to keep me quiet.'

'Well that's not quite so bad is it? We've got the mortgage and school fees to pay. You could stay and look around for another job.'

'That's just like my last job. I left there for running and owning a great company with my best friend. What Jonny's done is selfish, unthinking and wrong. I said I'd call him in the morning. When it all happens behind your back, you feel totally worthless.'

'Barry darling, get changed and we'll go down to the pub for a beer and baguette and then see the boys when they come home from school. I'll do what you like this evening and I don't just mean food.'

They did all of that, all of that.

Next morning, feeling calmer and more logical, he phoned Jonny.

'Can I come over to your place and talk this through? See you at eleven.'

The coffee was ready and the lounge straightened out for effectively a business meeting.

'Jonny, I recognise you are the boss in our work relationship but you and I go back a long way. How did you get drawn into this? It's like you've gone all secretive and plotting. Couldn't we have talked about it?'

Jonny was apologetic and apparently caring. He had had no choice. The business was going well, thanks to Barry, but loans were building up and past debts were being chased. He hadn't wanted to bother or disturb Barry with the non-operational side. He had been passing bits of cash and promises around all the chasers and eventually they had stepped in. Neville and Edward were put in as non-execs on their behalf and they and their backers spotted the company's strengths straight away. There was a massive carve-up of debts, loans, shares, board seats, and of course their own companies to grab some of the goodies. He knew in reality he had sold out but he had had no choice.

'So you kept me in the dark, sold the job to me under false pretences, got me to find a way forward and then cannibalised it. You've unilaterally broken up a partnership. Shame on you.'

'Barry, Barry, I kept your job, your salary and bonuses. It's the least I could do.'

'And the most you could do. That's like saying you can keep your Austin Allegro but the rest of the world is driving around in Jags and Beamers. The whole scenario is changed. Sorry, no I'm not sorry, I can't be part of it. Can you at least do your little best and get me the best pay-off you can, including notice, car, shares, bonuses, pensions, the lot, all in one lump sum and pay it by the end of the month? You owe me, you bugger.'

He left with coffee untouched and drove to work and started to tidy up a few loose ends and delegate the in-tray to others. That afternoon, he got a letter with figures in, assuming return of car, for payment at end of the month.

He left the car at work and walked the few miles back. The money came through on the last day of the month, tax deducted. It was less than expected because of bonus assumptions but still a good figure. Full and final settlement. No comeback. No disclosure.

Jonny and Barry were over.

THIRTY-SEVEN

James phoned Ellie.

'I'm in this French town where Molly phoned from. Have you heard anything more?'

'No, have you? What exactly are you going to do?'

'No. I'm going to call the French number and try to meet him. I'm going to look around the station; might go to the police to see if they have been contacted by our Drewett. Keeping my mobile fully charged and on.'

'Same here. Good luck.'

James had come via an early Eurostar with an onward local train from Paris. It was still just morning and he was sitting over some coffee in a square. He phoned the French number. He did not have good French.

'Bonjour, mon ami. Je m'appelle James et je suis un ami de la fille qui téléphone sur le train.'

'Et que?'

'Puis je vous acheter le déjeuner aujourd'hui ou demain?'

'OK. Où êtes-vous?'

'Place Charles de Gaulle à ce moment. Bientot?'

'Oui, dans l'heure, vous restez là.'

That was hard work. James kept the coffee coming; it was good stuff. Eventually a boy in his late teens approached cautiously with a girl. James thought he must look like a Brit.

'Bonjour, James?'

They conversed. He was Francois and this was his girlfriend Belle. James had no difficulty recognising their role was solely as bystanders caught up in Molly's capture. He thanked them profusely for helping Molly and asked them what they wanted for lunch and to drink. They relaxed. This Brit was not dangerous.

With language a struggle, Belle's English was the glue that made the dialogue work. James said he wanted to know everything, literally everything, about the incident with Molly.

He learnt that she was in her walking gear, not particularly smart, no make-up and hair a mess, and at first they thought she was asking for money. It was all about the phone. Francois was sorry he took the phone back off her when he realised she was calling the UK. Belle said she did not notice anybody with her, in fact she seemed to be avoiding everybody. They all got off the train at the terminus here.

James asked where she went but they did not see, nor whether anybody met her. The train had come in to platform 4 which was a branch line in from a remote country area. The line survived because there was no alternative for the rural folk to get up to town. James figured that meant Molly had been held in an isolated, remote part of the country. The veal and frites and beer arrived and conversation dried up.

'Is there anything else, absolutely anything, whether silly or not, that you noticed about Molly? Anything odd or not odd?' They continued eating in silence, evidently thinking.

'She had dirty fingernails,' this from Belle, 'and she kept looking round. You know, I think she was in fairly good shape, like she worked out. She was not tearful or upset. I think she knew what she had to do. She was not a begging woman, she was relaxed she wanted out of any fix she was in.' Belle was warming to this theme. *That's good,* thought James. *She's not damaged, she's escaped, she's trying to get home and get word to us.*

James bought them an ice cream to go and thanked them even more profusely.

'We meet again, yes? With Molly, yes?'

'Mais oui, au revoir, Monsieur James. Merci pour le déjeuner.'

James settled the bill and left for the railway station. He found platform 4 and made a list of all the villages that the trains serviced on that line. He asked some railway staff about the train arriving at around nine thirty last Thursday evening; did they see a girl looking like this photo? A Gallic shrug. He should come back at nine thirty tonight and ask again.

During the rest of the afternoon, he found a B&B and wandered about the town trying to imagine what Molly would do next when she arrived that night. It was a small town and she would probably have blagged her way into sleeping at a rough B&B. He asked at his own B&B where somebody without much money would have stayed. He even went there but they had no recollection of the woman in James's photograph.

Back at the station at nine fifteen, he asked some different railway staff about a girl last Thursday on the next train on platform 4. The train came in and he positioned himself at the barrier holding up his photo of Molly.

'Avez-vous vu cette femme, Jeudi dernier?' he spouted quaintly to every exiting passenger. No response until an older man, definitely in the final quarter of his life, looked more closely.

'Possible. Une jolie fille, mais oui.' He had wondered about asking her if she was all right in a foreign country but a tall young man met her off the train. They went off together quickly. James asked again if he was absolutely sure.

'Mais oui. Absolument. Anglais.'

James asked him for his mobile number in case he needed to get in touch but he only had a landline – which he freely offered. He was Gaston Blanc. He might possibly be a pervy old git but James thought not and that he was telling the truth. A tall man. Sounded familiar from the South Downs. Molly had escaped and been on the run; got on a train; they had worked out where she was going and met her off it. She had been captured again.

He went back to the B&B, put his mobile on the charger and phoned Ellie. It was an hour earlier in the UK so not too late. He recounted his lunch and evening endeavours.

'I'll give it to you James, I never thought you would get anywhere.'

'Well I haven't. We've gone backwards. They've got her again.'

'Mmm. They must want her for something. This is not a casual pick-up nor is it blackmail or ransom territory. We would surely have heard by now.'

'Agreed. I'll report all this to Drewett in the morning and ask him how to pursue this with the French police. How are your mum and dad?'

'They are carrying on as if nothing has happened. They've internalised it. There's no life in this place, they mope around, done another appeal with the local media. I tell them what you're up to and reports from Drewett. Now what about this HELL stuff, shall I tell him about it?'

'My guess, it's childish meanderings. Have another read and think how you would even explain it to Drewett. It doesn't seem to have any relevance to this adventure.'

They chatted on for a few more minutes before signing off. James didn't sleep; Molly grabbed again by the same lout. *They are not going to let her out of their sight a second time.*

THIRTY-EIGHT

The blindfold came off. She was in the loft space of a house. The roof lining went up at a steep angle and there was a single Velux window. It had been made into a room with panelling on the sides and a boarded up floor. It was past first light and they had driven continuously through the night apart from call-of-nature breaks. If they had started around ten, that was probably around eight hours on the road. They hadn't been on the motorway toll roads so maybe at least three hundred miles. Unless they had gone round in circles just to confuse her. No, they would not have wanted to perpetuate the journey any longer than necessary.

'Everything off. You're not having anything other than the clothes you stand up in.'

'I beg your pardon. I'm not a clown or a joke and I'm not stripping for you. Get me a large blanket and I will undress under that and I'd be grateful if you would look the other way after everything you've put me through.'

'Look lady, it's nothing personal, nothing we've not seen before. It's orders. You're not escaping again. Alain, fetch madame a blanket.' Said with heavy sarcasm.

They searched all her clothes and took the cigarette lighter kept hidden in an inner pocket. They threw the clothes to one side and motioned as to go.

'Excuse me. How do I wash, go to the loo, feed, or are you releasing me now?'

The tall man unlocked a side door in the loft to reveal a sink and a lavatory. Another pre-planned hostage place.

'We'll bring you food and drink twice a day until the Boss decides what to do next.'

'Who's the Boss? Do I know him?'

'The Boss is the Boss. We're downstairs all the time so don't think you can get up to your silly tricks again.'

They left. She was tired but it was light so she made a thorough search of her new address. The Velux window was screwed down and all she could make out were the roofs of other nearby houses. It looked more like a residential setting, so a second choice for them to keep her. The isolated farmhouse would naturally have been their first choice. So what was the weak spot with this one? The space was not cramped, extending over the full footprint of the house; the floor boarding and side panelling were not a bodged job, it had the makings of a good-sized bedroom in a normal house if there had been a dormer window and another Velux. The bathroom fittings were properly done; good quality taps; this was not some outhouse for the workers. The entrance was a lift-up hatch in the floor. This was locked on the other side and she had been shoved up the steps, one by one, before they took her blindfold off. She felt and tapped the sloping walls of the inside of the roof for any weakness. And what would she do if she found a way out on to the roof? Fly? She remembered a first flight of stairs so this was a two-storey house with a loft space. She could hear Sherlock saying, 'Watson, this is a two-pipe problem.'

She was examining the bathroom when the loft door went up and a tray pushed up and along. Bread, jam, milk, mug of black coffee. *Civilized,* she thought. *Maybe they have some respect for me, the mutual respect between wrongdoers. I will just have to escape again and then it will be scrambled eggs and smoked salmon.* She smiled to herself and thought of James again. *He will have gone to that town by now and won't have found anything to link me to here.* She devoured the bread and jam and pretended to herself it was the said SE & SS and resumed her investigation of the bathroom. Her experience of substandard flats in London was limited but plumbers always knew how to get at things to fix leaks and washers and suchlike. The boarding at the back of the loo and the sink was more makeshift, more like plywood than the thicker plasterboard or chipboard on the rest of the walls. It sounded more hollow and she could imagine her London plumber ripping it apart in seconds.

If the thinner panelling would detach then perhaps it might show some more roof space without boarding on the floor. Maybe just a few planks laid loosely on the laths, with insulation and ceiling plasterboard underneath. *Take care, old girl, don't get carried away. There's a plan there but it will take muscle (I've got those), no detection (very unlikely), gymnastics (maybe) and then escape.* Her thoughts piled small probability on small probability and even her elementary statistics told her this made the outcome remote.

'But not impossible,' she said out loud. *Think it through. Those boys are not going to come back up here until it's time to move me. The sole contact will be exchange of trays at the loft door.* 'So when there are noises outside, I can keep trying to dismantle the bathroom panelling. I don't need to restore it each time because they're not going to come up here.'

At the next exchange of trays, she said, 'As I'm cooped up here, I will be doing my exercises, bend and stretch, jogging on the spot. If you hear it, it doesn't mean anything and I'll do it in the morning.' They just laughed.

So that's what she did. Every time during the day whenever there were sounds of roadworks or lorries reversing or lawnmowers, she picked and kicked at the bathroom panelling. Even after a few days there was progress; she was on a mission.

THIRTY-NINE

'Mission accomplished, Guv. Target delivered to the house and secure in the loft room. Food twice a day. Strip-searched, with some modesty, and I can guarantee she has only the clothes she stands up in.'

'Good, well done. I'm still thinking through our next step, which might surprise you. That's not the thinking but what the next step is. Might be moving her in a week or two. Check she's OK each day and don't fall for any gimmicks. She's not stupid.'

'OK, Guv. Will do. She's already told us she does her exercises after breakfast so we hear the dance of the elephants every morning.'

'Bye.'

'Bye.'

Pete told Alain they might be here for two weeks.

'Better get the other one over here so we can do three shifts like before. Can you get him? We're here for the long haul and it's so bloody boring.'

FORTY

Drewett had received James's update with mixed feelings. On the one hand, he was obviously delighted that James had made progress with Francois and the old boy recognising Molly; on the other hand, shouldn't it have been him doing the sleuthing? James had asked about contacting the local French police and in the absence of anything from Knutsford, Clive had asked James to hold fire on that at the moment. He went into Knutsford.

'Sir, James Longton has had success in talking to the kids on the train and also found another man who makes that trip regularly and who says he identified Molly Otsworth coming off the train and being met by a male.'

'This girl might have done a runner, you know, to escape the clutches of her young man and her family. Wouldn't be the first time.'

'No sir, but I don't think it's like that. These are all sensible, stable people and Mr Longton thinks Miss Otsworth escaped from being held captive and this male at the station was her captor recapturing her and whisking her off somewhere else.'

'Well, that's just as fanciful, no?'

'No sir. Please may I contact the local French police there and get them to interview James Longton, who I am sure would be delighted to update them and work with them?'

'Yes, I've had clearance for us to do that. Was going to tell you later. Keep it at the factual, local level and no trips. There's no reason for you to go there on some speculative basis and we certainly don't want our French partners coming here. Heaven forbid. Keep me informed and don't make this a diplomatic incident. It's just a missing girl, who we have been relieved to know is still alive.'

Clive brought Mavis up to date. Since their interrupted dinner date, they had built up the makings of some mutual respect for each other. She had shared some of her training experiences with him and that she played badminton down at the leisure centre.

'You've got the go-ahead to call the local French police in. Go for it.'

'If the lingo gets a bit tricky would you help me out with vocab and what they mean in English?'

'Bien entendu, Monsieur, je vous aiderai aujourd'hui et demain et toujours!'

Clive thanked her and felt some reciprocal leg-pulling was needed later. He phoned the French number given and worked out with Mavis's help that they would find the right person to ring back. They interpreted that to mean an English speaker.

'Bonjour, Monsieur Drewett, Pierre Faure here. My English not good but I understand it good. How can we help?'

Clive went through the missing girl, the phone call from his town, the interaction with two students and one of the train passengers. 'The missing girl's partner was in his town and would very much like to see you. Please may I ask him to come in and see you?'

'But of course. Bon. Please ask him to go to the police station and ask for me, Pierre Faure on the second floor, and I will be here this afternoon. Au revoir, Monsieur.' And with that he was gone.

'Are they taking us seriously? That was short and sweet.'

'No worries. James will come over very well. And I think James has a much better insight into what Molly is like than we do.'

Clive phoned James who was delighted to be able to do something with somebody who might have authority to carry it out. Then they both went back to the names and searching on back records. It was tedious and after a further hour, Clive sat up straight.

'They've had Molly O for nearly two months now. No ransom; no blackmail; we know she's alive as of last week; and still they want to recapture her. Why would someone do that? Maybe Knutsford's right. It's obscuring the possibility that she's a girl trying to escape the humdrum life she's in.'

'Clive, no. I'm pretty certain that Molly and James are very devoted to each other. James's reaction, Molly's phone call, the closeness of the sisters, they do not point in that direction. I agree it's strange. What's that philosophical thing, the simplest solution is the most likely – Occam's Razor? We haven't got to the simple solution yet. Simple doesn't mean easy or obvious.'

'No, Miss.' They were all square now. He continued. 'When I think about this case, I keep coming back to why. It's odd; it doesn't fall into a pattern of other cases or like those ones in TV dramas.'

'Life is stranger than fiction.'

'Yes, Miss.' She threw a lever arch file at him. Knutsford put his head round the corner and reminded them that the traffic and bicycle returns for the week were overdue.

FORTY-ONE

Molly was making slow progress. Her farmhouse routine returned. What clothes she had were divided into two halves so she could rinse and let dry and alternate with the other half. Her own personal hygiene was a daily battle but she had convinced her captors that toothpaste and brush, loo rolls and her monthly supplies were not weapons of mass destruction. The tray swapping now included her personal rubbish. Then there were her exercises, making sure that pounding on the floor was well heard downstairs. She jogged, did push ups and pull ups, twisting and turning for a good half hour. Being ready for the great breakout kept her going.

And the bathroom escape route project, now nicknamed BERP, continued. It could be quiet outside for long periods so she had to be patient. When the lorries or delivery trucks came and turned round, she cracked on. For the very first time in her life, she wished some utility would randomly decide to dig the road up outside. Progress was slow. She had removed two panels through which she could see pipes angled for positioning towards the taps. Beyond the pipes was a void, just as she had hoped, with insulation laid down. With two more panels removed, she would be able to reach the insulation and pull it aside. *That's a day's work.*

FORTY-TWO

James arrived at the police station and asked for Pierre Faure. He was directed to the second floor and he walked up, mentally preparing his statement for Monsieur Faure.

Pierre had a natural, cheerful and approachable disposition and he made James feel comfortable straight away.

'Why don't you tell me everything about your young lady and what she has got up to?'

James kept to the essentials, particularly the train, the phone call, meeting Francois and Belle and the voluntary input from Gaston Blanc. Pierre wrote down all the names and numbers. He wanted to know how long Molly had been kept captive.

'I want to work backwards from the train station to where she might have come from. With no possessions or ID, I suspect she could not have been on the run for more than a few days, so that would place her prison say two or three days walk from one of the outlying stations. I can talk to my colleagues in that area for anything strange happening.'

'I agree. Molly would have been single-minded to get away and to a phone. Getting to a train and begging a phone off a passenger are consistent with this. Your English is very good, Monsieur.'

'Merci Monsieur! I once knew a very nice British girl but that is another story. I will talk to this Gaston Blanc to check with your description of the man in the 4x4 and to my colleagues at each station on that line. If you have no other commitments, please would you drop by tomorrow morning?' And with that brusque efficiency, the interview was over and James was back on the street. He made a mental note of how to improve his management of meetings back home.

He called Ellie and told her about the cool confidence he had in Pierre. Ellie then went on to HELL.

'I think we must tell Drewett. It might be absolutely nothing but I keep feeling we are withholding information that could be useful. We must do all we can to get Mols back.'

'Of course, agreed. You tell him in rough terms and that I had an IT geek at work who was able to print it out. It may be nothing. If Clive rings me, I can immediately confirm. But Ellie, have you mentioned it to your dad?'

'How can I do that? I do have secrets from my dad and I bet you do and everyone in the universe. If it's nothing, he'll dismiss it and tell me not to waste police time. If it's something, I don't want to be a part of it, I know I found it in Mols's stuff but it feels very private and I don't want to betray Mols in her absence. And if he's involved in some bizarre way, he'll dismiss it as well and tell me not to waste police time. However, I think Drewett should know.'

'OK, I get it. The printout is in my flat in town, I don't want a police search warrant on the flat so I'll get it to him when I'm back at the ranch. Take care.'

James had nothing to do for the rest of the day so he found a place with red and white check tablecloths, ordered a carafe of wine and made some calls. First Mum and Dad, who were pleased to hear from him. Next Paul at work to thank him again for compassionate leave and for a further extension – granted. Then Steve at the flat for any post or calls or anything.

'Hi James, it's really good to hear you. No mate, nothing at all. Dead boring without you.'

'Wish you were here in a funny sort of way as I'm enjoying the French scene and my bit of amateur sleuthing. We know Molly's alive but she could literally be anywhere. By the way, can you keep my room secure? Don't let anyone from outside wander into my room. Please, mate, could you put all the papers on top of my desk in the bottom left-hand drawer? Nothing incriminating but not anything I'd want to go astray or someone else to read. Thanks, Steve and I'll be back soon.'

'No problem, see you soon.'

He spent most of the rest of the lazy day thinking how he would tell Drewett about HELL.

FORTY-THREE

Molly was really getting somewhere. Two more panels had been detached. The insulation lagging, which she could just about reach, lifted off easily. She piled it up in a corner of the loft room. Her guess proved right, it was thin plasterboard which formed the ceiling underneath and, where a wire for a light fitting went through it, there was daylight. She could see immediately what the next problem was. Unless she was a Houdini, the contortion required to get into the loft void, make some gap in the plasterboard and then squeeze through was beyond her. She had noticed she had lost weight but not enough to squeeze through yet. Maybe in two or three months, she smiled.

So more bathroom panels would have to be forced off, the entry to the loft void made wider, and a strip of plasterboard removed. This last would depend on what was underneath. As it was the end of the loft, maybe it was a spare room or cupboard that was apart from the general domestic life below. She would have to listen, make a slightly bigger hole and watch.

'At least I'm not bored or kicking my heels with nowt to do.' She said this out loud. In case they might have heard below, she started singing a popular song.

At tray swap time, one of them came up the ladder and peered in.

'All OK up here? You sounded jolly earlier.'

'Well I have to while away the hours doing my exercises and washing so I might as well do a sing-along.' She had positioned herself between the loft hatch and the bathroom door. The insulation padding was covered with wet clothes.

'OK luv, as long as you're happy.'

'Ecstatic.'

'Enjoy the apples, they're fresh.'

'Thanks.'

Note to self: keep all the junk to do with BERP in the bathroom so they don't see it.

FORTY-FOUR

'Monsieur James, I have progress for you.'

It was the following morning and James was there early. He was shown straight in.

'Gaston Blanc's description of the tall man is the same as yours. So to go forward, we should assume they are one and the same.' James liked the statistical leap without heavy proof.

'Then I called each of our gendarmes on the train route for anything unusual. There was nothing until this tiny hamlet here.' He had a map and he pointed to a group of houses a little way off the line.

'A farmhouse was badly burned in the night. The owners or the residents there were not keen for intrusion by the fire services or ourselves. Their explanation was that it was some straw catching fire in a barn which had spread. One of their boys was a smoker. It's plausible but in my experience people usually make much more of a, how you say, a song and dance about it.'

'Yes, they would, I follow you.'

'And the student Belle, I was able to talk to her and Francois on the phone, she repeated that Molly had dirty fingernails, yes?'

'Yes, yes, and?'

'I'm going to make, how you say, a leap in the dark here. Monsieur, you are improving my English with this case. Your Molly was able to start a fire and then somehow she scrambled out. Is she that sort of girl?'

'Yes, she's fit and practical and, yes, she always carries an old cigarette lighter with her. Makes a joke about it being better than rubbing two sticks together. How they didn't find it on her, is another matter.'

'I like your Molly, Monsieur James. That all fits together. Now this farmhouse is owned by a British. You know how the British like to buy our isolated run-down properties here. It does so much to improve our countryside and keep our tradesmen busy. Thank you.'

James laughed. He had previously thought of doing the same himself.

'The entente is very cordiale.'

'Let me get some café.'

They discussed what to do next. Pierre would call Drewett and give him the address of the farmhouse and whatever they had on French files on ownership. They would put the farmhouse under low-level watch because one, it was largely burned down and two, it seemed very unlikely that Molly or anybody linked to the capture would return there but agents for the owner might. James took down that detail as well.

'If they've recaptured Molly, as looks likely, they would have to take her somewhere else. Might it not be another house owned by the same person or company?'

'My thoughts exactement. That is a very big task because you are saying search all the property ownership files en France. And ownership could be in a different name, like a wife or a previous wife or a mistress or indeed any made up company name. The link would have to be a British address or company in common and that is easily got around.'

James, with some awareness of IT know-how, could see that this would be a long and arduous task and out of proportion to the case.

'OK, I get that obviously. But maybe a simpler search, for example restricted to the areas that Brits buy in, or just in his name. When he, or she, bought their properties it is unlikely they would have thought of a future crime like this. Brits buy properties for holidays, enjoyment, capital gain, vanity.'

'Mais oui, you know your people well. I'll ask; there is some French interest in this. A crime has been committed here; the insurance company will not pay out till they are satisfied. Yes, yes, I'll ask. Au revoir, Monsieur James.'

Meeting finished as abruptly as the previous one. Noted.

James's work at the moment was done in France, even though he was sure that Molly was still here, a captive in some random house or outbuilding anywhere in France. He had confidence in Pierre though and didn't think the case would lie in an in-tray. Local train to Paris, Eurostar to St Pancras, back at the flat by the evening. Steve had been as good as his word and piled all the HELL output into his bottom left-hand drawer.

He called Ellie to say he was back and would tackle Drewett in the morning, then shouted at Steve, 'Beer and a curry, I'm back.'

They talked long into the night.

FORTY-FIVE

Clive Drewett felt the case was getting active. First, James on the phone to say the French police would call and it would be a Pierre Faure, decent English, to bring him up to date with French matters. James would call Clive later after that about another matter. Second, Pierre Faure called and they had a long chat about the fire, the escape, the train, the students, the old boy, the recapture and how lucky Molly was to have a good man in Monsieur James. He also gave Clive what few details they had of the ownership of the farmhouse.

'It will mean more to you than to us. The company, the names, the British addresses. We are also looking to see if this man and the company have other properties in la France but that is tres, tres long time.' Clive went overboard in his thanks and gratitude, mainly because he had something to go on. They promised to keep in touch and Clive was seeing bistros with red and white tablecloths, boules in the square, a carafe and Mavis sitting opposite. He reprimanded himself to not be such a stupid old romantic.

Nevertheless it was uplifting to recount these developments to and with Mavis. She often had a take on these things.

'Sounds like our Molly is a resourceful girl. She will certainly try to escape again but her captors will be more watchful this time.'

'Agreed. Trouble is she could now be literally anywhere in France.'

'Or the rest of Europe, with Schengen.'

'Let's not get started on Brexit.' He knew her views were at odds with his. 'Would you do the name and company search on the farmhouse property ownership, plus agents, other houses etcetera? And remember that Jones & Jones Bros mix-up the other month.' The Joneses had multiple properties each and jointly and with wives and the same initials, they had tied themselves in knots. 'Keep it simple.'

'Stupid.' Clive reddened at this unaccustomed banter. Some badminton at the leisure centre the previous evening had tested him round the court; it was quick and his reaction time took a while to speed up. Mavis in the bright white gear which set off her colour was lithe and fit; in contrast to his football stuff. The lager afterwards was very welcome and he said he would get the proper kit and play better next time.

'If there is a next time. Am I allowed another go?'

'Of course. Showing early promise. Yes, some new kit would look better otherwise the others I play with will wonder why I've come down in the world. Only joking. I've got chores to do back at the flat so must run. See you first thing and thanks for the game.' She touched his shoulder on the way out. Clive thought, *That's some progress,* and then dwelled on the second phone call from James which he had not yet shared with Mavis. Random writings from years ago while a teenager are not a solid foundation. Girls, and to some extent boys, have mixed emotions about lots of things during those years. Committing this stuff to a floppy disk is unusual, you would normally expect those sort of jottings to be in a fat diary with a clasp on. And holding on to it all those years? Though that could have been an oversight. His own relationship with his father had been formal and strained at the best of times. But Henry Otsworth was delightful with his daughters; you could tell he was proud of them and loved them properly as a father. At its simplest it could be a normal disagreement over a boyfriend, which Molly had got entirely out of proportion, wrote down some silly words and it all blew over within days. At another level, it could be a record of something ghastly that Molly had wanted to set down so as not to forget the surrounding people at that time. He had asked James to send over a copy, with dates, so he could read the originals. He didn't think their own IT support would do any better with an old floppy than this Fraser.

He walked back to his flat. A good day; lots to work at and think about; good exercise and even better social company. Properties and printouts in the morning should yield further progress. And meeting Knutsford.

FORTY-SIX

Two more panels were off now and Molly could squeeze through into the loft void beyond the bathroom. She did this straight after her exercises, pounding the floor so they would imagine her to be resting. She placed her weight on the laths and tried to peer through the slight gap of light around the wiring to the light below. There was no sound so she tried to pick at the edges of the plasterboard. It did indeed crumble but some of the crumbling would fall down and look like dust on the floor. If they looked up, she was discovered. What little she could see appeared to be sheets and blankets. If it were a store cupboard, good! It couldn't be an actual cupboard because there was light and it was a sunny morning. So the next best bet was that these blankets were on shelves, maybe floor-to-ceiling shelves in a back bedroom. From the little she had worked out about the geography of the house, that would be plausible because this loft void was right at the end of a roof or a gable to the house. If she was going to escape through the plasterboard, she would have to break through with her feet and legs, risk making a racket and an uncertain follow-through of being able to get out of the house undetected.

She speculated once more on her captors' thinking. They had not hurt her; they had not required her to make an appeal with demands for money; they had treated her almost with respect given the circumstances, for example fresh apples yesterday. They hurt James but their objective at that time was focused on whisking her away. *They can't want me forever,* she thought, *they must have some plan. After all, they are wasting a lot of time on me instead of their jobs or whatever other crimes they get up to. Should I try to befriend them; try to get on their side?* This seemed unlikely; these boys were acting under orders but surely even the Mr Big, if there was one, would want to move soon. Should she just go with the flow, do what they say and wait for the denouement? To all of these questions, Molly said no. 'I have a bias for action; James and my family would expect me to try to escape – but not to put me in danger. Pushing through the ceiling will be a big step into the unknown but if they haven't hurt me so far, then catching me below would merely be an irritation. I might be holed up more securely afterwards; but on the other hand, I could be running down the road. Yes, I'm going for it.'

But what time of day? The street was not well-lit viewed through her Velux window but the one on night duty might be dozing. It was a long period between tray-swapping at early supper-time through to breakfast. She could not risk daytime because someone would be awake downstairs and they would hear and then see her. It always had to be two in the morning. Other issues were that they had taken her watch previously, her cigarette lighter, her boots and her anorak. The replacements for these last two were flip-flops and a woollen sweater to keep warm. She could pile on all her clothes but 'all' would not make a difference. So lifting some items from a supermarket was pressing. *OK, if it's got to be tonight, get on with it, girl.*

She was chatty with Alain with the tray-swapping at supper-time; she thanked him for the apples, they were lovely. She asked how they all were, were they keeping fit like her and so on. She was overjoyed to hear that there was a football match on TV this evening, so sorry she couldn't watch it with them. Alain laughed; that would be cosy, it's just him tonight. A few more pleasantries and he was gone. Molly guessed this would be as good a time as any. She gobbled up the food and tea and listened at the loft hatch door for sounds. Eventually, after what seemed an age, she could make out cheering and the commentator speaking loudly over the crowd. Alain might not be dozing but the noise of the crowd and his intense concentration on the game would be good enough. She put all her clothes on, gathered everything she could put in pockets and a small bag and squeezed into the loft void.

First, a tentative push down with her feet. The ceiling board cracked and gave a little. She listened; still the crowd. Next a more positive shove and one foot went through. She listened; still the crowd. She peered through the wide gap and could see the pile of sheets and blankets. There must be a window because there was a little light. *This is it,* she reckoned. Both feet shoved down hard on the plasterboard next to the gap. The gap was big enough and she dropped through on to the blankets. She listened; still the crowd. The TV sounded a few rooms and another floor away so it was a safe guess that Alain had heard nothing. She slipped down to the floor and looked through the window. Flowerbed below in a faint light. In a rush, Molly threw all the sheets and blankets out of the window, climbed backwards out of the it, lowered herself as much as she could, clinging onto the ledge with her hands, took a deep breath, letting go and pushing out as hard as she could. It worked like a dream. She almost laughed it was so funny. She got up, ran round to the side wall of the garden, over into next door and out through their front gate on to the road. She ran along back roads, avoiding bright lights and traffic. This was a village, maybe a small town. It was mid-evening and it seemed as if the whole village was watching the football. She needed safety desperately and hesitated to enter either a home or a café/bar. Everybody knows everybody in these small places. If Alain had heard nothing and if he didn't go into the storeroom and if he didn't go outside, she would have a clear run till the breakfast tray swap or when the others came. These 'ifs' were all plausible, which meant that time for once was on her side. But what was she going to do next?

FORTY-SEVEN

James felt more empty than normal back in London. His flatmates had been pleased to see him back and he and Steve had caught up with everything during his first evening back. Steve was sympathetic to James's situation and tried reassurance at every negative put up by James.

In the office, Paul Williams was the same – sympathy and reassurance – but keen for James to get back to proper work. He had further reflected on those two phone calls he had had previously about Molly; even to the lengths of getting Rosemary to check his phone records for unknown calls to his extension at and around the approximate time he remembered. There were about two dozen and over a desk lunch he called each of them back. No go. They were either old client calls he had forgotten about or the numbers no longer existed or he was fobbed off with being told it was a wrong number. The name Julian did not register with any of them.

James's new assignment was outside London and commutable out of Waterloo. Train journeys are thinking time. The new assignment was to project manage moving two work sites into one, a third site, and then maximise the use or sale of the two redundant sites. There were recruitment, relocation and redundancy issues at the people level in addition to the logistics of physically moving operations while having continuity of production and servicing for the customers. It was a challenging brief and he could see that Paul had given him this to take his mind off Molly's disappearance. He did throw himself into the work and working with the joint team drawn from both sites given over to him. He could phone Ellie in the evening.

'I've sent the HELL output to Drewett; I'm not sure he places any value on it; he just said thank you and that would I put a hard copy in the post. He should also have heard from the French police by now.'

'Good, that will reinvigorate him. If you think about it, they've had nothing to work on since, you know, the beginning. I'm still puzzled why they took Mols. Now at least we know it was deliberate, I think we do, we've had no ransom demand or any other type of demand, not that Dad's that loaded or anything. I know this is not a staged way of getting away from family, Mols is not like that. Why have they taken her?'

'If we knew that, we'd know where to look. My line of thinking is that HELL is so unlike Molly that it must have a meaning but that doesn't mean it's connected to this case. Just 'cos two things are out of the ordinary in someone's life, doesn't mean they are connected. Keep at the Dad and Ken thing, but I agree with you, don't tell your M and D.'

'Yep, will do. Good luck in the new job by the way.'

Train journeys are also phoning time. Back at Waterloo, he returned to the flat via Molly's. Bee and Dee were also just in from work and were chatting inevitably over yet another pinot grigio.

'James, lovely to see you. Have a drink.'

'Thanks. Just passing through. I've a little news but have you anything, any strange post or phone calls?' They hadn't and James felt very uncomfortable when they raised the matter of the flat.

'We thought that if, sorry when, Molly comes back, you two guys are going to shack up together. Obviously not here so we wondered about the room. No pressure or anything; no hurry either of course but, you know, as time goes by.'

'Look, at the moment Paul at work is continuing her salary so the rent comes out of that. OK, I understand. If or when work stops Molly's pay, I'll cover the rent and we'll review it from time to time.'

'James, you're lovely and that's fine, thank you. It's not just the rent either, it's the company. For us weirdos, three's company, two is boring.'

'Well don't let any strange men in Molly's room. May I take another look?'

Nothing had changed since the last time and although he shook a few books, no notes or scraps fell out.

'Did Molly ever talk about strange doings with her dad or someone called Ken? It's only clutching at something she said months ago.'

'No, nothing comes to mind. We'll let you know if anything comes back to us. Now bring us up to date. You said you had some news.'

He filled them in on a selection of the French activity, not all of it, then made his excuses and left.

Fraser was waiting at his own flat when he got in.

'Hi buddy, good to see you're back. See you've got the Surrey job. OK?' James recognised that Fraser hadn't come round for a cosy chat.

'Thanks, it's fine, it'll keep me busy for months. What goes?'

'It's that floppy. Something is nagging me. First off, I've found the date that it was written. That might be useful. Second, the computer etiquette is very amateurish, just about the minimum required to save the text. This is not by an IT person or computer specialist, which suggests that Molly wrote it herself with guidance from someone else to get started and do the filenames, etcetera. She would have been a young teenager then and probably, I'm guessing, not accustomed to the filing conventions of that time. No offence, Molly didn't or doesn't seem like that sort of person.'

'You're right there.'

'So someone else helped her. Why would they do that?'

'Dunno. It could have been any friend who was geeky enough to muck about with it and muddle through. There's always one. The act of keeping it seems significant too. I agree it's puzzling but it might be nothing to do with anything. By the way, had a problem at work today about the number of routes across 3x5 rectangular grid between opposite corners. How many?'

'That old chestnut.' Fraser smiled. 'Let's call the 3 direction U for Up and the 5 direction R for Right. That's going from bottom left-hand corner to top right-hand corner. Then if you imagine a string of instructions there are eight of them and three of them must be U and five of them must be R. For example URURRRUR is a unique route across and any route you choose can be expressed in the same unique way. So it's how many ways can you choose three from eight, or five from eight, as they're equivalent. Go on, you can do that.'

Now it was James's turn to smile 'That's fifty-six, and it solves my problem because I said we would need over fifty whatevers. However, back to Molly. Let's assume it's a him. He helped her and she kept the floppy. Either it meant something in her words or it meant something in his words or it was a trial lesson or… what?'

'That's your business; but if you need any more techy stuff, drop round for some scotch anytime. Thanks for the contribution by the way, I did get some decent stuff.'

FORTY-EIGHT

'At last we've got something to work on. Better get on with it then.' Knutsford finished with this implied reprimand and Drewett escaped back to his desk in the open-plan, now opposite Mavis while they were on the case together.

The farmhouse in France was in the name of a Ms Mary Johnson, bought some years ago via agents in East Anglia and her address was shown as c/o the agents. Mavis had tried to track down the agents but they were no longer independent and their business had been absorbed into another firm in Norwich. No member of staff had transferred over and previous records were either in storage or been destroyed 'years ago'. Mavis had put in a police request for the previous papers in store and said she would be back to them in a few days' time. A search on the name and other official records yielded thousands of Mary Johnsons.

'How can we narrow down the numbers; what filters can we put on?' she asked Clive.

'Assuming she's a Brit, then the farmhouse is probably a second home so age and income level but it's not exactly a rifle shot. It could also be through a company. Do you fancy some sleuthing in Norwich? We've got the agent's former name, the dates, the name of the buyer. You might be able to cut through the search better with the files in front of you. You go.'

'On my own? Am I allowed?'

'Of course. You're more than capable. I'll clear that with the Knut and an early train will get you to Norwich in time for a full day at it.'

'Thanks Clive, I agree.'

'What did you make of this computer printout?'

'Bizarre. But I'm going to stick my neck out and say it's connected in some way. It's so weird, as is keeping it. Maybe you could confront the Otsworths with it, including Ellie.'

'And I agree with you. I'll go up there while you're in Norwich. Keep in touch. Now to get these two trips through Knutsford.'

This done, they each phoned through to arrange trains and meeting their targets at the other end. Drewett had had to promise Knutsford that the other day-to-day stuff would be up to date by this evening.

FORTY-NINE

Keeping to the shadows, Molly walked to the opposite end of the village. It was a big village, maybe a small town. There were shops, bars, restaurants and offices. She didn't dare go into any of these even though she knew there would be a phone. The risk of recognition and recapture was just too high. Finally on the outskirts, she found what she was most wanting – a crinkly shed supermarket open till ten. She sidled in, not wanting anyone to see her state of dress. There would be CCTV but she had to risk that any follow-up would be later. There were the typical late evening buyers, either going straight to what they had come in for or just dawdling around aimlessly looking for bargains.

First, shoes and clothing. With no experience of shoplifting, she had to make up how to proceed as she went. Brazen would be good; stroppy Brit with a 'how dare you' attitude would be good; and no labels or packaging would definitely be good. With these attributes well to the fore, she found some plastic shoes, thick socks, a sweater and what she and James called a day bag for walking. *Now how to escape from this supermarket?* she thought. *If I can get away from villains twice, this should be a doddle.* She picked up a wire basket and pretended to do some completely different shopping; cooking ingredients, packets of cereal, picnic plates and sausages. Some rations found their way into her day bag; some dirt in a plant pot happened to scuff her new shoes and the front of her new sweater; even the day bag got covered with spices. Now for it; she ambled back to the entrance, emptied her basket back onto the shelves and with a sigh and a practised Gallic shrug walked confidently into the street. No bells rang and she merged into other shoppers, some arriving just before closing time and others leaving with bags.

By now it was late evening and Molly knew she was at risk from the CCTV in the supermarket and the discovery of her disappearance from the supposedly safe house. Her first thoughts were to carry on walking or find a bus out of town but these would have been aimless routes. She needed to bed down for the night somewhere, eat her food and get sleep and think about tomorrow. She was on the edge of the town where along with the supermarket were some modern light industrial units and deserted utility roads. One of these had ordinary wooden fencing which she climbed over and went in search of shelter round the back. At school, these would have been the bike sheds; but for tonight they were her bedroom – with a couple of workmen's donkey jackets as her duvet. It seemed safe enough; not the sort of place search parties would necessarily search at night and there would be workers arriving in the morning. She tried to sleep and couldn't help herself thinking what a right little trooper she was becoming. Next stop, the SAS.

Sleep was intermittent and as soon as it was light she got ready to leave, before the early staff arrived. She ate some of her food, put the donkey jackets back where they had come from, straightened herself out leaving no trace of her overnight stay and set off cross country and at right angles to the main road.

Back at the safehouse and about half an hour later, Alain took up her tray before the other two came for relief.

'Allo, c'est le petit déjeuner et le café.' Not a sound.

'Allo, allo.' Not a sound.

He climbed into the attic room and saw the destruction.

'Merde! Elle ne peut pas...' He peered through the loft space and saw the damaged ceiling. He went down to the room below, saw the open window and looking down saw all the blankets and sheets spread out on the flower bed beneath.

'Donc, vous êtes une fille intelligente et mechant. Mais vous n'êtes pas sortir avec cette capre.'

He phoned the others who were furious and said they would be round straightaway. She had taken everything she could carry and there were no clues left. They got in the van and drove round all the town's streets, stopping now and again to talk to shopkeepers about a young woman dressed roughly and on foot. This met with some fruity ribald comments about how desperate were they – but they drove on. They even guessed that as she needed food, she would have made for the supermarket, which they did. The previous evening's shift had gone but the lady supervisor did offer to look through the CCTV some time.

'Maintenant, s'il vous plait. C'est important.'

She didn't want to argue with these three who looked somewhat intent on getting their way. She agreed but it would be five or ten minutes until her deputy came to work. They waited impatiently for all of seven minutes and then followed her upstairs to the office. She asked them the approximate time slot and scrolled back to late evening.

'C'est elle.' Alain recognised her from her gait and from what she had worn yesterday.

'OK, suivez la femme.'

By criss-crossing various cameras, they worked out all that Molly had done, what she had taken, what she was wearing and how she had sloped off undetected. The supervisor had noted what Molly had taken in preparation for reporting minor theft from her stores. Fortunately for the three men, she did not think the amount involved was sufficient to bother the police. Unfortunately for them, the cameras were not able to show her ongoing direction of travel. So they drove round all the roads on that side of town, again stopping to ask various contacts they knew in shops, houses, even offices.

'Elle a disparu. Merdre. Quoi?'

If she had followed her route away from last time, she would be heading for the railway station. But here, it was even deeper into la France profonde and the nearest station far too far for her to reach on foot. They worked out that she would walk, hitch or bus it away. She didn't know where she was so which direction? Sadly they would have to tell the Boss about their and his loss.

Molly, meanwhile, was making great strides in both senses. The fields were open, with gates, and walkable. When she had to cross a road, she listened carefully for any sound of a car, which could be her captors driving round. When silent, which it usually was, she crossed and kept going at right angles to the road. It was late autumn now and the brisk walk kept her warm. The shoes were sturdy enough for the purpose. The next need was food and drink.

FIFTY

It was ten o'clock by the time Mavis arrived at Norwich station. She had cleared that she did not have to travel in uniform as long as she had her ID with her. The train journey had given her time to prepare for her first trip out unaccompanied by a colleague or even Clive. She smiled to herself. Clive was a good man and maybe a little sweet on her. He was attentive, thoughtful and rather old-fashioned for his age. She had been used to the rough and tumble of homelife with four siblings, two older, two younger. Then college and the decision to go into the police; and then the equally rough and tumble of police training and her first brief posting in South London. The posting to Sussex had come up by chance as she was immediately available to fill the abrupt departure of the person she was replacing. The work was very different from South London where it was always a struggle to hold the line with many unrelated things happening every day. Down here, you had time to work at a case without too much interruption. This missing person case had definitely grabbed her, and Clive's, attention and the minimal clues so far pointed to something rather deeper and maybe darker than stolen bikes, car crashes and shoplifting.

One or more had deliberately taken Molly, whisked her over to France to avoid detection, was content to hold her without any hint of ransom or, apparently, harm. She had escaped and been recaptured and Mavis guessed that Molly would try to escape again, however securely she was held. Molly would by now have worked out that this was not about ransom or murder but something else. The absence of contact by the captors to James or the family was mystifying as well as intriguing.

The Estate Agent's offices were a ten-minute walk from the station. She introduced herself at reception and was taken to see a Renee Evans in a back room. She was a lady of an uncertain age but instantly recognisable as businesslike, dependable and probably never made a mistake. Mavis kicked off.

'Renee, may I call you Renee? You've had our request about this farmhouse purchase in France some years ago. All the French can find about it is that the sale was to a Miss Mary Johnson care of Messrs Overton and Smythe, now handled by yourselves. What have you found?'

Mavis found herself being called Miss Smith.

'Thank you Miss Smith, yes, we took over Overtons some years back and I was given the job of handling any queries relating back to them. These are now few and far between, no more than half a dozen a year, and the main problem is locating the files. They were handed over to ourselves in a state as one might deliver potatoes. We'll go down together shortly but was there anything else?'

'Not really until I've seen the file. Do you, I mean this firm, have any ongoing connection with this Mary Johnson? Please, do call me Mavis.'

'We used to be Robertson & Robertson when I joined quite a few years ago but the new owners wanted their change of name. Dear old Mr Robertson was such a gentleman, gave a lovely Christmas party every year, now it's a glass of shiraz and a mince pie if you're lucky. Sorry I do go on. Would you like a coffee to take down with us, er, Mavis?'

They went down to the basement clutching two plastic cups of instant decaf, Renee leading the way and putting the lights on as she went.

'This section from here to here,' she spread her arms widely, 'is all Overtons. Over the years, I have tried to put them in date order, so I am afraid the order is still approximate. Shall we try in the area of the date you have first and then fan out?'

They did that and for the next two hours there were only the sounds of sneezing from the dust, the emission of, 'Oh dear, oh dear,' from the despairing Renee and a strict police method from Mavis, who didn't want to do any part of this search twice.

'I normally get a salad and fresh juice from you-know-who over the road. Would that suit, er, Mavis?'

'Ideal, please may I join you? We need some fresh air back in our lungs and brains.'

An hour later, with more of the decaf they were back downstairs. Another hour later, they were about two-thirds through when Renee unaccustomedly screamed.

'Yes! Look. Johnson France; it must be the one. Wow!'

'Well done, Renee. Shall we just look at the files on either side to see if there is more than one?' There wasn't and brandishing the file as though it was an Olympic gold medal for file searching, they marched back upstairs to Renee's office.

The contents were meagre. There were the farmhouse particulars, drawn up in the style of the day. An appointment to view arranged with a local French agent, local solicitors handling the sale for the French farmer selling up, a local surveyor's report, a London solicitor acting for Ms Johnson and finally confirmation of money transfer between solicitors. It did not appear to be a contentious transaction and neither side raised objections. Renee thought that unusual. Mavis took copies of the complete file and the correspondence, which amounted to no more than ten sheets, put it in her briefcase, thanked Renee warmly and requested that if Ms Johnson emerged anywhere else in their files or in fresh correspondence or even on the phone, to get in touch with her straightaway.

Mavis got something slightly less healthy to eat on the train back. A good opportunity to digest the file for the follow-up questions from Clive and the Knut. When she was on the train she phoned Clive.

'Hi, it's Mavis. A good day and worth the visit. Got the property file which is a bit thin but some follow-up names to go on. How are you getting on?'

'Great Mavis, good to hear. I'm walking in treacle here, sensitive stuff which I don't want to talk about on the mobile. I'm going to have to have another go at them in the morning, it's a long story, so I'll be back tomorrow afternoon. You do what follow-up seems safe in the morning and we'll catch up with each other either late tomorrow or the next morning. Safe journey.'

'You too. And don't go overindulging in that real ale you go on about.'

'As if. It's local research. Bye.'

He sounded as though he had made some progress, if sticky. She settled down to absorb the brief file. There were bank details, a London solicitor, and not much else. The farm particulars showed details of the house and Mavis could make out the possibilities of an upstairs room being used for keeping Molly. Liverpool Street, crossed London, train down to Sussex and got in at nine. A stir fry then bed.

FIFTY-ONE

Clive Drewett also used the train out of Paddington to go over his thoughts on the printout of the floppy disk. At a coffee stall at the station he had ordered a long black only to be told he meant an Americano. He was not persuaded and resolved to keep up his mission on the better description. Was it really down to the American campaign in Italy in WW2? There were other forces from the English-speaking world there too. Mavis had agreed with him on this which pleased him. They were good mates and clearly, he thought, enjoyed each other's company. But he was the senior, she was female and the zeitgeist was no, not in the workplace. He knew nothing about her or her family so it would be a long game. Chat in the office, coffee and snatched lunches, and the occasional drink after work. And badminton, of course. He also occasionally played in a football team, swam in the police session at the local pool or went for a jog.

By now he was past Reading and he steered his thoughts back to the case. The printout from the floppy disk was input years ago and then kept in what appeared to be in a safe place. Why? The anger came straight off the page, as did her remorse in the accompanying file, which presumably was later with help from the same person. He wondered how he was going to initiate a discussion on this as he was aware that James had said he had only told Ellie. *I'll be meeting all of them together at first, then it will have to be separate individual discussions.* He had forgotten to arrange for a local colleague to join him; so he phoned the local station on his mobile and apologised for not getting through before. Could they spare someone this afternoon? No they couldn't but Neil Poole would be available first thing tomorrow. It would seem that the local boys had lowered the priority on the missing girl. Clive accepted this offer, having allowed for it with a few essential stopover things in his bag. Soften them up this afternoon when they are all together and then individual sessions in the morning.

His taxi drew up at the wide gate to the Otsworth's gravel drive. Mr Otsworth was striding down the drive to meet him as he left his taxi. *Must have been looking out for me,* Clive thought.

'Good morning, Officer. Good to see you again. Sorry you had to drag out here, but it was your idea.'

'Good morning, sir; no problem. I thought it was about time we brought each other up to date, face to face as it were.'

'Come in, come in. My wife and daughter are waiting with some fresh coffee and we hope you've some good news for us. The girls are missing Molly dreadfully and though the news that's she's still alive is what we want to hear, nobody knows where she is. Black or white?'

Clive indicated black and he could tell it was the real stuff this time. He was shown into the same drawing room and Annabel and Ellie were sitting in the same chairs as last time. He thought Ellie looked subdued and pale.

'Good morning Mrs Otsworth and Miss Ellie. Thank you for seeing me at short notice and I'll plunge straight in. You know about the phone call from France; well we have located where it was made from and our French colleagues have been very helpful. Indeed our contact there, Pierre, seems to have warmed to this case, probably helped along with how he got on with James Longton. He even remarked that Molly – may I call her Molly? – had a good man in James. By working backwards from the station and the few people Molly spoke to and some other evidence, we have traced the farmhouse where Molly was first held. Crudely, it appears she set fire to the place when no-one was there, escaped through the farmhouse and ran off into the fields. Then she made her way to a nearby station and got on a train. We have to remember she had no money and she must, somehow, have got hold of food and drink. We have a witness who saw her recaptured at the station and driven off. I have to say, first, that she is a remarkably plucky young woman and, second, she would appear to have some use to whoever wants her. She is bound to want to escape again and I am sure she will try – but we are reassured that whoever 'they' are, do not want to harm her. Does any of this make sense to you?'

'Molly was, is, always a resourceful girl.' Annabel, surprisingly, started first. 'Nothing was, is, ever a problem or a difficulty. I can hear her saying: We are where we are. This is what we do next. It's just a hiccup in the way. It's nearly two months now and I so worry about her health and strength. But she is a survivor.'

'My wife is absolutely right and I agree with all of that. She has already proved that as soon as she is able, she wants to get to a phone to call us or James. Our mobiles and landlines are never unattended. Why won't she go straight to the police?'

'We don't know. Being on her own in a foreign country with limited language skills, perhaps makes her unsure or even defensive. They could argue that she is an arsonist and try a counter claim. Miss Ellie, what is your take on what your mum and dad have said?'

'Totally agree. And please call me Ellie. She's a get up and go girl, nothing too risky mind, she would always think through whether a plan would work or not. On your police point, I agree she would be wary of just waltzing into a police station with a flimsy story.'

'OK, thanks. That does at least give us some hope for her next, let's hope, final escape. My colleague from our station is as we speak getting details of the UK ownership of this farmhouse, when it was bought and how. That should give us a direct line to someone here.'

It was all rather formal and polite; and going nowhere. Clive continued while they were all there about any connections to France, second homes, family holidays, any strange messages or phone calls hanging up. Nothing at all. Annabel got up and said she would make a sandwich or two over some more coffee. While she was in the kitchen, Clive lopped in. 'How has your relationship been with your daughter over the years?'

Henry was not startled but showed some surprise at the direction the questioning was taking. Ellie looked down at her shoes.

'Er, pretty normal I would say, in my limited experience.' He smiled at Ellie who smiled back thinly. 'British standard upbringing, local school, family holidays, extended family over at Christmas or Easter, then weekly boarding over the way and then to university. Got a social degree and after working locally for a few years announced she was off to London. Then James and you know the rest.'

'Sorry, I didn't mean a CV. How did, sorry do, she and you get on personally, family-wise, socially, time together doing crosswords or even having cross words?'

'Is this some sort of psychological assessment of my suitability as a parent? I'm a regular guy and I think I've been a good dad to her and to you Ellie, yes?'

'Of course Dad, no problem at all. Mols has had her moments with each of us at separate times but nothing that has any relevance to a normal family relationship. I'm sure Mr Drewett, you had your moments with your mum and dad.'

'Um, yes, I suppose I did. I suppose what I'm trying to... ' He was interrupted with Annabel bringing in everything she had promised, and more. Clive was glad to have a pause to think. '...Trying to get at, is there anything from the past that might have lingered on to the present? You know how some people bear grudges or hold a running sore about something or somebody.' He shut up and took a tuna and cucumber sandwich and a napkin. There was a small hiatus. Ellie, being aware, kept silent and carried on eating.

'Henry, darling, you've always been so loving to Molly. I feared she was your favourite and you took Ellie for granted. I know that's not true of course, we are so lucky to be blessed with two such lovely daughters.' Annabel gushed on and Clive didn't know where to look. He poured himself another coffee, letting them talk on.

'Yes, thank you my darling, but I think Mr Drewett wants something solid to go on, like in those crime dramas when there's a lightbulb moment. There isn't one. I love both my daughters equally, thank you, and apart from those teenage moments about money or clothes or homework or what time to be back home by, there is absolutely nothing out of the ordinary or to report to the police. Sorry. And, of course, I will do anything to get Molly back.' Henry's prickliness temporarily got the better of him.

It was only mid-afternoon but Clive felt it was time to withdraw and come back with 'Ken and Dad' tomorrow with each of them individually.

'Thank you, you've all been most helpful in what must be very trying circumstances for you all. I would like something formal from you each and rather than ask you all to come to the local station, I'll come back briefly in the morning with a colleague. Don't worry, no-one's accusing you of anything, in fact the opposite, we are wholly sympathetic to Molly's disappearance and want her safe return as soon as we can. Thank you for lunch, Mrs Otsworth, I'll see myself out.'

He went to the front door closely followed by Henry.

'Sorry if I sounded a bit heavy back there but this disappearance is getting to us all. Is there anything you know that you're not telling us?'

'Not at all, sir, our job is to keep you informed of progress and help get her back. I'll see you in the morning. Shall we say nine?'

He ordered a taxi on his phone and started walking. Air would be good. He thought that the conversation had been a bit of an act. The politeness, the courtesy, felt a bit false. Their elder daughter was missing for God's sake, where was the agony, the sadness? Why weren't they screaming at him for the police to get off their arses and do something?

The taxi came and took him to the local police station, got there and asked to see the Chief.

'So you're young Drewett. Knutsford and I go back a few years, which is a bit of a coincidence. How is the old charmer?'

'Very well, sir, and following this case closely. He's keeping an eye on me to get a result. Anything local cropped up on the missing girl?'

'No, lad. She's not lived round these parts for a few years and the appeal and the press coverage were blank and gone rather stale. The Otsworths are a pillar of the community round here, well-liked as well. I see Henry at some functions and we exchange pleasantries. I've commiserated with him over the daughter.'

'At first sight, he doesn't seem emotionally wrecked over the missing, Molly. Is there anything here about him or family going way back? We've looked nationally but come up with nothing.'

'You've watched too much TV. No, nothing and I've been here a long time. He was part of the local establishment before I arrived. Always helpful.' Clive didn't think it was time to raise his personal views on the establishment and corruption.

'Thank you, sir, most helpful. I'm borrowing Neil Poole tomorrow morning back at theirs just to take a formal record of our discussions. Better than wheeling them in here and giving all the wrong impression.'

'If you have to, lad, if you have to. A copy for you and a copy for Poole to put on file here. Otsworth will no doubt tell me what you've got up to; I'm seeing him at the Club next week. Regards to Knutsford.'

Clive had booked in at the same Three Horseshoes as last time and he ordered the same food and ale as before. He chatted to some locals over a pint at the bar, listened to what they said, dropped the Otsworths into the conversation and got nothing except how sad it was about that daughter.

The next morning he picked up Poole and continued on by taxi to the Otsworths'. Mrs Otsworth had got the same necessary coffee brewed for them. They positioned themselves in a side room and saw each of the three in turn.

Annabel had nothing to say. That didn't mean she said nothing. Happily married, happy family, everything she had ever wished for in life, so happy and now so sad to the point of despairing. It was all very human and believable and touching.

Ellie came in next, sheepishly.

'James told me about the floppy disk and the printout in confidence and I haven't breathed a word. You will respect that confidentiality, won't you? I don't like keeping secrets from Mum and Dad, well not secrets of that sort anyway.'

'That's fine Miss Otsworth, sorry, Ellie. Your mother has no recollection of a Ken or of any, er, uncomfortableness between Molly and your father. What have you thought about it since James first raised it?'

She had nothing. There were Kens around in school and at uni but not a boyfriend. Molly and Ellie shared all their boyfriend experiences and Ellie would know. Yes, there had been blazing rows in the family but they were always over the sort of things her dad had said yesterday.

Henry came in, feeling both awkward and annoyed at this unnecessary police formality.

'I think I said all there is to say on our family and my daughter's disappearance yesterday. I'll summarise it again and then perhaps I can sign and get on with my business.'

'Quite so, sir, that's fine. Does the name Ken mean anything to you? It could be a boy, a man, any age, and any connection with Miss Molly?' Henry sat back and thought for a few minutes. He appeared to be going through his mental card index.

'No, clearly like any name in common use I've met a few Kens and Kenneths. Nothing of significance and nothing in connection with Molly.'

'Did you ever have words, or an argument, with Molly about a Ken or a Kenneth?' Clive lent forward intently.

'Not that I can recall. Where did this come from?'

'Just a name that we can't place popped up in our searches. We have no direct connection with it having anything to do with this case or the kidnapping or the subsequent silence. Could I ask you to dwell on it, sir, maybe even search your own records and files, and if anything, and I do mean literally anything, would you please get in touch? There is the smallest chance that it might help our getting Molly back.'

'Yes, of course, it's the very least I can and should do. Leave it with me.'

Poole had typed up all the statements. He plugged in his little portable printer and printed them out. He asked each of the family to sign, finding Annabel and Ellie in the kitchen. They offered him a slice of fresh lemon drizzle. And a piece for Mr Drewett. There was some small talk waiting for the taxi, which delivered Drewett to the train station and Poole to the police station.

FIFTY-TWO

Julian Foxley was puzzled. He leant back in his standard Civil Service chair, gazed out at the London skyline and steepled his fingers. He was called 'Q' in the Department, not officially but as a nickname for the Bondish tricks and thoughts he had and was expected to have. His speciality was recruitment, specialist recruitment, for suitable operatives to work effectively in the intelligence underworld. Effective to him meant not only able to operate nimbly and discreetly in the field but also directly, bluntly and equally discreetly in the corridors of power. Departments were minefields and the ability to handle departmental crossfire deftly he considered was a skill up there with dealing with intelligence in foreign territory. He notionally reported to Colonel 'Buffy' Smithson-Smythe who was recognised on MoD charts but this line was largely procedural. As long as Q kept producing the goods, he was left to get on with it. He had a small staff of a dozen whose main focus was to help him identify and keep track of potential candidates.

Julian had approached MNO personally when she was at college. She had come to his attention through the combination of her interventions in lectures, her antics in amateur dramatics and a subtle captaincy of the ladies hockey team. They had had a brief chat. She had been quite straightforward with him.

'Sounds interesting but might not be. I want to do other things but please keep in touch. Don't take that as a fob-off.'

The fact that she had recognised that a simple cliché could have been misinterpreted stayed in his mind. He had wished her well. Back at the office, he had opened up an 'MNO' file and handed it to Percy with the request to follow this one.

Percy did and many years later Julian was able to call up an old contact, Paul Williams, joint chief of a services company on the City fringes, who had also done some background work for him.

'Paul, it's been a long time. Let's do lunch sometime. I just wanted to touch base with you about one of your new recruits. You know her as Molly, to us she's MNO.'

'You were always into acronyms, abbreviations, abstractions and apercus. Yes, Molly has been with us for some time now. It's curious that you've rung. I'm sensing a connection and then you're going to ask for something.'

'Alliterations should start with a consonant but, well done, you know me so well. I've become aware that your Molly has gone AWOL – ho ho – through a French contact. What more do you know?'

'She was drugged and smuggled over to France and kept captive for several weeks; then she escaped but her captors picked her up again off a train. They drove off with her. We can only assume she will try to escape again but undoubtedly they will try harder to keep her this time. I have not heard from James, that's JKL to you, whether the family have received any ransom demand or indeed any communication at all.'

'Yes, that squares with our updates. Anything suggestive on her file?'

'Nothing at all. If you find anything through, er, your channels, would you let me or the family know? They are quite distraught. If you lot are behind this, you would let me know?'

'As much as I can, yes. Lunch sometime, your club or mine?'

'You're the one with clubs, Julian. Give me a call.'

Julian closed his eyes. That had all happened a few days ago when Percy had burst into his office to relate that Pierre had phoned about the missing girl and asked if it was one of our exploits or were they real criminals? Julian had smiled and said to Percy to leave it with him. It did look horribly like one of our games with the obvious difference that they always told the employer in advance, once the employer was on-side. *Someone out there is playing our game. Who might that be?* He was fairly confident it wasn't another government department; it didn't smell like a European government activity either; companies don't indulge in that sort of thing nowadays, if they ever did. *We have to follow this one up, not only as a further test of MNO's capabilities but also to find what joker is behind this.*

He called Percy in and told him that this was now an active case and that Percy was on it.

FIFTY-THREE

Molly Nanette Otsworth was getting weary. The briskness of her walking kept her warm and the strange combination of her clothing was fine for this purpose. It was clear what to do now, keep walking across fields, cross roads cautiously and always proceed at right angles to roads. But to what end? It was OK for phase one of stage one of part one but as a Plan it somewhat lacked an objective. And she was hungry and thirsty. By midday, she reckoned she had covered over eight miles from her last prison and had no designs on being taken to her third prison. She needed a base camp to restore her strength, find a phone and get a train or bus to an airport. Maybe a village person needing work for lodging? It would be a risk by exposing her existence to her captors but risk was her middle name by now. At the next vantage point she looked out over the great empty expanse of French farming and countryside. She was looking for a village or some settlement roughly in the direction she was heading. There were some wisps of smoke coming from below her field of vision in the middle distance. So setting out for there as an immediate objective she again took to the fields and went in a semicircle towards this little bit of civilization.

It was a farming village with a few small houses clustered around a tiny square with a boulangerie and a café, both shut. Two houses had washing lines up filled with small clothes. Child minding? One had an old guy struggling to saw wood in a side shed. Housekeeper? Clattering sounds emerging from the back of the café. Washer-upper? This last was far too exposed to the public and gossip. The old guy might be a raving sex maniac. Help with the toddlers looked better, very back room and no exposure as the no doubt loving mum and dad would front up everything. Gingerly, she sidled round the side of the house and knocked on the back door.

'Bonjour, bonjour?' There was no reply and, as the back door was ajar, she went into what was a primitive kitchen area, highly reminiscent of some of the student flats she had been in and gladly departed from. There were sounds of labouring and crying upstairs; she went to the foot of the stairs and repeated her salutations. A woman appeared at the top of the stairs, hardly dressed from getting out of bed this morning and sounding stressed.

'Quoi? Qui êtes vous? Que voulez vous?'

'Moi, je m'appelle Molly. Puis je vous aider avec les enfants?'

'Venez ici. Occupez vous Georges pendant cinq minutes s'il vous plait.' And she thrust a two-year-old into her arms and pointed to a chair. Molly's child-minding days were in the future but she remembered doing some baby-sitting locally about fifteen years ago. Engagement was the key word. She talked and joked at him, pointed to things and photos, juggled him up and down, found a piece of bread to shove in his mouth and then a child's mug with some water in. Georges appeared to find most of this acceptable and gurgled and smiled at her. Meanwhile the French woman was wrestling with a younger child, more like a baby, doing washing and wiping and dealing with nappies before and after use. This baby was evidently Francoise.

The five minutes turned into nearly an hour and Molly was pointed to go downstairs while Francoise was fed. When she came downstairs, she made sign language that baby was asleep and put the kettle on.

'Merci, Molly. Moi Catherine. Je m'appelle Kat par tout le monde. Merci avec Georges. Thé ou café?' Kat had coffee so Molly did too. Molly asked if she spoke English.

'Non, non, un peu. Why are you here?'

'Je suis tres, tres fatiguée. I'm lost. Si je vous aide avec Georges et la nettoyage, puis je rester ici pour quelques jours, s'il vous plait? Rien d'argent.' Kat thought she meant she had no money and wanted some; Molly eventually convinced her she had no money and didn't want any. Kat would be more than kind to let her rest up, help with the house and the children and move on in a few days. She tried to stress that she wanted to get home to Angleterre but was left feeling that Kat thought she was a pikey and others would be turning up tomorrow.

Kat's young man was a merchant seaman and help for a few days would be very welcome. She was equally wary of parading Molly in the village as a hired home help. People talk. So: sleep on the sofa; do all the cooking and cleaning; look after one of them while she attended to the other; and they would share a bottle of wine each evening. They had a deal and each of them thought they had got the better of the other. Molly didn't quite know how to get over to Kat that she didn't want to be found and was happy to stay in the house all the time. She hadn't seen a phone yet but there was sure to be one if not just to phone her matelot.

The next three days flew by. Molly aimed to get the house clean from top to bottom and cook some decent food. The best treat of all was the hot bath. Heaven on Earth. She kept one eye all the time on the outside, observing passing traffic and the people walking by. It was very quiet. Nor did she appear outside herself or to the neighbours. Kat was entirely happy with this because with their earnings being offshore she did not want to attract any bureaucratic attention about unpaid labour or live-in staff. While most people seemed to be able to treat bureaucracy with abandon, there was always the risk of severe application and her children scarred for life. In the evenings after the children were put to bed, they put the telly on, ate what Molly had cooked with Kat murmuring approval and sank a bottle of local white or red. Not great but very acceptable. They laughed and joked in pidgin English and French and enjoyed each other's company. Kat did not make any mention of Molly going or staying.

The next morning while Kat was out shopping at a pop-up market in the square, Molly hunted for the phone. She searched the living room and Kat's bedroom. There was no wire to the house for a landline but there must be a mobile and a charger. She found nothing; in the evening Molly thought she better come out with it.

'Kat, puis je téléphone mon ami, s'il vous plait?'

'Ah ma cherie, non, mais mon mari utilise le téléphone de Monsieur Bertrand à son retour.' She waved an arm in the direction of a house over the road. Gradually Molly worked out from her that her landline had been cut off when the bills weren't paid and she didn't have a mobile. She could phone her husband from Monsieur Bertrand's house and he made a call to Monsieur Bertrand first to say please get Kat and then phone again ten minutes later. Only very exceptionally did this Monsieur Bertrand allow Kat to make other calls. Molly sensed this needed careful handling either to get to use Monsieur Bertrand's phone or for Kat to do it on her behalf. It had to be one or the other.

'Puis je parle a Monsieur Bertrand pour le téléphone?' Kat shook her head.

Molly wrote out James's number in full with the +44 together with the simple message: 'Hello James, I am friend of Molly, Molly is here, she is safe, come to village St Jean des Ponts, ask for Kat.' Kat read this over to Molly many times in English and in French until Molly was confident there were no mistakes. Kat did not know Monsieur Bertrand's telephone number and clearly did not want any call back. Molly was building up a picture of a somewhat brooding, grumpy and intolerant man.

Kat did not want Molly to go yet but it was clear that this James would be coming to fetch her. She was now a party to Molly's departure but neither did she want to be a party to harbouring Molly who may or may not have been wholly truthful with her. Reluctantly, she agreed to make the phone call when she felt Monsieur Bertrand would be in the right frame of mind to let her. He normally settled down after breakfast in his back room to read the paper and do any paperwork. Unfortunately this back room was where the phone was and he was always there pretending not to listen.

The time was now. Molly made Kat read the message over to her one last time and then Kat left. Molly watched her go over the road and knock on the door. After a distinct pause, the door opened and she could see a tall dark man with a beard, probably newly retired and living alone. They chatted on the doorstep for a while and eventually she was let in and the door closed behind them.

'Merci, Monsieur Bertrand, merci. C'est un court message a mon ami à Londres. Je serai tres rapide, merci.'

Kat dialled the long number, it was answered straightaway.

'Hello, James Longton.'

'Hello James, I am friend of Molly, Molly is here, she is safe, come to village St Jean des Ponts, ask for Kat.'

'What? Great. Where are you? Can you put Molly on? What is your number?'

'Excuse moi, c'est tout, au revoir, à bientôt.' And Kat put the receiver down.

'Merci, Monsieur Bertrand, merci, au revoir.' And with undisguised relief she slipped out of the room and out of the house over to her own house. Molly was all over her.

'Did James answer?'

'Oui.'

'Did you read it out OK?'

'Oui.'

'What did he say?' Kat gave her version of James's four questions as best she could and said he sounded a very nice boy.

Molly put the kettle on to make them both coffee and something for Georges. There was no choice now, she had to stay there and wait for James or someone to come. Mobilisation of trains or flights and then cars would mean at least two days and those hours would pass so slowly.

Over the road, Monsieur Bertrand picked up his phone and made a call.

FIFTY-FOUR

'Guv, there's no easy way to say this, she's escaped.'

'You plonkers. What the hell's going on? Three strong men can't contain a slip of a girl. You shift your arses and find her, soonest.'

'It was the day before yesterday and after last time we thought we'd soon get her back as there's nowhere round here for her to go. We've done the roads and shops and even seen her on CCTV at the supermarket, where she nicked some stuff by the way.'

'She's got more oomph than you lot put together; and why didn't you tell me earlier? Push off and find her. You're a fucking disgrace.'

Pete put the phone down and wondered what to do next. They had combed everywhere after the supermarket sighting but short of doing a house-to-house search what else could they do? There were no trains or buses within range and he reckoned Molly would not be into hitching a lift. So she must be hiding up somewhere, lying very low and scrounging for food and shelter. All they could do is ask around without drawing too much attention to themselves about a strange English woman wearing strange clothes.

FIFTY-FIVE

Clive and Mavis compared notes on the morning they were both back. Mavis had checked out the conveyancing solicitors and the bank which made the money transfers. The bank confirmed that there had been an account in the name of Mary Johnson but it had been closed shortly after the funds had been sent to a French account. Her address was c/o the solicitors. The solicitors' business had been merged into a larger firm of solicitors. This larger firm had closed all the files from the merged business and if there were any further business with those clients, new files would have been opened. They did not have a Mary Johnson as a current client. The previous files were in deep storage as it was 'years ago'. Mavis reminded them that this file was needed as a matter of urgency in connection with a current criminal case. They promised to come back 'shortly' when the storage location was found.

Clive's debrief was even briefer. They had to agree that they were no further forward other than adding to the thickness of files.

James came through on the phone. He was a torrent.

'I've had this call, from someone in France, Molly's there and is safe and OK, somewhere called St Jean des Ponts, I'm going, are you coming? Shall I call Faure or is that your job? We need to get moving, I'm booking a Eurostar and then another train out of Paris, it looks like there are at least eight St Jean des Ponts, how shall we cover them?' He stopped for breath and Clive got in next.

'That's good, sir, but can we take this one step at a time. Half an hour won't make any difference. First up, when did this call come through?' Clive had put the phone on speaker and Mavis pressed record.

James then went through the call second by second. It was a French lady ringing who had little grasp of English; it was rushed but he felt sure she was reading a prepared line dictated by Molly; it was short, to the point and probably said all that Molly knew about her situation. She had clearly escaped again as this was not a ransom call or anything sinister. She was holed up somewhere and she knew that someone or other would come to find her. Clive asked James where he thought all these St Jean des Ponts were.

'There's three in the middle roughly, two along the Seine, two along the Loire and one along the Rhone.'

'Well that's a tour of France. There's no point you going to seven wrong ones James, there may be others too small to mention. We'll check your phone records first for a call from France at that time and we'll check with Faure for calls from those eight locations to your UK number at that time. Please let's do that first before we lose you in the wrong part of France. If I can get Faure now, and he's available, he might be able to narrow this one down more quickly than you can get to St Pancras.'

James had to agree. 'Yes, you're right of course. But please get back to me as soon as you've found it.'

'We will, James, we will. Right, let's crack on.'

Mavis and Clive were relieved. At last, something real to go on.

'It could have been a hoax call, you know. But I don't think so. Press coverage has died away so it's not in the public eye at the minute. Anyway, can you do the incoming French call to James's phone and I'll try Faure.'

Faure was not available but a message had been left for him and a text sent to him to call Drewett, UK, as there had been an important development. By the time he did phone back, two hours later, Mavis had heard back from James's phone company about an incoming sixteen-second telephone call from France at the time James said. It checked out, but number withheld. As it was cross border, the phone company could not know the specific number.

'Bonjour Monsieur Drewett, it is a pleasure to speak to you again. How may I help?'

Drewett gave a police version of James's statement and then said it was from a French number which had been withheld.

'Bon. There are many St Jean des Ponts but we can try each area for a phone call to the UK at that time. We may be able to access the number but even if not the chance of more than one call to the UK from those areas at that specific time must be tiny. Leave it with me. Au revoir, mon ami.'

FIFTY-SIX

James had phoned the Otsworths' house to tell them the good news. They wanted every breath and syllable of the call. James said that they were convinced it was not a hoax call and the police were treating it as real and trying to trace where the call was from. Annabel was overcome that Molly was alive. Even Henry betrayed some emotion. Ellie was up to going.

'James, when you go, I'm coming with you. I'll come up to town now and stay in Molly's room and link up with you re transport.'

'Are you sure?'

'Yep. Mum and Dad will man the phones here, you and I will have mobiles, she needs both of us there.' That was the plan then. It might be tomorrow before they knew which part of France, then there was getting there, and bound to be in a remote area like the farmhouse had been.

Ellie called Bee and Dee and gave them her version of the news; no problems with them and she would be there later.

James awaited news from police. He gave Paul a ring at work. Thrilled.

FIFTY-SEVEN

'Alain?'

'Oui.'

'C'est Bertrand.'

'Oui?'

Bertrand said he knew where the missing English woman was and it wasn't here. If it was important for them to know where she was, then it had to be worth something. Did they have a figure in mind? Because he did. Bertrand suggested they got back to him soon because birds can fly.

Alain was with Pete who was wondering who this call was from.

'Who is this Bertrand? We should go and do him over.'

'Non. He has his own boys. He lives in little St Jean des Ponts and has his fingers in most pies. One of his contacts will have seen this girl tramping somewhere. He will want the money. How much?'

'Sod all he's getting from us. Let's go over there and try and get him on his own. The Boss would expect nothing less.'

They piled into the van and drove to St Jean des Ponts, went up to Bertrand's front door and banged on it. They made such a racket that Molly looked out of the window and saw her captors. Index finger to mouth, she crept down low and motioned to Kat that she would hide upstairs and she was not to let them over there in here.

Bertrand had seen who was outside and immediately made a local call. Two healthy-looking farm workers miraculously appeared from next door and confronted the three of them. Two metres is taller and bigger than six feet.

Alain had to translate threats and commands from one group to the other. Pete and his two mates gesticulated and swore violently.

'You'll be hearing from us you… faggot.' And they slunk back into the van and made off.

Pete reported all this in a phone call to the Boss.

'Sorry Guv, there was no way we was going to get the better of them. Thought I'd bounce it off you first before we go back.'

'No worries. Give me that phone number and I'll give him an ultimatum. He wants cash and we want the girl. There's a deal there.'

He finished the call and keyed in the French number; it was answered on the second ring.

'Bertrand.'

'It's Alain's boss here and this is going to be in English, OK?' It was an instruction rather than a question. 'I hear you've been messing with my boys when they were very civil with you. You know where the girl is so why don't you say so and stop friggin' about.'

'Whoever you are, whatever your name is, and thank you for being so rude. I am in business and I have information which is valuable to you so it has a price. You sound like someone who recognises business situations. In language you might understand, a brown envelope filled with notes – euros or sterling or dollars, is fine. Say, enough to pay my living expenses for the next month. Do we have a deal? If it doesn't feel the right thickness, my associates will no doubt urge me not to accept your initial kind offer.'

'I hope you live frugally, squire, but a brown envelope stuffed with notes is what you'll get and only in exchange for the exact info of where this woman is. Understood?'

'Perfectly. Goodbye, Monsieur Boss.' Both slammed each phone down.

He did not want to be held up by some petty fogging deal and four weeks' grocery bills with a bit extra for wine was a drop in the ocean. He called Pete back.

'OK, I've done a deal; it's a brown envelope stuffed with notes. Hand over only when you've got the precise info of where this girl is. You know that debit card I gave you? Well go to the nearest ATM and get the max out allowed on the card. It's OK, I've set a limit on it, and put it all in a brown envelope. Make it look thick, OK? You three get paid on completion of the French project so don't dip into it; we can't risk not getting the girl.'

'Understood, Guv. We'll go down to the town in the morning, get the dosh and do the business by the end of the morning. Will confirm.' Both ended the call without farewell formalities. Pete was on edge and frayed. He had not slipped up on any previous project with the Boss and he needed this to go well to restore his reputation. They went into the café and ordered three beers.

FIFTY-EIGHT

Pierre Faure was also getting a little frayed though his professionalism did not allow it to show. There were eight St Jean des Ponts that he could find and there were multiple phone companies in each of the areas. It was slow work, bureaucratic, and painstakingly explaining his identity and authority in this matter with each of them. As a police force, it was no problem to get through to each company but then his request, more accurately his instruction, got stretched out down the line and he was not prepared to let them get away with vague promises to ring him back.

Eventually, and into early evening, he got his result. A brief +44 call made to the UK number at the time Drewett had said. The phone company wanted more authority to give out the undisclosed number but the confirmation of the telephone area in which there was only one St Jean des Ponts was sufficient for Faure. He looked it up and it was a tiny hamlet, just a few houses, a shop and a café, and disappointingly deux cent kilometres away. The local police had minimal out-of-hours staffing and phone calls went through to regional headquarters. Frustratingly, Faure realised he couldn't do this by himself with say two colleagues; it would have to be concluded by the local police there. He left a very full message for them, leaving his number, which would be on all night, and asked if they would get on the case first thing in the morning. Before calling Drewett, he put in a call to Julian, or at least the number Julian had given him to leave messages on. It went straight to voicemail and Pierre left a brief message giving the update and the timing and the place. He didn't have a codename – he was merely PF.

He phoned Drewett who sounded out of breath and in a place with an echo. In truth, he was enjoying an energetic badminton evening with Mavis and two of her badminton friends. They had a full exchange and debrief which included saying that there was no point in him or any UK team coming over. The local French police should be able to finish this off in the morning.

'James will want to come and when I tell him and the family after this call, he will be on the first Eurostar out of London in the morning.'

'Of course, I think so. It will take him all tomorrow to get to Paris, cross Paris, and get out to St Jean des Ponts. If, and it is an if, it is all concluded tomorrow morning, there will be a nice reunion. Very happy. Tell him to report to the local police station. Au revoir, it's late.' Drewett thought Faure was an old romantic and very touching it was too. He was not even close, not a good word, to any romantic meeting with Mavis who was bashing the shuttlecock all over the court. He called a timeout and took Mavis to one side.

'They've found the right St Jean des Ponts. It's miles away. Deepest France. They hope to spring her early tomorrow morning. We have to sit and wait. Shall we leave the other two to it while I phone James and the family?' Clive got through to James on the second ring and brought him up to date.

'Right. Ellie has come up to London so we will somehow get on the first Eurostar out of St Pancras in the morning and find our way down there. It will be early afternoon at the very earliest but thanks for the info and we'll get moving.'

James phoned Ellie and then Mr and Mrs Otsworth. All were very happy for James and Ellie to go first thing in the morning. All mobiles fully charged and all promised to keep in contact.

FIFTY-NINE

Molly was now in a fix. She had watched the confrontation over the road from the edge of an upstairs window. She had to assume that Bertrand knew she was there and local gossip or know-how had connected Bertrand with her captors. They must have put word out about a strange missing English girl; it could be made to sound worthy. Then why did the two farm workers turn up followed by a muscular stand-off? Surely they would be back, that was guaranteed. But that had to be balanced against James, and therefore the police, knowing where she was in this tiny village. If she stayed, her captors would come and find her first. If she ran off, the police would not know where she was. She tried to discuss this with Kat. After a mixed-language interchange, Kat finally understood this dilemma. Her own safety was at risk too, because if Molly fled, her captors would bear down on Kat until she would have to tell them where Molly had gone.

Bertrand would eventually tell her captors that the missing girl was over the road at Kat's house. Fact. If Molly stayed, she was gambling on the police coming to St Jean des Ponts first. Possible, maybe probable, but not a risk she wanted to take. She had to go and Kat must not know where or in what direction. She hugged Kat and Georges and kissed Francoise in her cot. She put food and drink in her rucksack, swapped some clothes with Kat's wardrobe suitable for the chilly nights out. Then she slipped out of the back door over the back wall into the big field at the back. She had told Kat not to look which way she went and Molly did not look back either. It was dark but still early evening. There was time perhaps to skirt the village and find a late bus or even hitch a lift. Desperate times called for desperate measures.

There was a farm at the other end of the village and she circled back to it. A farmer or a farm worker, not one of Bertrand's gang, appeared to be setting off after work in a small car.

'Monsieur, Monsieur, puis je venir avec vous à la prochain ville ou village?'

'You're OK, Molly. Hop in, luv.' A beaming British smile. She smiled back, heaved her rucksack off her back, climbed in with it and off they drove.

SIXTY

The following morning three things happened at the same time.

James and Ellie met at St Pancras for the first Eurostar to Paris.

Hortense and Henri arrived at their police station to hear long messages on the office phone and the phone ringing from a Pierre Faure.

And slightly later, Pete and his two mates drove into their local town to try to find an ATM.

SIXTY-ONE

Ellie had got to Bee and Dee's the previous evening and spoke to James.

'James, I've arrived and packed ready to go in the morning. Tickets OK?'

'Hi Ellie. Er, a bit of a bureaucratic hassle which I can tell you about on the train but yes, two tickets to the nearest town, changing in Paris, and arriving just after midday. I didn't get return tickets because of how Molly would be coming back, but if I quote a reference number, I had some vague reassurance that they would treat the journey back as a return on ours. Anyway, moving on. See you at St Pancras 6.15 in the morning.'

Which he did. Both admitted to a restless night but were obviously excited about the likely outcome of the day to come. They had coffee and croissants, 'to get in the mood' James said, then queued up in the departure area until released about twenty minutes before departure. James had secured tickets with a breakfast thrown in. Over their second breakfast, James outlined what the day might be like.

'We'll get to the local town about 1.30 and then I suggest we phone Faure for an update, then take a taxi to St Jean des Ponts – all dependent on their finding Molly. We have to assume they will. No doubt there will be police procedures and debriefing; but I'm hoping we can all stay at the best hotel in town to celebrate. Phone round everybody and plan the journey back.' Always logistics with James.

'Yes, it's a plan but actually we don't know what we'll be facing there. Better be flexible in our thinking.'

'Sure, of course, you're saying I'm being too optimistic. I just have to be positive about getting Molly back.'

They chatted away until they were drawing into Gare du Nord. Then the RER across Paris to their next mainline station where they stocked up with generously filled baguettes for lunch later. Their train was a TGV with limited stops and ninety minutes later they were stepping off it at precisely 1.30. James called Faure.

'Bonjour Monsieur James, welcome to France again. Molly's case is now with Hortense Alphonse near where you are now.' He rattled off her number and wished them well. James phoned Hortense.

'Bonjour Madame Alphonse, je suis James Longton avec la soeur de Molly. Comment vous portez vous?'

'Bonjour, Monsieur mais pas maintenant. Restez ou vous êtes et je vous telephonerai plus tard. Bonjour.' And the lady Hortense was off.

James told Ellie she was very brisk and to the point but they had to stay here and await developments. *At least we're here and I hope all is well.*

'Prepare for plan B, James.'

SIXTY-TWO

Hortense Alphonse was old-school. Everything by the book. Her training and considerable experience had taught her that it was always for the best. This message from a Pierre Faure, deux cent kilometres away, was odd. Why had they not been briefed before? Where was the paperwork and the evidence? Henri was younger and more flexible. He led her through it. There was this missing British woman, who had by now been on the run for two months, and who had been able to phone to say where she was and it just happened to be on their patch. It could have been anywhere but it was here. They were in the privileged position of being able to find her, release her from her captors and by the way claim some good local credit with the press, their superiors and with it a chance of a move or a promotion earlier than would otherwise be the case with chasing stolen cars, bikes and pigs, speeding offences and marital distress.

'Bon, bon. OK, je comprend bien entendu.' She instructed him to speak with Faure first and then they would go off to St Jean des Ponts and meet up with the area gendarme. Henri got the full gist of the case from Faure and was excited to be following up this wonder woman who had escaped from capture.

They drove into St Jean des Ponts and parked in the tiny square. There seemed to be quite a commotion between two houses on opposite sides of the road.

SIXTY-THREE

Pete drove the van straight up to the ATM at one of the banks in the main street of the town. It was later than he would have liked but the beer and then wine last evening had led to a late night. He prodded the other two to get up, brewed some coffee and kept yelling at them to get a fucking move on. Eventually he had goaded them into the van with the final ultimatum that 'we have a job to do and get paid'.

Pete took out the Boss's card entrusted to him and shoved it in the slit. A screen full of French screamed at him.

'Oi, Alain, gettez vous ici.' Pete had clearly done some French before leaving school. Alain took over but Pete did not want him to see any figures so as soon as the numbers screen came up he shoved Alain away. Pete clicked down to the Autres box and input the figure the Boss had given him. Sure enough, the Euro notes were revealed in a thick wad. Pete retrieved the card and put the notes straight into a brown envelope, sealed it up and buried it in his anorak pocket.

They drove directly to St Jean des Ponts coming to a sliding gravel stop right in front of Bertrand's door. Pete banged heavily on it. After what seemed like minutes, Bertrand came to the door and miraculously at the same time the same two farm workers strolled up alongside. Pete started the dialogue.

'We've got an envelope for you as agreed. Where's the girl? And can you tell these two monkeys to get back to making hay or whatever they do?'

'Let me count the money. I spoke with your superior and we agreed a figure. I need to see you have not taken anything for yourselves.'

'You can have the money when you tell us where the girl is. We don't want to go through every house in the village but we will if we have to.'

'I understand. Open the envelope and spread out the notes so I can count them. Then, you pass me the envelope with the notes in and I will point to the house. Then you go. Clear off, understand?'

'We'll go when we feel like it, thanking you all the same. OK.' Pete took the brown envelope out of anorak pocket, fanned out the notes in order of rising value so Bertrand could peer at them.

'I suppose that will have to do. Let me grasp one end of the envelope then when I indicate the house, you let go, otherwise my dear friends here will help you.' He even smiled.

Pete thought none of them wanted a fight so he put the envelope roughly halfway between himself and Bertrand, grasping it very tightly and waited for Bertrand's gesture. He nodded at the house directly opposite. Pete gave him a quizzical look as if to say 'are you sure?' and Bertrand repeated his nod.

Pete let go and with the other two went over to Kat's house. He noticed that the two farm workers went into Bertrand's house and the door was firmly shut.

Pete was not going to do any formalities. He tried the side door and it opened and they all marched in.

'OK, game's up. Where's the Molly girl? Do I have to search everywhere? Save yourself and us some time. Come out right now.'

There were domestic sounds from upstairs where Kat had just finished feeding Francoise and settling her down for her next morning nap. She could hear these foreign sounds and she picked up Georges and went downstairs.

'Where's the Molly girl? Come on, don't hang about.' Kat understood the one word, 'Molly'.

'Molly va. Molly n'est pas ici. Ne comprend pas.' And she did sign language to mean 'she went, I know not where'.

'Search the house from top to bottom, boys, and next door both sides.' They did and found nobody. By now both Georges and Francoise were crying and Kat was urging them to go and leave her and her family alone.

Pete squeezed Kat's arm, not in a friendly way. 'When did Molly go?'

'Hier ou la veille. Je ne comprends pas. Allez, allez, s'il vous plait.'

Pete could see this was just a simple rural cottage with a single mum struggling to get by. Molly must have offered to help her and this poor woman was glad to give her shelter in return.

'Back to Bertrand's.' The three of them crossed the road and Pete banged on the door. The three of them opened the door and Pete held out his hand as if for a gift.

'Wrong, wrong. No Molly. You're giving us the run around. Money back right now, Monsieur Bertrand.'

'The contract has been fulfilled; I've done my part. If you can't find her, that's your problem. Maybe she has gone for a little walk.'

'And where might that be to, sunshine? We've no Molly and you've got the money. The contract is null and void.'

'She was there when I spoke with your superior and we agreed terms. I cannot be held responsible for the actions of a young woman. Goodbye.' Bertrand tried to shut the door but Pete was ahead of him, putting his foot in it – in more ways than one. The farm workers emerged from behind the door and onto the street. They started to pull them off and push them towards the van. Their wrestling had moved to the middle of the road when the police car drew up with three officers inside. They all stood up separately and acted as though nothing had happened.

Charles, the area gendarme, knew the two farm workers and Bertrand slightly from past indiscretions though he had never connected them together.

'Voila, Que ce que c'est?' Bertrand stepped up and assumed command. He said it was nothing, just a little disagreement over some bad language that did not happily translate. With his bilingual skills he had sorted it all out and the men were just apologising that they didn't mean it and they will all be going to the café later when it is open for some beer.

Charles did not think this gathering looked like a mutual love-in of apologies. And it might be connected with Molly. This time the articulate young Henri stepped up.

'We are looking for an English woman by the name of Molly. Have you seen her or heard of her round these parts?'

All six of them gaped open mouthed with a bewildering sense of astonishment. How could this backwoods policeman know about Molly?

'Non, pas du tout.'

'Mais non.'

'Non, certainement.'

'No mate.'

This rapid agreement was in sharp contrast with the apparent disagreements of a few moments ago. Henri persisted.

'Thank you, gentlemen, for confirming you do. Now boys, where is she?'

'You heard what my colleague said, how you say, spit it out.' Hortense was thinking she should be in charge of this whole situation.

Bertrand was thinking maybe the police could lead this rabble to Molly and so protect his brown envelope from further attacks.

'We did hear some gossip, of course there may be nothing in it, that a visitor might have been staying over the road.' And he inclined his head in the direction of Kat's house.

'Everyone stays here and one of us will go to speak with that house.' Henri, leaving his superior Hortense in charge with Charles, went over to Kat's house. He returned in a few minutes.

'Yes, an English woman stayed with Madame Kat for a few days but left some time yesterday. She did not leave a note or say where she was going. In fact she just got up and went and Madame Kat could not say what time she left.' In fact Kat had told Henri a lot more besides but this group in the road did not need to know that.

'OK, break up, you lot. If you are going to, how you say, kiss and make up, then off you all go to the café and we'll take your details and statements there.' Bertrand motioned to go back inside his house; Charles followed him inside and took down his statement. Hortense told Henri to follow the five of them down to the café, buy them some coffee and take down their statements. She herself went to Kat's house.

Kat repeated what she had told Henri, that Molly, she confirmed her name, was a young English woman who had been held captive twice by this gang and escaped twice. Kat said she found Molly a heroine. Resourceful, kind, considerate, lovely with her two children and therefore she believed everything she had told her. Molly had seen the gang turn up opposite the previous day, when some strong words and threats were available for all to hear. Molly had worked out that Kat's phone call had been traced to the house opposite and the gang would be back again. So reluctantly, because she had also worked out that the police and her boyfriend would turn up soon nevertheless she thought the gang would be back here first because they were more local. For Kat's protection, Molly did not say when and where she was going and Kat reckoned she didn't know either but had to get away. Hortense was sympathetic to Kat and, because of her straightforwardness and openness, was inclined to think her honest. Hortense took down further particulars of dates and their talk and the note Kat had read out on the phone; then she left to join the group at the café.

At this time, James phoned. Hortense told him to stay in town and she would phone him back. It was a developing situation and that was the picture she wanted him to have.

Henri had finished with the two farm workers in short order. They were Bertrand's muscle and workers. Their account of both meetings with the gang tallied and they had no insight to what was happening. They finished their coffee and were glad to get away. Charles rejoined. Hortense decided to separate the three of them on separate tables, as there were no other customers, and get an account of what these three were doing in France and where they were from. Hortense told Henri and Charles to keep to this and see how the Molly mission emerged, without mentioning Molly at first. She ordered more coffee and for the next half hour, there was a gentle buzz of three conversations.

With no actual crime being evident or reported locally, the police could not detain the gang. Hortense made sure she had got all their personal details, their UK addresses, why they were visiting France, where they were staying in France, what their movements had been, whether they had received instructions from anyone else and so on. She required them to present their passports to her police station in the morning and had kept an open mind whether then to just retain their passports or detain them for further questioning. The gang was dismissed and they drove off in the van.

The three police compared notes and statements. The gang said they shared a house in a nearby town and were merely a group of lads doing odd jobbing wherever work took them. The work they each described was consistent – builder's mates, shifting old furniture to the dump, clearing up rubble, delivering anything and so on. This all seemed plausible. They would visit the house unannounced later. Reference to 'the English woman' or 'Molly' produced blank expressions all round. Never heard of her; who are you talking about; we had heard that Bertrand had got some work for us to help his workers. And so on.

SIXTY-FOUR

Hortense phoned Faure for a complete debrief, including ownership of the second house, but effectively told him that because all the action had shifted here, she would be running the show now. Reluctantly, Faure passed on Drewett's number as the UK contact and wished her well. He had wanted to conclude this case himself. He phoned Drewett who was out and had a pleasant chat and flirt with Mavis, whose French was impressive. He also left a message on Julian's number.

Hortense phoned James back and gave him an overview. It looked like the police and the gang had converged on St Jean des Ponts at roughly the same time earlier this morning. There had been a dispute with the tip-off about which house Molly had been held but Molly, in any case had fled yesterday, probably late afternoon after she had seen the gang in the village looking for her. There was no evidence that the gang had either captured her or even found her. A local source had sheltered and hidden her for a few days. She appeared safe and in good health and optimistic. She must be nearby.

'What shall we, that's Molly's sister and me, do? What can we do?'

Hortense said she would formulate a search based on likely scenarios and a local appeal on radio and TV. James and Ellie should be part of that and they could show pictures of Molly. They should present themselves at the station first thing in the morning.

James did not like what he had heard and was far from relaxed about the proposed action. Why not now? He decided to hire a car and go to St Jean des Ponts for himself and talk to this Kat. Ellie agreed.

'We've got to do something.'

Kat was slaving over housework and children when they knocked on the door. James introduced themselves with difficulty though Kat recognised something of Molly in Ellie's face. They cuddled the two children and let Kat talk away. She really did not have any idea where Molly was going or would go; she had no clue. James asked how had Molly been in herself and felt better for it on Kat's reassurances. The three days here had restored Molly to normal food and sleep and she was in good shape setting off. James left some euros under a jug on a sideboard and they left. They drove around for the rest of the day while it was light and then back to their hotel.

SIXTY-FIVE

Hortense and Henri easily found the house where the gang said they lived. Alain was cooking some stew in the kitchen when they barged in. Protestations about search warrants were wafted aside as it was not their house. They found the loft and Molly's escape route. There were even some sheets left on the flowerbed uncollected. The ceiling tiles had been replaced roughly and it all looked very recent. Molly's damage in the loft room had been left untouched.

Hortense decided that she would detain them all for questioning when they reported in with passports tomorrow. She reminded Alain about the passports. He grunted. He knew that Pete was out somewhere private phoning the Boss and was guaranteed not be in a good mood when he came back.

The next morning, everyone turned up at the police station. When the gang turned up, they were shown into separate rooms, cautioned and questioned. Each, separately and unanimously, said holding the Molly woman was just a silly prank; that it had got a little bit out of hand; no-one was hurt and they had looked after her well.

'We didn't know who she was, no, never seen her before, seemed like a well brought-up kid and maybe we could have taken some dosh out of her bank account but she had nothing on her. We were just playing for time. No harm done, Guv.'

Hortense and Henri recognised a sieve with holes in it and gently but firmly persisted all day.

They took a break mid-morning to do the radio and TV appeal with James and Ellie. This came over very well; both filled up sincerely and naturally; and the interpreter did her level best to portray their feelings as well as the meagre facts. A recent photo of Molly would be shown on TV that evening, and repeated every few days, and on posters in the town and the villages surrounding St Jean des Ponts. Any information or possible sightings was to be reported to this police station or a dedicated telephone number.

The questioning continued throughout the day. They stuck doggedly to their story, denying any involvement with the owner of the two houses. They had merely rented them, in cash, for a few weeks odd-jobbing in various villages. Hortense kept her feelings to herself but she was inwardly seething. There had to be more to this story than just a casual capture of a young woman. It did not appear to be sexual and open questions to each one to the effect that were either of the other two involved with her met a complete blank. They admitted chatting to Molly and Alain was relatively voluble about the football conversation before he remembered that was the evening he slipped up.

Hortense thought a night at the station might make them think this game was a bit more serious. Pete insisted on a phone call and put it through to the Boss. The number was one of the emergency anonymous mobile numbers the Boss had given him before they left. Its only trace would be to a phone shop in London for a cash sale.

'Guv, the frogs are keeping us in for the night in the hope we say more tomorrow. We are sticking to the plan and although I don't think they believe a word of it, they have nothing on us apart from holding her without her say-so. Without the girl, there is nothing as even they acknowledge she has escaped from us as well as her family. Providing we get our freedom, we can find her before they do.'

'You're all silly buggers. Brewery, piss-up, organise, can't. It's now a three-cornered hunt – you lot, the boyfriend and sister, and the police. You better win this one and hole her up somewhere while I work out what to do next. It's getting hot round there and it might be clever to ship her over back to the UK where there are more secret house possibilities. You find her and get a ferry back to the UK. Any port will do. I'll find a local solicitor to be there in the morning.' He clicked off without formality and Pete was left in no doubt about the rows that lay ahead.

James and Ellie had left the police station straight after the interview and media appeal. They were in an emotional state and did not say much until yet more coffee in the square. Ellie started.

'I know Molly's mind inside out, and so do you by now. I totally understand that she had to take off but what will she do next? I mean, it's getting to be a habit, this escaping and swanning off into countryside. I hope she's not getting deluded.'

'No. Think about it. Everything she has done has been a logical next step. If you are captured, you attempt to escape and luckily for her, and us, successfully so. She has found food and shelter and a friend in Kat. Furthermore, she has avoided further capture by seeing them and being ahead of them. She has phoned twice and she must be desperate to phone again whenever she can get hold of a phone. She left the afternoon of the day before yesterday. It's not long and I'm very hopeful of a phone call soon.'

'And I'm supposed to be the cool logical one. By the way, I thought you, and perhaps me, were superb on that appeal. Anyone seeing or hearing it would have been especially moved. If anyone knows of or sees Molly, they will report it.'

'Thanks, you were great. Let's keep our phones charged and drive a complete circular tour around St Jean des Ponts. Might also go to train and bus stations, just for something to do. Agreed?' They left to drive around and have a late lunch in one of those calendar picture French villages en route. They had to live.

SIXTY-SIX

Clive and Mavis were deep into properties. Faure's debrief to Mavis had gone down well to which she added to Clive, 'He's got a twinkle in his eye, that one. Bet the girls in his office keep their distance.' Clive ignored this. The French case had moved on to Hortense and Henri miles away, near Molly's last sighting. They had pinned down the property where Molly had been held, together with limited ownership details.

It had also been purchased by a Mary Johnson c/o a different firm of solicitors, and via different agents from Robertson & Robertson and their successors. It was a few years before the farmhouse, so Ms Johnson had progressed from a modest house on the edge of a village up to a farmhouse out in the country. Clive asked Mavis to follow these up just like for the farmhouse.

This time the agents and the solicitors still existed. The agents were not helpful.

'If it was a foreign purchase, we would have dealt through the French agents. And it was ages ago. We've kept nothing from that time and any papers would have gone to the solicitors or the French agents or to the buyer. Sorry.' And rung off. Mavis recognised 'nothing to do with us, Guv.' Maybe follow up later.

The solicitors pretended to be more helpful. They would find the papers and report back in a day or two.

'We do keep literally everything so you will understand we will have to search through a forest of papers.' Mavis had this fantasy in her mind of a forest being turned into wood into paper and then back into a forest. Follow up in two days.

'Why would someone want to keep property transactions hidden?' Clive initiated.

''We don't know that. Could be totally legit. Look at our old records, imagine the questioning the other way round.'

'Fair point. But this is the second. What's that quote about once is a misfortune, twice looks like carelessness?'

'Importance of Being Earnest. Seen it?'

'Long time ago. It gets repeated; must watch it again sometime. But what if this Ms Johnson is deliberately concealing her identity and her purchases? If we do a search on Ms Mary Johnson on all the accessible national files, we might easily get ten thousand.'

'And the rest; and the name changes and immigration and emigration. She could be living on Costa Whatsit, in another of her properties.'

'Quite. We need an address or a bank account or a pension or something, anything. Shall we do badminton tonight, yes?'

'Sorry, got a sore ankle after a twist the other evening, when you were away, and I don't want to risk it too soon. I'm cooking something native, which would be nice to share with someone. Want to come to mine for a plateful?'

'Is that OK with you?' Clive thought he could settle for 'someone'.

'Course, we can speculate on this case. You've got the Knut in the morning so you need to be up to date; 7.30, bring a bottle, gone by 10, OK?'

SIXTY-SEVEN

Molly had gratefully accepted the lift just to get away from the village. It was a big surprise he was a Brit.

'Who are you? You're not connected to the gang, are you?'

'No I'm not, Molly.'

'What! How do you know my name? Who are you?'

'Relax, it's OK. I'm Percy by the way, and vaguely connected to the authorities back home. My boss knows your boss and we've been kept in touch with your emerging developments over the last few weeks. Quite a journey, if you don't mind me saying. You're going to come to a safe house this evening and then we're inserting you back into the field so that it appears you have been found by the French police and your friends. We're all rooting for you.' He said this with a big smile as though it was all a big joke.

'Well that's just fine for your parlour games but yours truly here is pretty fed up with being on the run. Why can't you just take me to the local police and my friends and we all meet up? And bang up the gang before they escape your clutches.'

'All very understandable, Miss, but I'm not supposed to be here, not supposed to be picking you up like this and not supposed to have anything to do with your release from capture. Here we are.' And he turned up a narrow farm track that in a few hundred metres revealed a typically French rural cottage, complete with a fire, a housekeeper and the smells of something nourishing.

'Can you prove this? Have you got any ID? Do I believe a word of what you've said?'

'Here you are.' And he produced a London season ticket, a well-known loyalty card, membership cards to a small amateur dramatics society and to a golf club.

'OK, I believe you,' was all she needed to say. He opened a bottle of wine and put it near the fire.

'Why don't you go to your room and freshen up, plenty of hot water, then come down to dinner with Therese and me? I fill you in some more and outline tomorrow's activities.'

She was glad of that and even more so to find some wearable clothes hanging in a large rustic wardrobe. She took her time if only to compose where she was, and not just geographically. James and probably Ellie would be somewhere round here; the gang must still be wandering around unless they had been picked up by the police; and she had to assume the police would have been able to identify where her phone call from Bertrand's was. She was nearly safe but not yet. Nor did she like the sound of being 'inserted back into the field'. That's what happened on day one. Feeling much refreshed, she went downstairs and was handed a glass of wine by Percy who directed her to a large and deep sofa.

'You're probably feeling somewhat confused but don't be. We've got it all planned out. When we knew where you were, I flew out to a little military airfield near here and picked up this car. I've been driving round St Jean des Ponts unobtrusively ever since. I observed the stand-off outside the two houses and with a bit of scouting was able to see you emerge from the back of the house and get a rough idea of the direction you were taking. Fortunately, after circling the village you got back to the road and we met up there.'

'Why? What is all this? Are you in competition with the police? Why this cloak-and-dagger approach?'

Therese came out of the kitchen holding a large soup tureen.

'Let's eat and talk, yes?'

Therese had set out a pretty table with napkins and glasses. Molly recognised civilization the first time for a very long time. It was all very welcome. Percy continued.

'You may not remember meeting Julian at college. You had been selected as a strong possible and he invited you to join the service. Your answer impressed him, effectively you said maybe later. So we've followed your career with interest. And it's been very interesting lately. What happened to you was just the sort of training exercise we would have put you through, perhaps without the drugs and manhandling James, and we keenly want to know who is behind this. Is it a similar organisation like us, possibly commercial, or is it more sinister?'

'That's easy. It's sinister and they are criminals and they need catching.' Therese added further ladles of soup and handed round fresh soda bread. Delicious. Percy continued.

'You're probably right and you are not in any danger from them anymore. We still want to know who's behind this. There are camp sites round here and I've found a party moving from one to the next tomorrow. They are the sort to give lifts to people, especially a woman on her own. You'll be positioned to hitch a lift from them in the morning. It's what we call normal field operations.'

'I suppose I should say thank you. What if the gang turn up and nab me?'

'They won't, trust me. There's some stew to come; they don't call it stew here but it is.'

They brought Therese into the conversation in halting English and French. She had been widowed and answered an advert to cater and host special guests for a British organisation, no questions asked. The locals thought she ran a B&B business and was left alone. Her weekly trips to the supermarket took care of most supplies. The rest of the time she gardened and visited friends and family. Molly imagined discretion was her middle name.

As the evening progressed, Percy kept asking Molly for any ideas on the gang; had there been anything strange in the days and weeks before her kidnapping? No clues at all. The wine finished, the local French cheese complimented, it was time for bed. Percy laid down the time for breakfast and when they should be off in the morning.

Early next day, Therese somehow produced fresh croissants and coffee that tasted as good as their tempting wafts. Percy produced some walking gear and some supplies in a day bag that made Molly look more credible. She had also had a word with Therese about swapping some clothes, which Therese accepted with a wave of her hand. 'Mais oui!'

Percy and Molly left by car just before nine and after two kilometres drew up at the side of the road.

'See that gateway? Lean over the gate and hitch a lift at the first camper van that is going in this direction. Goodbye Molly, good luck and maybe see you in London in better circumstances.' He gave her a wave and was away with fierce acceleration.

There was not much traffic and all of it drove straight past. Eventually a camper van stopped and waited for her to run up to it. They were a Dutch family, beaming smiles, welcoming noises.

'Oh, you're British. And on your own?' She said she was between groups, which was technically one hundred per cent true. They chatted about usual stuff and it was soon so friendly that Molly thought they liked her. And she liked them and their wholesomeness. *Is this Famous Five go camping (again) or not?*

'We're just doing this area and going where Emily takes us. Emily is our camper van and we're very attached. We're aiming for the camp site down by the river and we've a spare sleeping bag in the girl tent. Why not join us for a few days until we move on? You don't sound in a hurry and you can tell your mates you're here.' This was Heaven opening up before her very eyes and ears. It sounded safe, good company and absolutely perfect for phoning James when the time was right. Molly had worked out that if Kat's phone call had been interpreted correctly, then this was probably the day the police and, she hoped, James, were approaching the vicinity. Also, let it be said, the day when the gang would be back in force to take out Bertrand. Molly hoped neither the gang nor Bertrand's heavies would endanger Kat and her two children.

'You are so kind; I have nothing except what I stand up in; I will do all the work for you; it would be a pleasure to come camping with you.'

'Agreed?'

'Agreed.'

Molly was actually light-headed having not spoken conversational English for two months, until yesterday. Their English was perfect, of course. The camper van was immaculate and Emily sailed along these French back roads, following signs to the camp site. The site was a picture. It had facilities; it was on the banks of the river. They secured a suitable pitch, with Molly apologising all the time for not having any money, and then they all helped out to pitch camp. Two tents, one for the dad and son, one for the mum and daughter, now increased to three with just a little squeeze. It was now mid-afternoon and Mum was starting to prepare food for the evening meal. Molly helped, wondering about asking to make a call. In accounting for her 'situation' she had not made it sound either desperate or urgent. And it was both. Her upbringing told her that it would be rude to ask to make a phone call straight away; the following morning would have to do. While helping Mum with the food, she asked if they would mind her taking a shower at the central facilities.

'Of course not, dear, you go and then you can do the fish nearer the time to eat.'

'I'll do more than that. You can all sit down together and I'll be your perfect waitress.' She laughed.

'Done.'

Even the showers were perfect, though her critical faculties were weaker than they used to be.

The late afternoon and evening were so pleasant she had to keep pinching herself that she was still Molly on the run from a gang, and probably from the police and trying to run into James. She had to dismiss the previous evening as an aberration; it was difficult to believe Percy's account of himself but she couldn't fault anything he said.

Wine flowed and went straight to her head, the second day running. Even the fish was fresh from the market that morning. They chatted and laughed over supper and then played silly games till nearly ten, by which time they were half asleep. They piled into their sleeping bags and that was the day gone.

SIXTY-EIGHT

'James!'

'Mols?'

'Yes, it's me, Molly, is it really you?'

'Yes, yes, it's Ellie. I'm with James. He's driving but we're both here. Where are you?'

'I'm at a camp site on the river, it's a big one, the river and the camp site; I think it's downstream from St Jean des Ponts. Can you get here? Where are you?'

'Yes. Oh Mols, we were driving around looking for you. Yes, we'll be with you as soon as we can find your camp site. Any clues? Are you safe?'

'Yes, very, please come quickly and safely. Look for the signs for the camp site on the river. Must give phone back now. Can I speak to James?'

'Here I am. Great to hear your voice. See you soon. Wow!'

'Get here quick. Must give phone back. Kiss, kiss, my darling.' And she was gone.

They had all slept long after first light and out of all of them Molly was first up and out fixing the gas stove for coffees all round. The family was probably going to stay at this camp site for a few days so they were keen to fix tents and the camping gear properly for the next few days and evenings as top priority. Breakfast was next priority and from the food produced from the camper van it was going to be a brunch 'so we have the rest of the day to do things'. All very logical but Molly was itching to get this brunch over with so she could politely ask Mr if she could borrow his phone for a few seconds to get in touch with her pals. Over brunch they discussed what to do. The choice boiled down to doing local churches, going canoeing, or enjoying a walk along the river. The first two choices won out and it split along age lines. Mum and Dad were not getting into a canoe at this time of the year. While they were clearing up and washing up, Mum piped up.

'What about you, Molly? Are you coming with us or joining in with the kids on the river?'

'Either is fine by me of course but I was wondering if I could possibly borrow your phone to get in touch with the group I'm supposed to be reconnecting with? You've been so kind and it has been a real treat to share in part of your holiday.'

'No problem. Of course you must. Why didn't you ask before?' Good question.

Mum went to the camper van glove compartment and took out a mobile phone and handed it to Molly.

'James!'

After that conversation, Molly beaming from ear to ear handed the phone back.

'It's wonderful. Thank you so much. They are quite close. They're coming here to pick me up. How do I look?'

'Come here, you lovely thing,' and Mum fixed her hair, sprayed some stuff on her, and put a dash of pink on her mouth. 'If he's important, you look gorgeous. We'll be sorry to lose you.'

Meanwhile James and Ellie had been driving around in an approximate circle centred on St Jean des Ponts after recording the TV and radio appeal. There was not much traffic and there were no particular villages or hamlets. Just roads with fences and hedges. They had chatted about the media recorded appeal and how effective it might prove to be.

'People do have radios on in the background and don't pick up on anything unless they are personally affected,' was James's view.

'Yes, but people do look at the pictures of a missing person. They might not take in any detail but they would remember whether male or female and approx. age.'

'Right. And how good looking the girl is. That's helps because Molly's got a lovely face, in my slightly biased opinion.'

'Of course she has, James! But she might be a quite dishevelled by now, she might look like a homeless person.'

'She is a homeless person.'

James's phone jangled in between them. Ellie picked up.

'James!'

After that conversation, James pulled up at the next gateway and looked at the map. St Jean des Ponts – big river – camp site by river – could only be one place. It was about ten kilometres downstream, plus two kilometres more to get to the right side of the river. Twenty minutes max.

The climax was an anticlimax, except obviously it wasn't. They drove to the camp site, drove up and down till they saw a woman waving like mad and running straight in front of their car. The next few minutes were indescribable. Hugging, kissing, tears, silly words, more hugging, more kissing, more tears, more silly words. All three of them, Molly, James, Ellie.

Eventually, eventually, order was restored and Molly introduced them to the whole Dutch family, together with a very abbreviated version of the last two months. The Dutch had by now worked out that this was some sort of mad British celebration and Dad produced a bottle of sparkling wine from the fridge. There was just enough to go round the seven of them in little white plastic cups.

James knew that they would have to do something official next but first he took name, address and email address of this kind Dutch family. Then they sat round the table and got official, while Mum and Dad brewed up more coffee. The kids had had enough of this strange meeting up and announced they were off canoeing. They were waved off and told to be back 'no later than four'.

James, Ellie and Molly were all talking over each other about what had happened. Then James held up his hands.

'We have a hotel room in the town, so we are OK for tonight. We must phone your mum and dad, we must phone French police first, and we must phone Clive Drewett back home.'

'Yes, James!' They both giggled.

'Yes, really. It's not a joke.'

'No, James!' More giggling.

James cracked up and laughed.

'OK, I'll go over there and make the phone calls while you two

FOUND LOST

catch up. I'll tell your parents that Molly is quite, quite safe with us and you'll phone tonight.'

He phoned Hortense and Henri, who requested, meaning ordered, them to report to the police station straightaway. Like now. They did sound pleased though.

He phoned Henry and Annabel and reassured them that the call was real and not a hoax. Molly and Ellie were in deep discussions and would not be coherent to phone them until this evening. He promised.

He phoned Clive Drewett, who was absolutely and genuinely thrilled. Clive said there would be formalities and he would first liaise with the French police depending on the action taken. James and Clive agreed they would keep in touch.

Back to the camper van for more coffee and thanks and then their farewells to the Dutch. James swapped phone numbers with the dad and said it was probable that the French police would want to verify Molly's version with them. Dad said they would be here for two more days and would leave the phone on just in case.

'Come on, girls, back to real reality; it's off to the police station, pile in.'

Goodbyes all round and they were off.

SIXTY-NINE

Drewett put the phone down and announced that Molly had been found and was with James and her sister Ellie. He punched the air and Mavis said that was wonderful. They were stalling in their own detective work with the French properties and the British owner and this was the best possible news. Earlier that morning he had been reflecting on the supper evening with Mavis. Maybe reflecting is the professional word for day-dreaming. The evening had gone well; it was social, enjoyable, good food and wine, and friendly in the sense that they were relaxed and happy in each other's company. He had left at the appointed hour and had stolen a peck on the cheek on the doorstep. He hadn't been rebuffed but it felt like it. Nothing was said then or since.

'There will have to be the formalities with the French police, identification of the gang, and no doubt a whole load of sworn statements. I wonder how pernickety they will be?' Mavis didn't know either but she thought Faure, now being detached from the main link in France, would be a good source of French procedure. Also, he had made her laugh with his French charm. Clive was not like that.

'No, me neither. I'll get in touch with Faure as he has good English and tell him we've heard. He can tell us what to expect next. Is that all right with you?'

'Yes, no, you go ahead, that's fine. Let me know.' Drewett was torn between wanting to do exactly that himself and, as Mavis was capable of doing that perfectly well, letting her do it. Leadership and delegation he found difficult to balance.

He returned to the feedback from the two solicitors. Ms Johnson and Ms Mary Johnson seemed to be the same person. The solicitors confirmed that her address for the banks was c/o themselves and she had directed that all correspondence relating to the property transactions should also always be via themselves. Without an official request from the authorities, it was their duty to comply with their client's wishes. The letter concluded with 'if we can be of any further assistance in this matter, please do not hesitate to get in touch'. Drewett thought, *Yeah, right,* and trotted in to Knutsford's office for an update and to get this authority.

Knutsford was all for clearing the decks.

'Well she's found now. Our esteemed French colleagues will do their bit and the family will get her back home. Tidy it all up, Clive. Pink ribbon, case closed.'

'With respect, sir, a crime has been committed on British soil as well as French and we think the instigators of this caper are British. We've tracked down the name of the British owner of the two properties but she is hiding behind solicitors' addresses and further personal information. Please may I do an authorisation for your signature to force them to tell us everything they have on file, sir?'

Formality can work.

'OK, Drewett, I understand but keep further time on this resolved matter down to absolute minimum. That's you and Miss Smith.'

He went back to his desk trying to hold back a smile.

'He'll sign the authorisation for those two solicitors and then we'll have addresses and phone numbers. The British end is unravelling. Oh, and he said we've got to wind this case down as it's been resolved. I know, I agree, it isn't, but while we can respond to any French comeback, I think we can press on with our end.' Mavis nodded and said she had tried Faure but he was out and would phone back later. His office knew that Molly had been found.

SEVENTY

The three of them decided lunch in France was a serious enough matter to have it. They stopped at a village café en route and James did not order wine, 'Because we don't know what we're going to have to face with Hortense and Henri.' The girls were relaxed and agreed, sort of, as they had the rest of the day to celebrate.

They arrived at the police station at two thirty and were immediately shown into a room where Hortense and Henri were expecting them. James knew the wine decision had been the right one.

There were introductions and welcomes and congratulations all round; then Hortense called the meeting to some formality.

'Let's get professional now, everybody. Now, Molly, may I call you Molly?' Molly nodded. 'Now Molly, you have been away for over two months and I have written and signed statements from James and Ellie. We have records of your escapades elsewhere from Monsieur Faure and we have had the incident at St Jean des Ponts. What I need to do is compare these accounts with what happened from your point of view. James and Ellie will not object to hearing this again from you but I'm afraid it is right back to the beginning en

Angleterre. In your own time.'

Molly first thanked everybody for their help and for finding her and her hopes of bringing the gang to justice, adding, 'And finding out what all this is about.' She then gave a long account of what occurred from being smothered near the South Downs right up to being with the Dutch family. She left out the evening with Percy and Therese and blandly covered this up with finding a shed to sleep in. Easily said but it did mean that until it was all over, she was keeping secrets from James, Ellie and the British and French police. She was uncomfortable with this.

There were constant interruptions by Hortense and Henri to clarify detail, particularly whatever the gang got up to. Henri produced a large scale map of the two areas of Molly's roaming and with a soft pencil marked the approximate route of Molly's journeys. They were all staggered by the length of her route winding around villages and avoiding main roads until she had to.

'Why did you not turn yourself in to the police?' This from Henri.

'I know but I wasn't sure how my story would go down. By the way, I never came across any police station in my rural routes. I had committed arson at the farmhouse, I had stolen from a supermarket chain and, while I was confident enough to find my own way out, I'm sorry but I was not that confident how a strange account from a foreigner with two crimes behind her would be accepted. I am probably wrong because you seem fair people and I mean no offence.'

Even Hortense smiled. 'I understand you, Molly. You would always be OK here but I can think of other places where you might be right. I don't think we, the police, will be pressing charges on your French criminal record,' here Hortense had a very big smile on her usually stony face, 'but of course the owner of the property might do, or their insurance company, as might the supermarket chain. I hope when they know the facts, they won't.'

Molly completed her account and answered their further questions. Hortense led to the next part.

'We are holding the three of them here and we would like you to confirm that they are the three who held you in both places. After that we will ask you further questions about them in particular.' Molly nodded and they were led down to a basement where the gang of three were held. Although there were officers and a local solicitor present, Molly and the gang were only two metres apart. She looked carefully at each one. Pete was expressionless, Alain smiled at her, which was not returned. They were led back to their cells, with the local solicitor demanding their freedom. The five of them went back to the interview room.

Molly formally acknowledged that these were indeed the three of them at both places.

'I must say, in all fairness, they looked after me well, they responded to sensible requests, they fed me well-ish and provided an adequate bathroom, and they did not harm me in any way apart from the drugging right at the start. I'm not defending their actions but I'm convinced that all the time they were carrying out orders.'

'Yes, we think so too. We have to find the chain or the links of the chain right back to Angleterre. We have the name of your policeman – Clive Drewett – is that still right Monsieur James?' James nodded and said he was still on the case when they left for France.

'You are free to go now but we would like you to stay here tomorrow just in case we have further questions. We should be able to free you to go home the day after, as long as I or Henri can phone you at any time for further questioning. If there is a case here, you will have to attend. You are staying at the hotel in the square, n'est ce pas?'

James got up and thanked them for all their help and that of course any of them would be happy to help with enquiries or a court case. He wasn't sure about this; but if they were to get back to the UK soonest, better to say these things.

On the way out, the local solicitor for the gang buttonholed Hortense and Henri, demanding the gang's rights. He was shown into a side room.

'Let's go,' James, Ellie and now Molly said in unison.

SEVENTY-ONE

Drewett phoned each of the solicitors for Ms Johnson, telling them that the necessary authority was being emailed to them with hard copy in the post. They should now start to assemble all available information on Ms Johnson in their practice and files relating to the property purchase and any other transactions any of their partners had had at any time in the past or indeed the present. He laid it on as thickly and as urgently as he could. He could have predicted their icy response which was to comply, to stonewall and to refer to their client. He asked Mavis to chase in two days' time and how had she got on with Faure.

'I said he's a charmer, that one. He had heard about the release and the gang being held. They liaise well, there. The sole French case would seem to be that they had held Molly against her wishes twice, having first brought her into the country by some means. The gang and their solicitor were arguing that they had looked after Molly well and she had burned down one property and effected serious damage to another. They would be bringing damage claims against her. Faure thought that providing the abduction was proved, a court would dismiss these damages as wriggling compared with the greater crime of abduction and held captive. We have to nail down the abduction because it happened first and it happened here.'

'Otherwise, they could make it look like a silly prank with three boys having so-called fun with a single girl wandering around France. It's back with us now, Mavis, despite what the Knut thinks, we've got to get the links of the chain between Mary Johnson, the gang of three and an apparent random hostage. What do we do next?'

'Want to brainstorm round the pub afterwards, Clive? I've got a load of ironing and stuff to do later but an hour off now would be just right.'

'Yes, fine.' Clive was taken aback.

And five minutes after leaving the station they were in the better bar of the pub it was OK for them to go to; Clive with a pint of Old Slack & Gravel and Mavis with some pink wine. No comment. Clive thanked her for what a great plate of food it was the other evening and asking, yet again, what was in it. Mavis said, yet again, 'It's a family recipe, something Mum would dish up for all of us.'

'The puzzle to me is why, oh why, has nothing popped up on this side of the Channel? It's all so civilized. No sordid ransom, no reason for a ransom, fairly well looked after, looks like a random seizing but clearly it isn't.'

'It could still be a random one. If no-one is popping up as you say, maybe it's for fun. Stranger things have happened.'

'Yes, but the recapture, the fact that they've looked after her, all that fuss with Bertrand. If it was just for fun, surely they would have said by now, "Yes, OK, we know we can do it, now let's get back to the real job." And what business have those three guys in France? They aren't earning any money, despite their claim that they're odd-jobbing for their holiday.'

'Which all points to them working for a Mr Big. They have their orders, Pete is told what to do, he is told to drive her to the other house, and look how quickly that local solicitor appeared at the police station, according to James.'

'Yes, I agree. Our job, as I said back at the office, is to find the links of the chain. And the reasons. We have all that Ken and Dad stuff which is incomprehensible. Is it connected? In which case Ken and Dad are in the link. If not, it's just the ramblings of a teenage girl. Which is more likely.'

'Like you rambled on when you were a boy.'

'Probably. And you. Nuts or crisps? Feeling peckish.'

'No, not for me. I'm off. Back with a clear thinking head in the morning. I feel like going to those solicitors' offices and reading the files before they choose what to send us. Can do a round trip in a day. Is that OK with you, boss?'

Clive had to agree and maybe this woman would achieve more than him with his more formal style. He agreed provided she could do it in a day and he would get it past the Knut as part of getting the case closed more quickly.

Mavis left; Clive ordered another pint of OS&G to go with the cheese and onion.

SEVENTY-TWO

The evening for the three of them was perfect. Molly phoned her mum and dad for a long conversation. Both Henry and Annabel were most concerned and attentive that Molly was unharmed.

'You haven't been abused in any way, you know what I mean, have you darling?'

'No, Mum, no, Dad, I'm fine, all in one piece, very healthy. James and Ellie say I've never looked better. Fresh air, no alcohol, outdoor living. I'm in good shape in both senses.' They rattled on while James and Ellie continued with the fizz.

Then Ellie took over and told them how they had found Molly on a camp site with a lovely Dutch family.

'They're such family people aren't they, the Dutch?'

'Yes, Mum.' After an hour on the phone, James started waving his arms like an umpire ruling that his Out decision had been overturned upstairs.

'Right, you lot, let's get cleaned up, put some decent clothes on. I've booked dinner for three at the starred restaurant across the road. It's all of thirty metres max.'

They arrived at the restaurant to find some commotion outside.

'Mademoiselle Molly, how does it feel to be free?' and other questions. The TV and radio news and press were gathered round a bank of microphones stacked up on a table outside the restaurant. Some collusion, James thought, and then he recalled that he had told the police where they were staying. It would be big news in this corner of France. They had to go along with this game. After the police questioning, they had already established their position and trotted out as harmless replies as they could. They were photographed every which way, photographed hugging and kissing, photographed posing to order. Eventually, James had to step up.

'Thank you all, you've been very kind, but it's been a long day and many weeks and Molly especially is very tired. It's our first evening together and we want to enjoy your lovely French hospitality over dinner and a good night's sleep. Please, that's enough now.' And from nowhere, Henri appeared, as if by guilty conscience, and started to shepherd the journalists and camera men and women away.

'Thanks, Henri, I thought they were never going to go.'

'You understand this is big story for our town. Give them what they want and they'll be on their way. Have a very good evening and congratulations!'

They went in to the restaurant somewhat overcome with emotion. James apologised to the maitre'd.

'Mais non, Monsieur, ce n'est pas un probleme. C'est tres bien pour le restaurant d'avoir les photos!'

He backed this up with a welcome drink of champagne. 'On the house!'

They chose well and many. They talked over each other, all trying to get a word in edgeways. Beer and wine flowed and James recognised this had to be a money-no-object gathering. He was ecstatically happy and so were Molly and Ellie. Molly was not used to rich food and frequent glass refills and by the time of the puddings after the cheese she was starting to fade. They virtually had to carry Molly back to the hotel over the road, then up to bed. Molly fell into the bed and was asleep in minutes. James had to laugh to himself; no, in truth, he hadn't expected a romantic sexy night. There's time enough for that. He took a beer from the small fridge and lay on the bed next to her. There was a text on his mobile from Hortense. 'Please report to the station straight after breakfast.' Yes, she had said that that was a possibility. They all wanted to get the train back up to Paris and then to St Pancras as soon as allowed. Then he fell asleep.

SEVENTY-THREE

The Boss watched the late news on TV and saw a small item at the end of the programme; the British woman Molly Otsworth, who had been captured and escaped twice, had been reunited with her family in France. There was a picture of the three of them hugging outside a French restaurant. He picked up the phone and punched in the solicitor's number.

'Gustav? Boss here. Yes, make the charges in the morning, get bail for Pete and co, report back on whether Molly and family are allowed back to UK. I'll be doing something this end if they are. Bye.' And he replaced the phone. This was getting out of his customary control. Plan C or D would have to be more subtle.

SEVENTY-FOUR

Mavis had got up to Paddington by nine and caught a train to Reading for the house purchase solicitors. Better to do them first as it had been bought before the farmhouse. Then she would train it to Oxford for the other solicitors for the farmhouse, back to Paddington, cross London and eventually back to Sussex. As soon as it was nine, she phoned each firm of solicitors to say she was on her way and the necessary authorisations were in place. She received the legal equivalent of a grunt followed by, 'We look forward to seeing you.'

After her concentrated police training following university, she had come to recognise how lucky she was to fetch up in her Sussex station. The Knut and Clive could not have been better to work alongside; the Knut was old-school, grounded in formality and what was right, Clive more go-ahead but still formal and correct. Clive had shown he could think outside the box and he seemed happy to delegate stuff to her that she could not imagine getting in her previous station. Clive was protective to her and she speculated again that he was a tiny bit sweet on her, making her giggle on the train. Passengers were looking at her, so she took out the file and re-read all the data they had on Ms Mary Johnson and her transactions. It was very sketchy, almost as though this Mary wanted to cover her tracks. But why would she do that? She would not have known that many years later, these two properties would be used for holding a young woman captive. Another angle was that the documentation had been weeded many years later, when for example someone somewhere realised that these two properties would be suitable for holding a captive or for other sinister purposes. She, Mavis, had always thought there was a Mr Big out there controlling events. The gang would not be up to that, nor owning or renting these two houses.

Reading Station, 9.45 and the offices three streets away off the main shopping area. Messrs Gilpin & Gilpin had the first and second floor offices over a travel agent at street level. She was shown into a side office and after a discourteous delay, a young Mr Andrew Gilpin came in, introduced himself as a grandson of the original Mr G and opened a file. 'Have you had coffee, Ms Smith?'

'Er, no, straight black please. Thank you for asking.' He went outside and she heard him question why the guest hadn't been offered coffee. He came back in looking pink.

'Sorry about that. On its way. Now, you want to know about our client Ms Johnson, yes?'

Mavis gave enough of an outline of the case without mentioning either Molly or her being held captive. It was really all about trying to trace the current owner of the property so as to continue enquiries with that person.

'Which may or may not be Ms Johnson as she may have sold on. But our French colleagues have confirmed that a Ms Johnson of the UK is the current owner.'

Young Mr Andrew stroked what would have been his beard had he got one. He looked at his file again.

'We have no record of Ms Johnson subsequently selling the French property but she could of course have used another firm of solicitors or even a local firm if she were selling.'

'Mr Gilpin, please may I read your file and any other file involving

Ms Johnson?' Mr Andrew was taken aback at this full frontal request and dithered.

'I have and you have the necessary authorisations for your firm to release copies of files to assist the police with an ongoing enquiry. If you could fetch me the files, I can decide what copies we need to save you doing the lot.' Suitably armed, Mavis felt she was able to take control of the situation.

'Yes, yes, of course, let me see what I can do.' And he made to go but Mavis butted in.

'I can start with the file in your hand; it will save you time.' Said with an irritating smile. He handed it to her and went off. He returned a quarter of an hour later with three more files.

'I think that is all.'

'Are you quite sure?'

'Yes, quite sure. These other files are where Ms Johnson is involved but not directly involved if you see what I mean.' She didn't but thanked him kindly for the files and took them off him. He said she could use this office to read the files and then let him know what copies would be needed. The coffee came in, complete with a dark chocolate digestive, maybe as an apology.

Mavis shut the door and set to. The files were thick and who knows what nuggets would fall out.

The going was tedious and largely procedural for what seemed a perfectly normal transaction of buying a property in France. There were to-ings and fro-ings with the French solicitors and permissions and searches, all apparently normal and procedural. What she wanted were UK addresses and any other contact points. There was an address in Nuneaton; but only one. Mavis was suspicious that it had escaped the obliterator's attention. She noted this page for copying. The other three files were small property sales of Johnson people, maybe parents or siblings or other relatives. Mary seemed to be the beneficiary of these sales and as they pre-dated the house purchase would seem to be the source of funds to buy it. And the farmhouse subsequently. There was scant information on these three sales, resulting in a bank transfer into Ms Johnson's account with a c/o Gilpin & Gilpin address. She asked for Mr Gilpin and requested certified copies of the Nuneaton page and some of the pages of the three small property transactions.

'It would appear that Ms Johnson inherited the proceeds of these three small property transactions from the extended Johnson family. Do you have any files for them and were they clients?'

'No, Ms Smith. That was one of the reasons I took so long to recover them as I wanted to check any cross-referencing. It would appear, to use your phrase, that our firm did not act for them. We merely received the funds for our client, Ms Johnson.'

'So you have no other Johnson, of this family at least, as a client?'

'No, I can assure you of that. May I assist you with anything else?' He was politeness itself.

'Thank you, no. You've been a great help. As this is part of an ongoing police investigation – and I must emphasise that no-one is accusing Ms Johnson of anything; this is just background stuff – I would request you not to contact Ms Johnson regarding this search. I know that professionally you act for your client and you may be unhappy about it, but the authorisation for access to these files remains confidential to the police and your firm. Is that OK?'

'I suppose it'll have to be; but we do have to reserve the right to consult our client in the final analysis.'

'Understood; but please cross-check with us first – either me or my colleague Drewett or our superior, Inspector Knutsford. Sorry to sound heavy but we believe this is the best approach at the moment.' She handed him her card and wrote Drewett and Knutsford on it.

'Equally understood, Ms Smith. I'll get these copies certified right away and show you out.' *And see me off the premises,* she thought.

That had not taken all morning. She walked back to the station, picking up a baguette and coffee on the way, and found a train to Oxford. These were frequent and took about half an hour. Thus it was 1.30 when she walked into reception at Messrs Pratt & Matthews, on the second floor of a Victorian street building just a few yards away from one of the more impressive colleges. They were expecting her and she was shown into a side meeting room, this time with an offer of coffee, which she declined.

'Good afternoon, Ms Smith. I'm Rachel Critchworth assigned to your enquiry.' Rachel was a young solicitor, dressed in black top and trousers, all very sharp and business-like.

Mavis repeated the substance of her enquiry, backed up with the authorisations signed by Knutsford. Rachel studied these closely.

'Thank you, yes, we have located a couple of files in connection with the French farmhouse purchase. There's not much, I'm afraid. Would you like to peruse them here and decide what you need to take? Copies obviously.'

'That's absolutely fine. Have you completed your search for the Johnson files? Is she, or any member of her family, a current client? Do you have an ongoing client relationship?'

''Fraid not. There are no other files for Mary Johnson or related Johnsons. I can't speak for a different married name if she hadn't told us of a previous transaction. And, no, we don't have a continuing live file for Ms Johnson. These two files were archived years ago. I'll leave you to it; please shout for tea or coffee.' And she left.

Mavis wearily went through the files. It was all depressingly familiar. Procedure, searches, enquiries, liaison with agents and the French solicitors, culminating in the bank transfers similarly with Ms Johnson's address c/o Pratt & Matthews. Then on a scrap of paper was written MJ, a Nuneaton address and a telephone number. It was the same address as at Gilpin's. Mavis wrote these down in her notebook just in case the formal Rachel said it was nothing to do with the file. She went out to reception and requested certified copies of a few letters. Rachel re-appeared.

'All done?'

'Yes, thanks, you've all been very helpful. Just copies of a few letters please.' And she repeated the low-key formality of not contacting their client, at least not without prior clearance from her or Drewett or Knutsford. She handed her card to Rachel.

'Cannot see any reason to at this stage. If she contacts us, which would be highly unusual for merely an old property purchase, that may put us on the spot to mention your interest.'

'I'm sure you can stall until you've got in touch with us. I agree it's a remote possibility. Thank you and I'll see myself out.' Mavis waited for the copy letters to come through and made her exit. That also had not taken long; so she strolled through a few colleges, comparing (and contrasting) with her own university days at an upgraded polytechnic. She smiled at the thought of how young the students looked even for those few years. She had worked hard at her studies and badminton, making the first squad, and had dallied with a few boys. Nothing serious of course; more like her own social studies experimental practicals. Girls could be silly, boys were hopeless, and occasionally one had special memorable times. Yes, she could remember just a few. Some others got into terrible complications; fortunately she emerged unscathed and wiser. *I'm a police officer, with a good job, interesting work and sound colleagues,* she thought, *but I would like some excitement. Clive? I don't think so.*

Her inner ramblings kept her going to the station. Paddington, cross London, Victoria, home. She phoned Clive from the train and said it would all keep to morning. Back home, hot shower, on with the leisure wear and big fluffy dressing gown, warmed up remains and with a glass finished the bottom half of a bottle. Sank in front of yet another crime drama on TV. 'It's never really like that; real life's better but with worse cars.' Said to no-one in particular.

SEVENTY-FIVE

The three of them reported to the police station the following morning. There did not seem to be any urgency about anything so they had enjoyed a leisurely breakfast, plenty of coffee and fresh croissants to follow the scrambled eggs and smoked salmon, specially requested by Molly. They told the hotel reception they would be back shortly to check out and collect bags. It was, however, a frosty Hortense waiting for them, frowning and looking at her watch as if to say 'what sort of time do you call this?' James apologised profusely for all of them, claiming special circumstances.

'There's been an unexpected development which I need to discuss with you. Please come this way.' They were shown into a side consultation room just off a corridor leading to the back of the station. The four of them sat round a table in a featureless room.

'A Monsieur Gustav Bontout, a solicitor from the next town, has appeared acting for the owner of the two properties in which Molly was held. He claims Molly was a guest and accuses her of wilful arson at the farmhouse and unwarranted damage to the ceilings and walls at the second house. The insurers are not paying up as neither was an accident and his client seeks the full cost of restoration to both properties or the equivalent, which bizarrely he claims would be met by the return of Molly to his residence.'

James spluttered his outrage, Molly just smiled weakly, Ellie looked bewildered. They all voiced, 'How could they?' James started.

'Well what about the counter claim about Molly being abducted, held captive, denied her freedom, exercising her right, nay, duty, to try to escape. And all of that over an extended period of two months. It's a damn cheek and I could say a lot worse.'

'I'm sure Dad would happily pay for the damage, of course.' This from Ellie. 'Can't we phone home and put Dad or his solicitor in touch with this horrible man hiding behind his solicitor?'

'I'm sure that's the way forward. This is now a French dispute on French soil. The counter claim would have to prove that Molly was being held against her wishes. I do not see that as difficult but it will require briefings, witnesses, time and resolution. Your British police are pursuing the original kidnapping of Molly but we do have the connection that both of you recognise the man called Pete and he is involved in all three places. He is guilty naturally but I think we all think that the gang are carrying out instructions by someone else.' Hortense paused for everyone's benefit, including her own.

'Here's what we'll do. You three phone Molly's father and see what he says about the money. Here is what they are claiming from the insurers,' and Hortense handed them a copy of two insurance claim forms, 'and whether he wants to deal direct or via a solicitor. You can phone from here and come back to me. If there is agreement on that, you are free to go after a further statement here. If there is not agreement, then it is a dispute here and I will try to get it heard in a few days' time in our local court. You would have to stay here in the meantime. We will charge this Pete and the others with holding Molly against her will. I will do my best to detain them here until a similar hearing in a few days' time. You will also be required to attend that as the injured party and as witnesses. It is all very messy but we want to get rid of this silly episode as quickly as you do.' Hortense leant back, pleased with her summing up but still showing her irritation at what she clearly thought was a tiresome diversion.

The three of them trooped out to another room where there was a phone and called home. Annabel answered.

'Hello my darlings, lovely to hear you all together and safe and sound. When are you back?' Ellie took over and asked for her father, who was already by his wife's side.

'Hi Dad, it's Ellie and I'm with Mols and James. We need to prevail on you as things have got a bit curious here.' And she went on to relay everything that Hortense had outlined to them over the last half hour.

'Well obviously the money would not be a problem if it gets you back here. I don't see why I should pay to rebuild Molly's prison. The key thing is your freedom to come back here and total resolution of this sorry business. Tell your policewoman that in principle we will pay in full and immediately whatever is legally due after these two court hearings. I want them found guilty of holding Molly in two places in France as well as the continuing case here of kidnapping down in Sussex. I'm obviously happy to talk to your policewoman and brief a local solicitor whatever works. I don't like this being strung out and nobody knowing where they are. Love to you all and here's your mother.' They continued chatting for a short while then went back to brief Hortense on Henry's promise.

Hortense said she would put this to Monsieur Bontout in another room. She returned a few minutes later.

'They will not drop their case against Molly without full payment now. They know they are up against a court hearing shortly and are prepared to fight it for the reasons already given. It looks to me like they want the money because they are going to lose the case. It's a see you in court thing. Go and have some coffee and come back after lunch and we will see where we are then.'

The three of them, not in the best of spirits and weary of this tedious stuff, crossed the square to the café.

SEVENTY-SIX

More than twenty years earlier, Barry was making coffee for himself and Sylvia. The previous evening they had drowned their sorrows rather heavily and, with no work to go to, had slept in. The boys romped around in their bedroom with computer games and morning TV. Sylvia was reflective.

'Look love, it's not the end of the world. You're fit and healthy, got a gorgeous wife and two boys, a lovely house and, by the way, a fat bank balance. Count your blessings.'

'You're not wrong. Of course all of that's good and if you ignore the past I'm one of the luckiest of men. It's the loss of the future that bugs me. We could have been literally rolling in it.'

'Well we're OK as we are. The past is gone. The future's all to play for. Do one of your famous thought experiments. What if you woke up one morning next to a gorgeous girl, in a lovely house, with two great sons to play football with da di da di da... what would your next move be?'

'I'd roll over and make passionate love to her.'

'Well?'

They did and the coffee went cold. So he made some more. He looked in on the boys and told them it was going to be a lazy day today, perhaps they could go over and play with the neighbour's boy and girl. They were roughly the same age.

'The thing is Silv, I've lost the spring in my step.'

'I didn't notice.' He laughed, she was great.

'The thing is I'm not good at doing nothing. I'm an action man, I need a project, something to sink my teeth into, work hard, play hard and earn some serious dosh.'

'I don't see what's stopping you, you big softy, the money gives you time and that time is to phone round all your contacts, get something – anything – and get back in the saddle and something'll turn up.'

'You're right, Mrs Micawber. I'll hit the phone this afternoon, we'll take the boys out to supper and then come back and watch rubbish TV. Appointments with coffee don't start today.'

They showered together and emerged downstairs to see a note from the boys saying, 'Next door, back later.' Barry phoned next door to check it was OK and for them to come back no later than 5pm. No problem.

Sylvia did a full English and a pot of coffee and sent Barry into his study with it.

'Now, get on with it. I'm going to see what I can do working from home and we'll catch up with each other on the sofa when the boys are in bed.'

Barry smiled to himself. A man with a good wife is the luckiest man in the world. He hoped he lived up to her expectations. Life had actually been good so far and this was his first reversal. Could he turn it round into a springboard into the future? He reached for his address book and switched on his desktop PC. He methodically sorted all his business contacts into divisions. Division one: could be very promising; division two: possible but unlikely; division three: very unlikely. Then the same with friends and family; this was quite short as he didn't want to mix business and pleasure but some of them might be able to recommend contacts. Then what to do about approaching head-hunters? His CV was not in a good shape with the short-term nature of his last two jobs and no actual achievements. Merely getting that company ready for the great step forward he didn't think deserved a mention of an actual achievement to show off to others. Leave the head-hunters for a while and see if anything turned up from his contacts.

Fresh coffee and he spent the rest of the day on the phone. Many had to be rung back at a specific time; most said they couldn't talk now but asked if he could phone back next week; a few wanted to gossip; and three actual coffee/beer-after-work meetings were fixed. *Until they are cancelled,* he thought.

He meticulously recorded the names, what they said, when to phone next. He got through all of division one by the end of the day and decided to leave the rest till tomorrow.

The Appointments section of a national daily was filled with apparent vacancies, all couched in a precious language of looking for someone who could walk on water before lunch and go to the moon and back in the afternoon. Any sort of liaison role was never for him; he wanted project work with a start, middle and end and serious money. He did find a couple of these and put them aside to phone in the morning.

The boys came back on time; Sylvia had prompted Helen next door to pack them off when, not if, they were too much. The four of them walked down to the village to the boys' favourite diner, one up from a greasy spoon and one down from a gastropub. Just perfect. The boys devoured the house 'mixed grill' which meant everything on a plate with bread and butter, Sylvia and Barry had steak and chips and trimmings with a bottle of Valpolicella. Then Black Forest gateau, two slices shared between four worked just fine.

Two hours later, with their feet and legs up and intertwined with each other, Sylvia and Barry compared notes.

'I've gone through all my address records and contacts. I've three actual appointments, fifteen people to be phoned back, twelve not available to try again, and a couple of adverts out of an appointments section. It's trying work, I don't like saying I've just left you-know-where and then they say why.'

'Sounds good for four hours' work, love. I remember you saying once that if there are twenty lots of 5% chances, the chance of at least one success is over 60%. I thought it was a good analytical way of saying that one about throwing mud at a wall.'

'You're not just a pretty face, ho ho, fancy you remembering that. What thoughts have you had?'

'Well I'm sort of housebound at the moment but I think I'm fairly good with people and also on the phone.'

'I second that. Can you be my secretary?'

'No, and they are called PAs now. Before you and I got together, I used to run the tenancies for a property company. It was working with people, it focused on the start and end of each tenancy, you know – references, rents, the inventory and the final clean-up inspection. During the tenancy, there were things like the washing machine had packed up or calling a plumber or electrician. Most of it was by phone with occasional visits. I thought I could try picking up where I left off and, if it works, think about setting up my or our own agency. It would really amount to no more than kitting out my study as an office and it's nearly that already. Is that OK, Barry, darling?'

'Sounds OK to me. Not much downside. Why don't you suck it and see?' Silvia gave a flirty, suggestive smirk.

'Wonderful, I'll do that as well.'

'Husband invests in wife. Well I guess I invested in you from that weekend in Swanage. Remember?'

'How will I ever forget? Those pyjamas just had to go.'

'OK my darling, get in touch with them and set the ball rolling. No rush and be cautious and careful.'

'It wasn't like that in Swanage.'

SEVENTY-SEVEN

Julian heard Percy out, wanting all the details made very clear during his debrief.

'So MNO has absolutely no idea who is behind this?'

'Nope. Nothing. She reckons the gang, that's the three of them, are working for someone behind the scenes.'

'Almost certainly and all contact will be via untraceable mobiles. Could it conceivably be one of our other departments or a commercial competitor to Paul I wonder? It doesn't seem in the style of Edinburgh, Cardiff, Belfast or even Brussels for that matter. Could you have a word with Pierre to see if our cunning French cousins are not behind this?'

'OK, but it would seem counter-productive to me, if they were.'

'Quite, that's why it would be cunning. Let me know. And how did MNO appear to bear up in handling the various situations?'

'A natural, if you ask me, Q. Aplomb should be her middle name.'

'Mmm. It's Nanette. Thanks for that. I'll give Paul a ring.'

With Percy gone to call Pierre, Julian phoned Paul.

'Rosemary, how nice to hear your charming tones. It's Julian. Is Paul there?' He was.

'Julian, you've heard the news on Molly?'

'MNO is in safe hands and appears to have handled herself well – so well done on your training.'

'That means I have to say well done on your identification of her.'

'Thank you, that's nicely symmetrical. Have you had any intimation at all from anybody as to who is behind this?'

'None at all. Have you?'

'I couldn't possibly comment but no. Lunch at my club, I'll be in touch.' And he was gone.

SEVENTY-EIGHT

Mavis was in before Clive and she was prepared for him. Clive made his coffee and offered same to Mavis. 'Thank you, white, no sugar and the red mug.' He had been brought up to date by Hortense and Mr Otsworth about the French developments. It was boring down there and he wanted Molly and James and the gang back here to conclude the case of the original capture.

Mavis told him all about the Reading and Oxford visits and the slip of paper with a Nuneaton address and phone number.

'It could be a lead. Shall I follow up or do you want to take over?'

'No, no. See where you get, you know the all innocent vague enquiry, no-one is under suspicion, etcetera.'

'Yes, yes, I get it. I'm used to those.' She had a smile on her face. 'The news from France is not good?'

'Well they are free but not yet free to come home. There's a

French equivalent of a magistrates court the day after tomorrow. It appears the other side is playing silly buggers either for negotiation or for money or both. I'm hoping Magistrate Grenouille will boot them into touch.'

'You could be reprimanded for that.'

'I never said a word.'

Mavis phoned the Nuneaton number. A woman answered.

'Hello, who is this please?'

'Good morning. My name is Mavis Smith and I'm calling from a police station in Sussex. There's absolutely nothing to worry about; we are just following up some other enquiries and your phone number came up in a file. You are in Nuneaton, yes?'

'Yes, dear, this is a Nuneaton house,' and she gave the address which tallied with the solicitors file, 'and I'm Janet Wright and I've lived here for years. What do you want?'

'I'm sorry to bother you. Do you rent or own the property?'

'My husband and I own the property and have done for years. We've paid off the mortgage now. What is this about?'

'Well done on the mortgage. We were wondering if you know or know of a Ms Mary Johnson, maybe you bought the house off her?'

'Oh dear, that's going back a bit. My husband does all the paperwork and he might have kept a file. Can he call you back? His name is Neville. He gets called Never Wright.' And she laughed saying it.

'OK, please ask him to call as soon as you can.' Not a great lead but you never know. The phone went in another minute.

'Hello Ms Smith, it's Never Wright here. You are right, by the way, we did buy off a Mary Johnson way back. It was a very clean purchase. No meetings. We viewed the property, liked it, put in an offer, accepted straight away and moved in a month later. Unimaginable these days.'

'Did Mary Johnson live there or was she a remote owner?'

'Difficult to say. Everything was done through solicitors. When we viewed it, it was empty, there was no subsequent post, we were just happy to take up an uncluttered residence. And still happy here as well.'

'That's nice Mr Wright. If you have anything, literally anything, about the previous ownership, I would be very grateful if you could send them on to me.' They exchanged final pleasantries.

'Clive, Mr Never Wright turns out to be always right. But no further forward. I have a feeling our Never Neville will turn out all his files for any scrap of the elusive Mary Johnson.'

'We need another break through. It's all gone stale again. I've never known a case like it. Badminton this evening?'

SEVENTY-NINE

James, Molly and Ellie had been kicking their heels for two more days now. They had had coffee in every café in town and taken wine in every bar in town. They had even done the local museum. Ennui was definitely settling in. James had phoned everybody connected with their case – Drewett, Faure, his mum and dad, Paul at work, Steve at the flat, Henry and Annabel again – all to the effect that he and they hoped the hearing tomorrow would be conclusive. Henry had instructed a local French solicitor with passable English called Philipe Montand and James and Molly had spent all their time in the cafés and bars with him going over the complete story from Molly waking up in the dark in the farmhouse. He had spoken to Kat and was optimistic that her man, now back from the seas, would drive her over in the morning. Gaston Blanc could not be tracked down but messages had been left with whoever it was that answered the phone.

The four of them had a quiet supper at the hotel. They were fed up with being holed up down in deepest France; they were fed up with going over Molly's escapades for the umpteenth time; and they were fed up not knowing when they could go home. Philipe and James tried to keep the atmosphere light.

'There are no weak links in your story because you are telling the truth. Yes, the magistrate will point to your crimes but the justification is strong. Everyone has the right to escape. He might want to set an example of your, er, misdemeanours, but you should not read guilt into that or be pessimistic about them. The key thing is what he says about them and their implicit master. That Gustav is a vicious little man and will not rest. He is used to doing dirty cases in a dirty way. Not nice.'

'If you've met him before, then you'll know his dirty tricks. The trick is to see them coming.'

'Yes, Monsieur James, it is. But there is always the unpredictable. Let's move on and enjoy this evening. I am so lucky to have the company of two such lovely ladies.'

They finished the wine and the cheese, James put the bill on his room and they all turned in for an early night.

Molly and James relaxed in each other's arms and after some serious kissing Molly was the first to state her feelings.

'Let's not enjoy each other too much until we really can, eh? Our minds are all over the place, you agree my darling?'

'I suppose I do; agreed, of course, it's just wonderful to be back with you. Times will be better soon. Looking forward to them!'

They laughed, stripped off and held each other tight in bed before sleep and snoring.

They all coincided at breakfast and got a corner table for the four of them. Philipe announced that the hearing was set for 11am which meant either a quicky and over by lunch or a lunch break and on for the whole of the day. James and he knew it would be the latter but said nothing. He had messages that Kat was on her way and that Gaston Blanc would do his best. Expenses had helped both on their ways.

Philipe told Molly to look drawn and tired but to let her natural good looks be very apparent. No make-up and plain, well-fitting clothes.

'They have to believe that you have been held captive and on the run for over two months now. And Monsieur James and Mademoiselle Ellie, you should show the strain of having missed your dear partner and dear sister.'

They both butted in and said it was their natural look these days.

After a final check-up at ten thirty, the four of them crossed to the far side of the square and entered the court house.

The magistrate and two wingers emerged at 11am prompt. Monsieur Jardin presiding was a Gallic emperor.

'Good morning all. Today unusually I speak in English as both sides in this dispute are British subjects and it will thus be more efficient. On one side we have Mademoiselle Molly Otsworth who claims to have been held captive in two places and on the run in between and subsequently from her captors. She is represented by Monsieur Philipe Montand.' They bowed very slightly to each other. 'And on the other side we have Monsieur Peter Ruff, plus two, er, colleagues, who claim no ill intent to Molly and claim significant damages by Molly on both of the two properties. He is represented by Monsieur Gustav Bontout.' They also very slightly bowed to each other. James thought the second pair of bows were a few degrees nearer the vertical.

'As Peter and his associates have been held at our local police station, would the police here please show these gentlemen into my court room?' It fell to Henri to escort Pete and the other two into a separate area. Not so much a dock as an enclosed area facing the body of the court.

'This is a dispute and it is not my wish to elevate it to a higher court unless I'm forced to. I will hear both sides and their witnesses and then my two colleagues and I will retire to consider our judgment. This may take a little while and I reserve the right to question anyone again. If both sides accept my judgment, this is all over. Either side may contest my judgment and the consequences would be a higher court in time measured in months, more solicitors, more money and no guarantee of achieving their desired outcome. The higher court will take full recognition of everything disclosed today and would not lightly change my judgment. Indeed, without fresh evidence, the outcome is almost always the same.' He paused. James reckoned he had said that set piece before many times. 'Monsieur Bontout, please commence.'

The hearing dragged on. Molly listened intently and wrote notes for Philipe whenever her version differed from Bontout and Pete's account. It would be good to contest their account. They broke for lunch at 1.15 and Molly was thrilled to see Kat with her partner Abel outside. They hugged and Molly asked after Georges and Francoise.

'They miss you!'

Gaston Blanc arrived after lunch and introduced himself to Philipe.

The hearing continued well into the afternoon until, with Monsieur Jardin's final request whether either side had anything more to offer or to ask, the three magistrates retired.

EIGHTY

Mavis's intuition about Neville was spot on. He phoned the next morning.

'May speak to Miss Smith please?'

'Speaking. It's Mr Wright isn't it? How nice to hear from you so soon.'

'Well I couldn't rest after our conversation and I determined to turn out my files. It's never wrong to do some decluttering, is it, and in a way I was pleased to do it. Janet too. We got rid of two big boxes of papers, thank you.'

'Don't thank me, I hope you found something and didn't throw it away.' She knew he wouldn't.

'No, far from it. I found the house purchase file and particulars and it brought back some happy memories. But I must get to the point, it was so nice of you to phone yesterday.' Mavis kept quiet.

'The thing is, it was empty before we bought and we viewed it as empty. But after we had been in a few weeks, what must have been a previous occupant came round and knocked on the door. We had him in for a cup of tea as you do. He wanted to know if there had been any mail for him because he had left well before the sale and he thought he might not have told everyone about his change of address. I let him ramble on,' *I know the feeling,* thought Mavis, 'and Janet did find some bill for him and a letter to Ms Johnson, whoever she was. So we gave the bill to him, I forget his name, and I popped round to the agents with the letter for Ms Johnson. They seemed to remember her and I distinctly remember the nice young girl at reception saying, "Thank you Mr Wright, I'll forward it on to her. She's a Brigg now." Yes, it's a clear as anything, I can hear her saying it. So Miss Smith, either your elusive lady has gone back to a maiden name or she's a Mrs Brigg or maybe on to other names by now.'

'Thank you so much, Mr Wright. You've been helpfulness itself. You are right in both senses, a new name is always good to search on. Good luck with your decluttering and let me know if anything else turns up. Bye now.'

'Can I get you a coffee, Clive? I've just had an earful, but we have a new name. Brigg. Mean anything?'

The badminton the previous evening had been good. Doubles and they made up a friendly foursome. Clive had suggested they all do something together at the weekend and it seemed to go down well. He wasn't sure what and now he was agonising over what would be just right. Maybe something original would come to him. They finished with a lager and Mavis determinedly left on her own, citing she had to get some milk and collect the dry cleaning.

'Yes, thanks, black with nothing else and mine's the blue mug.'

'I know. I'll start all the usual searches on Brigg plus marriages around those years. OK?'

'Yep. Do court cases as well.' He was receiving updates from France from Henri and Philipe and like them awaiting the outcome of the hearing that day, which he would not expect to get till the morning. He went into Knutsford to tell him about the court hearing and the new name Brigg.

'I suppose it's progress but you can't see it or smell it or touch it yet, can you?'

'No sir. I feel there's some momentum building now and the hearing plus solid police work will give us new leads.'

'I hope you're right. Keep me up to speed on the hearing tomorrow.'

'Sir.'

There was a stand-up comic at the local AmDram. Could be tawdry. Theatre. Could be pretentious. A combo at the local pub. Definitely not. Cook in at his place? Could be disastrous and/or set a precedent for returns back. Tricky stuff, this socialising.

EIGHTY-ONE

Magistrate Jardin plus the two sidesmen re-entered the room. All stood up. It was gone five and they had been out for over an hour. He raised himself momentarily to his full height of 1.92m, bowed slightly and indicated for all to sit.

'This has been an interesting case of claim and counter claim. Fortunately the facts are not in dispute apart from the contention by Monsieur Bontout that Miss Molly was a temporary guest at his clients' lodgings while she travelled in France seeking friends and work. The combination of this upright woman and these three workmen does not fit the account of Miss Molly, the conditions of her accommodation at the two lodgings, nor even some of the accounts of Monsieur Peter and his two friends. The recognition by Monsieur James, Miss Molly, Monsieur Blanc and Miss Kat that Monsieur Peter is one and the same as the captor of Miss Molly is irrefutable evidence that Miss Molly was held against her will throughout. This is not contentious and my written notes to a presumed higher court would rule out any other interpretation completely. That is quashed, Monsieur Bontout, completement.' They affected a gracious bow between them.

'Next we come to the damages to the properties. As Miss Molly was being held against her will, it is entirely justifiable that she should seek to escape. You might argue it would be her duty to do so. It is clear that Monsieur Peter and his associates bore no ill will towards Miss Molly. Indeed Miss Molly has been gracious enough to state that under her prison conditions, they looked after her well, fed her well and acceded to her many requests. That does them credit and, in that respect, they were gentlemen. We cannot surmise on the reason for their holding her captive however strange it might appear. The damages are stated as serious: consequential fire damage at the farmhouse and superficial plasterboard at the second house. On this second item, I dismiss it entirely. Miss Molly was held captive and she effected an escape in a manner direct and straightforward. These three self-described workmen will have no problem restoring the house to its original state. I can see that Miss Molly in her mission to escape from the farmhouse could not have given any regard for the consequential damage to it. Nevertheless, it was foolish of her to select an escape route that wilfully destroyed much of the property. One could not expect an outlying farmhouse to have defensive fire equipment such as sprinklers or anything automated. If such a fire had started by accident, the insurers would naturally pay up and to me it is significant that in this case they are not. Our decision on this, on which I am happy to go to arbitration, is that Miss Molly and her family are liable as to two-thirds of the cost of re-building. I understand that Miss Molly's family have paid an initial deposit into court at the wish of Monsieur Bontout and I am directing that the amount is held here pending resolution of any arbitration.' Jardin paused because all sensed what was coming next and even he wanted his moment of theatre.

'Finally we come to the outcome of these cases. I have already adjudicated on the financial settlement and I am satisfied as to the financial promises made by Miss Molly's family that the agreed amount of settlement will be met by the deposit paid into court plus any additional amounts. I have said that Miss Molly was detained unlawfully and she and her family are free to go from this place with our best wishes for their future.' He smiled at Molly and she bowed and mouthed 'thank you'.

'These three men have wilfully captured and detained Molly on British and French soil. The French detention was a continuation of the original British kidnapping and I rule that Monsieur Peter and his British friend are returned under police custody to face proceedings in Britain. Monsieur Alain, who is French and acted under instructions, will be detained here for three months plus one hundred hours community service for the good of this fine town. I also request my British legal friends to determine who was behind this silly game. He or she or they are almost certainly British and should be brought to justice. Case determined.' He and his colleagues rose, bowed and marched out. Henri marched the gang out. Monsieur Gustav Bontout bowed to Philipe and marched out. Everyone else hugged each other, quite a few times.

EIGHTY-TWO

James, Molly and Ellie filled up and the tears overflowed down their faces. Overjoyed would be an understatement. James invited Kat and Abel, who had no English at all, and even Gaston Blanc back over the square to the same restaurant, where predictably the local press had gathered again. Even a British tabloid team were there. Molly gave out predictable sentences, thanking everybody, James exuded relief that it was all over and they were looking forward to getting back home to a normal life. Philipe and Henri issued what might be called the official version, praising each other and the local system down here that had worked splendidly for the benefit of this family and the immediate neighbourhood of the town. The tabloid team persisted longer and they and James came to a garbled understanding about a UK exclusive. Cards and phone numbers were exchanged all round.

Finally the press went; Henri and Philipe lingered for one more glass, wished the extended family well and left. Gaston Blanc, who didn't know anybody, was in it for the wine and then the last train back to Paris, had found a fellow imbiber and they were happy to be left alone. Kat couldn't stop crying and kept inviting them all back to St Jean des Ponts; Abel's seamanship included another sort of drowning and he had found a B&B round the corner for him and Kat to sleep it off later.

And then it was just the three of them. It was an hour earlier in the UK and they had phoned the Otsworths and the Longtons. James phoned Steve to say hoped to be back tomorrow. They aimed to catch an early train to Paris in the morning and a Eurostar back to St Pancras. James did what he could online for a booking.

'What now, you two?' said Ellie.

'I think we'll be boring for a while. No trekking for a while. Maybe City walks and Hyde Park. Don't forget work. We owe them as they have decently kept our pay going all through this. I'm not going to ask about holidays yet.'

'And I've got to get different parts of my brain working. I'll be hopeless for weeks. I'll be trying to work out how to escape from work and scrounging for bread and coffee. Isn't Kat lovely? I'd love to go back there sometime to see Georges and Francoise. I'm sure they would remember me.'

'Well it won't be tomorrow, my darling. It's trains and back to the flat. Bee and Dee have been missing you and your mum and dad will be desperate.'

They turned in. After a quick breakfast, then check out, down to the train station, train to Paris, crossed Paris on an overflowing RER, queued for ages to get their Eurostar, zoomed to St Pancras, walked out to the full reception committee of Bee, Dee, Steve, Henry, Annabel and even Fraser was there.

EIGHTY-THREE

Gustav phoned the Boss.

'Not good. I did my best but the evidence was too overwhelming. I had nothing to fight on. We got two-thirds of the costs of putting the farmhouse back together. I don't think we should ask for more – one, because I don't think we'll get it and two, most of it has already been paid into court in order to get his daughter back. Pete and his mate are being sent back to the UK to face the original charge of abduction in Sussex. Alain got three months plus community service here.'

'No, not good. The money's fine. Formally accept and get it paid please. I've got other guys in the UK so it's not the end of the story, not by any means. This is an irritating interruption, not the finale.

Your end's finished now, Gustav, apart from getting the money. Send me your bill when you've got the money.' And the phone clicked dead. Gustav sighed; no social manners, that guy; just straight and functional. He phoned the Court and agreed the timetable and conditions for the two-thirds to be paid. Move on.

EIGHTY-FOUR

Clive and Mavis were in with Knutsford going through the outcome of the hearing.

'That's cleared up now. The two of the gang will be back shortly in custody. We'll arrest them for the original kidnapping and consequential events in France and the CPS will take them to Court. Should go down for a few years. End of. Well done in your liaison with the French side. Take closing statements from James and Miss Molly and I think we can close the files.'

Clive and Mavis didn't know which of them would speak first. Mavis deferred to Clive.

'Thank you, sir. Yes, it's good they're back safely. We, er, I think I can also speak for Miss Smith, think there is a mastermind or a Mr Big behind this and we are on the trail through ownership of the French properties. We would like to continue that lead and also grill these two when they're back in custody here. There could be a trade-off between their sentence and revealing their backers.' Mavis nodded her agreement with this.

'Mmmm. Life's not a TV crime drama, you know. Don't get too fanciful on this one. OK, you have to interview these two anyway so you can try that on. The property trail? Not optimistic on that, all a long time ago and could be a poisson rouge.' They produced weak smiles for his attempt at humour. 'So keep it running but not too much time on it, mind. I want you next on this car scam down at Evans's Garage. He's undercutting service and MoT charges and letting lethal cars out on our roads. Local people's lives are at risk.'

'Yes sir.' Said in unison. They knew a partial victory when they saw one.

Clive had already linked with Hortense and Faure when Pete and Martin would be back in the UK. The French wanted final interviews with them too so it would be two or three more days yet. They would not be held here at their station but at the bigger police premises at the next town. He had also contacted there to arrange for him and Mavis to interview them over the original abduction, now more than two months ago.

With that on hold for a few days, it left some time for the property trail. Mavis had started all the usual police searches for a Mary Brigg who may have been before or afterwards Mary Johnson. Brigg was rare and there were hundreds of Briggs, which could easily have been misheard by the estimable Neville Wright.

'We need to come up with a methodology that focuses on the most likely. The facts are Nuneaton, two in France, Mary Johnson and Mary Brigg or Mary Briggs.'

'Yes, Morse, we do. Can you give me some time to wade through this please Clive?'

'Yes, of course. I was wondering about our last badminton game with Sue and Matt. What do you think about asking them to make up a foursome to go ice-skating at that rink on the coast? We could eat out on the way back?'

'Do you think they're up for it? I know it was nice and social etcetera, but away from the leisure centre, they, and we for that matter, might not work so well?'

'Could you phone Sue and try her out? If you two girls are happy, Matt and I'll be fine.' Mavis was not sure about this casual use of 'girl'. Times were changing on that one.

'OK, leave it with me. Can I get on with some work now? You heard what Knutsford said.'

'Yes, sorry. Over to you. Thanks.'

Clive went back to his desk and got the file out on the computer disk and the Ken thing. Now all the parties were back in the UK, he could interview Molly on her own. He tried James's phone but no reply. They would be on the Eurostar.

He went over to the central desk and asked for the Evans's Garage file. Two inches thick.

EIGHTY-FIVE

Henry and Annabel had booked a room at a central London hotel as well as two other rooms. One for Ellie and one for Molly and James. James recognised that this meant he was finally accepted into the inner circle of the Otsworth family. Henry had really stepped up to this one and had booked a well-known restaurant for all nine of them. He hadn't been expecting Bee, Dee, Steve and Fraser but if they were good enough to turn out for his long-lost daughter, a phone call quickly extended the size of the table. They were all good company too. Bee and Dee and Steve had taken what little luggage the returning travellers had back to their respective flats and brought back minimal essentials for James and Molly for the night. Henry was as expansive as his daughters had ever seen. 'Order what you like, no boundaries everyone.' Ellie speculated to herself that this was what it took for their father to recognise his latent love for his daughters.

Henry drank a little too much, rose to make a speech, 'just a few words' which he did and then ended up crying and sat down. To cheering applause, James did slightly better. He thanked everyone for their continued and trusting support throughout and he was so happy. Dee stood up, towering over all of them, and said how much they had missed Molly. 'Some things you never know how special until they, in this case she, aren't there.' Finally Fraser, claiming total independence, said his observation was that James wasn't James without Molly and now he is James again.

It did end. It was all of a hundred yards to the hotel. Bee and Dee got a tube to their flat, Steve to his and Fraser to his.

At the hotel, head to pillow to sleep was a matter of seconds.

The assembly for breakfast extended over an hour. James and Henry did the full English.

'It's back to reality now everyone. We've all been on a massive trip,' announced James. He was not wrong.

James phoned work to say he and Molly would be in later.

James and Molly went to their flats to change clothes.

Molly ordered a new mobile.

Henry and Annabel and Ellie got a taxi to Paddington.

Clive phoned James to arrange separate interviews with him and Molly.

The Boss phoned Doug to meet 'soonest'.

EIGHTY-SIX

Doug was different from Pete. First, he went back further with the Boss; second, he hadn't been inside; and third, there was a lot more in the brain department. After the phone call, they met the next day over lunch in the back bar of The Prince of Wales. It had a faded elegance but more importantly it was tucked away behind the High Street and the alcoves were discreet and discrete.

'Hi Boss, how you doing?'

'Could be better, thanks; how are you and Celia keeping?'

'It's our twenty-fifth next month and hoping to get away to Spain for a few days. The south; warm.'

'Well done, old chap; we're thirtieth next year – God knows where I'll be.'

'What's all this about? You said something about plans being disrupted. I'm guessing you want a hand from me. Nothing physical this time and not too far off being legal if you don't mind.'

'You'll be OK, I'll see to that. I want a certain person picked up, kept safely for a few days and then delivered on. The important bit is that I want as little press coverage and involvement from Her

Majesty's as possible. Just for a few days with all the busybodies thinking it's a brief trip away, all innocent.'

'Like visiting an old aunt, for example?'

'You've got it. A text on the mobile might just be enough.'

'When?'

'What's keeping you? I'll give you personnel details, you may want to catch up with recent events so maybe leave it a few days yet. Usual terms, all in cash after delivery and a bonus on top if there's no interference from the busybodies. Now, the beer's good here and the steak-and-kidney is home-made.'

An hour later they went their separate ways.

EIGHTY-SEVEN

Julian was in thinking mode. Percy had spoken to Pierre, who was totally convincing that this was absolutely nothing to do with the French. 'It's not how we do things here. If it's a game, it's a British game, like your cricket.' Percy had related this back to Julian together with an account of the trial and its outcome.

'The two Brits will be back in a few days and interviewed by the police down in Sussex.'

Julian took all this in and wondered what to do next. There was no need to do anything. It was a simple crime and the police and the courts would find them guilty and they'd be off to jail. But his tidy, slightly autistic mind wasn't happy with just that. Those two ruffians couldn't be bothered to do all that without some serious cash and no ransom had been demanded. So the cash was from elsewhere. His professional interest was who or what was behind it. He had identified Molly and so had someone else. They were competing for the same resource. He decided to have a word with the Police Chief heading up the investigation, see where they had got to and pull rank if necessary.

EIGHTY-EIGHT

James and Molly reported for work at twelve noon. There was a standing ovation organised by Paul and Rosemary and their desks were covered with cards and banners saying 'Welcome Back'. They were overwhelmed and said some customary clichés. When it quietened down, they went into Paul's office. He poured three coffees.

'You've both been through a lot, you in particular Molly. And I expect you've had some riotous celebrations on both sides of the Channel. We're delighted you're back of course, but I am concerned about suitability for certain types of work until you are back into the normal swing of things.'

James thanked him for keeping their salaries going and promised they would do their very best to give something back.

'What work did you have in mind? Are we being put down a layer? I was in the middle of that merger and I'm looking forward to getting back into it.'

'No, no, no worries. I know you'll make up a bit of time and work hard at whatever you're given. No you're not demoted, don't be silly. We just think that for a while you should not be in client-facing work. One, you'll be a distraction with questions from everyone wanting to know everything, even minor details, especially from you Molly as a young woman. Two, undoubtedly there will be press coverage and more so when the prosecutions take place. Three, the police will be interviewing you again anytime soon. Four, for your own pastoral sanity, you both need to get back to normal life, domestic stuff and the rest. It will all settle down, I know, in a few weeks. Therefore, we propose putting you on separate teams, which you were before anyway, and working on internal projects here in this building. This does not mean filing or data prep by the way and I have some interesting stuff lined up for you. You can phone clients and outside people but I suggest you each adopt a new name for external purposes and say you've been transferred internally from another department. It happens all the time anyway and no-one will be bothered and the quality of your work will be unaffected. As for the press, we would like you to do whatever you're going to do off the premises and we would allow a bit of time for that by coming in later in the morning and/or leaving a bit earlier in the evening. We'd rather not have the press on our doorstep and please check with our Legals for what you can or can't say about the firm.'

'I can see you've thought a lot about this re-entry to work. Maybe we hadn't given it any thought at all, thinking we would just resume where we left off. Molly, do you agree with all that Paul's said?'

'Yes, I think I do. It's very caring and pastoral and I'm not a 'Look At Me' person. I think as long as the work is challenging and I can sink my mind into it, it'll work a treat for a few weeks. I'll be glad to use brain again if I'm honest; but I do want to get back out on site. It's what I do best.'

'Yes, yes, all that's fine. I've got separate internal projects to give you now. Think of your new names, not James Bond or Molly Maguire please, something unexceptional. Then we'll meet again after a week to see how right or wrong I've been. Geoff's totally with me on this by the way. I've even got you a sandwich so you don't have to go outside. Hope you like my choice.'

They thanked him and left his room.

'You happy with this? I think it's driven by caring but maybe they think we might be psychological nutcases.'

'James, now it's me being bossy. If that were true, we wouldn't be here now. No, I think they value us and want to do the best for us without actually knowing what to do. That's why we're meeting again in a week. For me it will be rather nice to get back to reading files, doing spreadsheets, and writing up summaries. Can I be Jane Jones? You can be John Brown.'

'Get away!'

EIGHTY-NINE

Doug reviewed the material given to him, scanned the internet coverage, got the geography in his mind. Work was on the edge of the City; the flat was West London; commuting was by bus and tube; boyfriend similarly and they did not live together – yet. *It won't be long after all this,* Doug thought. Straightaway, he had pretended to be the police and phoned the flatmates for Molly's new mobile number. He thought it would be pretty clumsy to bundle her in the back of a van and drive off to the house he had in mind in Berkshire. Shades of what Pete would do. He needed her to go somewhere on her own initiative and then pick her up. He'd got two boys to help with the grab, that wouldn't be a problem. *The only people she's likely to want to see are friends, police, solicitor, press, clients.* None of those sounded remotely plausible for her to go out of her way for. *Ah!* His brain went ping. *The medical. She's been away and handled roughly and struck out on her own over fields and whatnot. The police or work or family would want her checked out, wouldn't they? Young girl, anything could have happened to her. As she appeared to be fit and in good shape and suffered no after effects, there's a good chance no-one would bother to fix a medical. And a health centre medical could be anywhere, couldn't it? Yes, that's the one. Get everything else in place first, then a nice friendly phone call to Miss Molly.*

NINETY

Clive had fixed up to see James and Molly the next day in the lunch hour at police premises near their work. His objective was to get the precise picture of Pete and Martin's actual involvement going over old ground for the Sussex capture for James, but with an entirely new perspective from Molly. Also, getting confirmation that her captors were one and the same at every stage in France, terminating at the hearing. The hidden agenda was gleaning anything that may transpire about the so-called Mr Big. Who was behind all this? Pete had stuck rigidly to his line that they were jobbing workers in France looking for work and had rented a couple of places. He would get to speak to them eventually but their journey back to the UK had not been disclosed yet. He peered over Mavis's shoulder.

'How's the search going and have you spoken to Sue?'

'Which first, Clive?' Mavis was full of concentration on her screens.

'The search?'

'I'm narrowing it down. Funny thing is, it's like a trail covered with leaves and other detritus and then it reappears further on. I may be paranoid on this but it feels like someone is trying to cover their tracks all the time to prevent someone like me tracking them down.'

'So are you getting warmer then?'

'In a way I am. The key is to cross-check with various databases – National Insurance, DVLA, Register of Births, Marriages and Deaths, HMRC, police crime records, I could go on.'

'I'm going up to town tomorrow to interview James and Molly so you'll have the place to yourself. And Sue?'

'It's a lovely idea, Clive, and nice of you to think of it. Thing is neither Sue, Matt nor me have skated before and we think we'll all end up on our bottoms.' Clive was about to make a smart remark and thought better of it.

'So why don't we meet up for badminton and then back to mine for something? Sue says she'll bring a pudding and you and Matt can bring some wine and cheese, yes?'

He readily agreed; everything was so effortless when she did it. He wondered if men tried too hard, or were they just hopeless?

'So the day after tomorrow, I will hope to conclude my searches from all the files accessible by the police and we can review your interviews with James and Molly. That should keep Knutsford happy. Good luck tomorrow, by the way, might see you first thing.'

'Yes, briefly. May your searches be conclusive. Bye.'

Mavis stayed on a bit. This search was going well; she felt she was getting the better of this Mary Johnson and some of it was surprising. Clive was a brick really.

NINETY-ONE

James and Molly were in different departments and the morning had gone uneventfully. Molly liked the unthreatening nature of the work, the chats to old colleagues, answering questions as blandly as possible. James on the other hand was unsettled. He wanted to be up-and-at-'em and found this audit trail and profitability assessment for a client he'd never met to be unabsorbing. These next few weeks were going to be like a prison.

Legal had laid down strict guidelines about their talking to the media. It was in order to say who they worked for and that was about it as far as the company was concerned. The capture and all the incidents in France and the return to the UK were all private to James and Molly and had absolutely nothing to do with the company. 'Keep it all separate from us' was the clear direction from the in-house solicitor. She also said they should have a solicitor with them for their meeting with the tabloid. That meeting was provisionally set up for the next day in an office near their work. But today it was Clive Drewett at a City police station. They met up in reception at noon and walked over, grabbing a sandwich to have on the run and trusting that the police would be offering coffee.

'Hello James, again, and I think this is our first meeting, Miss Otsworth?' Clive directed them into an interview room straight off the entrance where a young colleague was already seated with a file in front of him. 'I've ordered coffee, if that's OK with you. Part of this will be you two together and part will be just with Miss Molly.'

'Should I get our solicitor?' James was struck by the formality descending on the meeting.

'I wouldn't have thought so at this stage and you are not about to be charged, obviously. We have not yet interviewed the two who are being sent back to the UK so we have not finalised our thoughts on the actual charges that may be brought. This is our opportunity to get Miss Molly's version of the last two months or so. If you feel uncomfortable without a solicitor, please say so.'

'James, it's fine, don't worry, love. I'm just going to tell them what happened.' Molly felt relaxed not being held captive.

Clive started right at the beginning. The lift they hitched. They confirmed without any doubt whatsoever that the two in the 4x4 were the Pete and Martin throughout the French part of the story. Clive said formal identification would become necessary after charges were made. He pressed them on the 4x4, any description, any clues, anything they could remember about the car. No, they could not remember anything. Clive then asked James to leave the room; there were newspapers and a TV on the news channel next door, 'And the coffee machine's not bad.'

'Will you be alright on your own? Shout if you need me.'

'I'm fine James, I've been over two months on my own.' James left and Clive tried to make the interview a little less formal.

'We've received accounts from a Monsieur Faure and Madame Alphonse about your stay at the farmhouse and the house, your escapes and various people you bumped into. Would you mind going through all that in your own words, any perspective you've got on the dialogue you had with the gang, any clues for a possible reason for your abduction?'

Molly knew that was coming and had given lots of thought to it during the whole period. No, nothing. She said the gang came and went at both places as though they had something else to do, maybe even the work as they had claimed. She had heard no phone conversations and she stressed that, given the circumstances, they looked after her uncommonly well. She felt their behaviour throughout was under instructions but had no idea who from. They were decent to her.

'Sorry to put it like this, and say if you would rather talk to a WPC, but were you handled in any way, if you get my drift?'

'No problem. Apart from the drugging right at the beginning near the Downs, none of them approached me in any way that you mean, not sexually, not suggestively, not remotely anything that could be called harassment. It may sound odd to you but in that respect, they were perfect gentlemen.'

'OK, that seems very clear but if you recall anything different, please let us know and a WPC can be arranged immediately. Now, Miss Molly—'

'Molly, please.'

'Thanks, Molly. Now Molly, while you were away, and do not reproach them for this because we didn't know where you might be or what you might be up to, James and Ellie came across this floppy disk from years ago slipped into a book or a diary in your room. It was old technology but we managed to get it printed out. Most of it was just references to people and personal events but one part of it was a fairly strongly worded piece about "Dad" and "Ken". Have you any recollection of this?'

Molly rarely blushed but she did now.

'I'm going a bit red because I remember writing about, er, becoming a woman and, er, losing my virginity.'

'That's OK, we all do things like that. I didn't mean that one; I meant the one I referred to previously.'

'I remember writing something like that about a boy. It could've been Ken. The hot blood had gone, I assure you; it's quite funny in retrospect. Ellie and I despite our age difference were fighting over this boy, like who fancied him more, who saw him first, who he wanted to go out with. Great teenage stuff by the way. Dad had to intervene it was so bad. I've never seen him so angry and I don't think I've been so hot-blooded since. That's the only time he ever did and that's the only time Ellie and I had a set-to over a boy. After that, we never laid any claim on each other's friends. You must see that and how she and James tracked me down. They could not have done more.'

'Why would each of them separately have no recollection of this incident?'

'My dad would have just moved on; he always has been busy with the business and the community. To him, it would be just another HR issue solved.'

'And Ellie?'

'She might have internalised it. More likely is that each of us moved swiftly on to other friends and maybe another boyfriend.'

'Is there any lingering, er, poison, between you and your father? My sole interest is clutching at anything that might give us a clue as to who was behind your kidnapping.'

'You think my dad is behind it? We are devoted.'

'No, of course not; but we are intrigued by the apparent lack of any motive or ransom and by the relatively soft way you were looked after.'

'Can't help you there. I agree it's odd. I'll keep talking to James and family for anything strange or remote in the past. And college.'

They talked some more about the gang's behaviour in the various situations including her ringside seat at the confrontation with Bertrand in St Jean des Ponts. Clive showed her out. James had left a note at the desk to say that as there had not been any further need for him he had gone back to the office. *See you there.*

NINETY-TWO

Doug had changed his mind. Couldn't risk any further time delay nor a tube or bus ride out to the suburbs. He had followed them to the police station, seen them go in, then James come out. *Perfect,* he thought, *she's on her own.* He was parked up a side street with an eyeline to the cop shop, with two associates. That's what they were called these days.

He phoned Celia as soon as Molly came tripping down the steps.

'Now.'

Molly heard her phone ping as soon as she switched it back on.

'Is that Molly?'

'Yes?'

'Oh good, I'm glad I've caught you. It's Becky from the health centre following up the police. It's just routine, love, but after what you've been through it's standard practice for you to have a brief medical. Twenty minutes tops and for a fit young thing like you, should be shorter.'

'Oh, er, thanks but I'm fine and no-one's mentioned it.'

'Nah, they never do, always leave it to us. Where are you? In the City by any chance?'

'Well I am actually but can I get back to you?'

"It needs to be done as close to your experiences as poss, my dear. Any chance you can head to London Wall and look for the health centre? It's a garish-looking building, bright lights with a tree in the reception area. Leave your mobile on and I'll direct you. Honest, it'll all be over in a jiffy.'

'Oh, OK then. I'm turning right up Wood Street and can see London Wall ahead.'

'Lovely. Keep going and you'll soon be here.'

Doug saw Molly change direction. He moved his smart saloon towards Molly's path and speedily drew up alongside. The two associates were out and bundling her into the middle of the back seat of the car before she realised what was happening. They grabbed her mobile off her and gave it to Doug. She wriggled and shouted a lot but, summoning up all her considerable captive experience, then sat back and tried to think what to do next. They did not respond to her questions and after quarter of an hour just sat back and took in her captors and her route. At least she was awake.

Doug pulled up in a service road in front of a row of shops. His other car was there and they shoved Molly from the back of one car into the back of another. Celia took over the first car and drove off to her mother's in East Grinstead. Doug settled into the second car and texted James on Molly's mobile "called away to friend Gwen, seriously ill and only a few stops on tube, all OK, talk soon xx", threw the SIM card out of the car window, drove off heading for the M4, past Windsor and then into rural Berkshire where by then it was dark. It appeared to be a deserted country house with one light on in the hall.

Molly was bundled upstairs into a seriously quality bedroom with an en suite. Everything was locked and she wasn't the least inclined to escape tonight. She could now assume, if they were from the same stable as the gang, that she would get an evening meal and some bathroom essentials. She did.

Downstairs, Doug called the Boss.

'Package delivered here. No problem. What's next step?'

'Well done Doug, assuming no trace on mobile or car, lie low tomorrow and I'll work out what to do the day after. No discussions with her. Bye.' And he was gone.

NINETY-THREE

James read the text wide-eyed. *What?* He called Molly; the phone was dead. He phoned Clive, who immediately launched into thanking them both for their help.

'She gone again.'

'Eh?'

James read out the text.

'Who's Gwen?'

'Never heard of her. I'll try Ellie, the family, even Bee and Dee and get back to you.'

No-one had ever heard of a Gwen and thought it extremely unlikely that Molly would go off on her own having just got back. He phoned Clive back and told him so.

'The time of the text is very shortly after she left the police station. I'll order the CCTV. Every inch of the City is monitored so we should be able to reconstruct her path. There's nothing you can do at the moment, stay at work or home with mobile on and charged.'

Clive had not left the City station and got straight on to the department controlling CCTV. He told them the time, place and type of incident and they tracked it down quickly. Clive could hardly believe his eyes – there was Molly leaving the station, then putting her mobile to her right ear, then changing direction, then a car swooping in and two of them grappling with Molly and pushing her into the back of the car, which drove off speedily. They were able to follow it going west out of the City but lost it shortly later as it went into side streets. The number plate was too fuzzy to read completely.

'They will change cars anyway en route to wherever they're going. We can put a track on her phone.' That came through later showing up finishing in West London and the phone dead.

'Looks planned to us; dealt with the car and phone tracking. We can put out an alert and description but let's face it, they could be anywhere.' Clive shrugged and had to agree. This was worse than Snakes and Ladders, one of the cruellest games in cupboard back home. He made a few phone calls and got a commuter train out of Victoria. Home by 7.30, had a beer and crashed out on the sofa till late.

NINETY-FOUR

Sylvia put the phone down and shouted for Barry.

'Yes!' She had at last been accepted at a local agency for references and CV checking. Not great but it was a job she could do at home and would keep her occupied and bring in enough for food and drink in the week. Barry came down from his study upstairs in old jeans and a sloppy sweater.

'Sounds good, whatever it was, yes?'

'Yes, I'm underway. How've you got on?' Barry had had mixed experiences over these weeks. His networking had produced a few assignments, mostly interims while companies got a permanent person. He had hoped that at least one would stick and they go for him as the devil-you-know rather than the lottery of the open market. It seemed like head-hunters had got the market sewn up.

'It's OK; been on the phone all afternoon; tiresome but got another interim next week. It's a fifty-mile drive which actually I don't mind. It sort of separates work from home.'

'Well done, my love. As long as you keep producing results, something'll turn up.'

'You're my Mrs Micawber. Actually I'm having lunch tomorrow with my best contact and he's really a good friend now. Two of my temp jobs have come from him.'

'You buy him lunch and don't quibble. He's not going to waste his time so maybe it's serious. And while you're in that kit, go for a run and then straight in the shower. We have to put up with you. It's a packet Mexican tonight.' Barry thought better of making a cheap joke and disappeared out of the back door and down the lane at the bottom of the garden.

Barry had known Frank since his first job. Frank had effectively been a mentor to Barry all his working life and had followed his progress, the ups and the downs, throughout. He liked Barry's ability to get things done through people yet still be a doer alongside any team he was in. They met at half twelve at a reasonable restaurant in the next village but one. It had a fair reputation and Barry was more than happy to go there to talk. No eavesdropping there.

'Frank, good to see you.'

'Barry, the pleasure's mine. How are you?'

They soon caught up with each other's news and families and went straight to the table in the window overlooking the road. Neither wasted any time ordering and, after drinks delivered, Frank started.

'Cheers Barry. Always good to meet up like this. I've been following your recent assignments, as they say "with interest". All very good and they tell me good work too. But it's not you, is it? What are you looking for?'

'You're right. I throw myself into things but there's no finish; I'm not building anything; each new assignment is a starting from scratch again.'

'OK but you are building up experience and skills and everything new is a new experience. But not building big bucks, no?' Frank smiled as he said this but he knew it was true. It had been true of himself too and, although he had kept several directorships, he didn't need to work again.

'If you boil it down to the essentials, that's spot on. Wife dabbling in a little job from home, private education, private health insurance and then plenty to retire on and do the golf thing. It's not happening yet; but I have some funds left over from that incident.'

'Well, building is the word. I'm on the board of a building construction company. It's not fashionable and we have to fight to find sites. They're not always suitable and then we're stuck with getting rid of it and we'd rather not sell to a competitor. The one I'm talking about is about ten miles away, you may know it, it's currently a scrap metal business called ScrapCash run by the Davidson family.' Barry nodded that he did, without much enthusiasm.

'Well old man Davidson wants to sell up, his boys aren't interested unsurprisingly, and as it's a fair sized footprint we had agreed to buy the site subject to clearance. Now we're no longer interested and we would be prepared sell to you at a slight discount rather than let it go to a competitor. Davidson will accept a bit less to save himself clearing the site; and maybe you could wring something out of the business and do something with the land? What do you think?' Said with a big smile.

'Well, it's entrepreneurial, I'll give you that. Can we talk figures and accounts? Yes, I'll look at it. You're not doing me over and playing me, are you?'

'Sincerely not, Barry. As I say, you'd be doing us a favour as we should never have touched it. We could discuss the scrap thrown up on the other sites we have to clear. There's always scrap, trust me.'

'OK, I'll build that in. If you can send the dox, I'll get back to you within forty-eight hours. Let's enjoy lunch and this plonk.'

They did and then parted, Barry picking up the bill. He drove back via Davidson's and was surprised at the full extent of the land. It went right back to a railway line and he could see that it would not be at all attractive for any residential development or even a customer-facing business. Possibilities were whirring through his mind.

Sylvia was waiting for him and over coffee they sat on stools round the kitchen table to compare notes.

'That was an eye-opener, Silv. It's a scrap metal business going nowhere at a discounted price. I'll see the figures later and maybe it turns in a profit. The nugget is the land at the back. No perceived value at all but it's land. They're not making it anymore. With the pay-off and a bit of borrowing, I might be able to stretch to it.'

'Sounds good. You'll have your eyes open to avoid a repeat performance of last time, yes? I'll have mine open for you. Good luck, boyo.'

Barry took a delivery of Frank's papers and went up to his study. Frank had biked them over as soon as he had got back from lunch. Barry rang him.

'Frank, it's Barry. Great lunch by the way. Nice to see you; and thanks for sending over the papers. I'll get back to you soonest.'

'I thought you would be interested so I had them ready. I could have brought them with me but I reckoned that was presumptuous. Don't read anything into our keenness.'

Barry absorbed the papers. All rather sketchy, as expected. He decided to pop round in the morning and have a chat with old man Davidson, perhaps even take some metal bits and pieces out of the garage.

Davidson was rather weary. He was having a flask of tea off an upturned crate and motioned to Barry to a detached car seat. At least it was real leather.

'I'm talking to Frank from the company that's interested in your site. What's your take on it, Alan?' Barry had done his homework.

'Barry, lad, I'm pushing seventy and had enough. The boys don't even come here and the wife can't wait for me to be shot of it. I just need enough to live on and keep her and me together.'

'You're making a profit but it gets less each year. Did you have a figure in mind?'

'I've got my state pension and we've got the house. Annuity rates are high at the moment and I've had a quote from one of those big names. Something around this should be OK for us,' and he wrote a figure on a paper bag from what looked like yesterday's lunch.

'Let me see what I can do.' The figure was well within Frank's suggestion. If Barry could get Alan a few per cent more, he reckoned he would get something extra on the handover. They shook hands, Barry saying things would happen quite quickly now. Alan gave him a cheery wave.

Back home, he had a final look over the figures and phoned Frank. It emerged that their deal was midstream so Barry's offer was to break their deal and agree what to pay Davidson without him having to clear the site. Fortunately for all, the solicitors were relieved there was now a solution and they could go straight to completion. Davidson shed ten years when he heard he was getting 6.5% more.

'Silv, I own a scrap metal business and a patch of land.'

'Come here, big boy.'

NINETY-FIVE

Molly woke up in a very comfortable bed and used the very well-appointed bathroom. Hot shower, fresh towels, *What the hell is going on?* she puzzled. *Yes, I'm used to being captured and held against my will by now but this is weird, even suspicious.*

Someone she had not seen before knocked on the door and delivered a breakfast tray, all very civilized.

'Hello. Where am I? What am I doing here? What's happening next?' All good valid questions but no response and he locked the door behind him. The windows, which were very well secured, looked out on to woodland with no sight of any paths or houses or farm buildings. This is rural Berkshire, Thames Valley, a well-to-do area and much desired by the seriously rich. You got privacy for the price.

She decided to sit this one out. There was not much alternative anyway and she could catch up on the pile of society magazines, like in a dentist's waiting room, left on the side. *Someone somewhere has a plan for me,* she thought. *I'm not in apparent danger. James and co. are in touch with the police and the tabloid which was going to run the French story will now be doubly interested. Or maybe fed up with waiting. The quality of this house and my new prison cannot be permanent so something is going to happen very shortly.* This was how Molly reasoned. There was a screen in the corner of the bedroom but not connected to TV. A DVD player and a pile of DVDs next to it were suggestive of how she might fill the time. It was all so quiet; she could not hear any signs of activity and escape was not an option. She just had to occupy herself and await developments. Molly did not think she would be there for more than a few days.

NINETY-SIX

Clive was unsettled. He felt responsible for letting Molly out of his clutches and had not anticipated anything like this happening. In the station he briefly told Mavis what had happened and then hit the phone. First, the London police station who said the car had vanished and they did not have enough letters to track down the registration number. The congestion zone readings showed entry points and were no help. CCTV had petered out when the car switched down some side streets. Second, James, who he partly blamed for letting her out of his sight. James in his defence said they had not been warned to be wary of possible follow-up action and they might have done exactly the same as they did by the South Downs and removed him and taken her. Clive relented. Third, the Otsworth family. Had they received any communication from anybody? No, they hadn't and were not best pleased about this turn of events and, if anything, blamed the police. Clive was conciliatory. He had to turn to Mavis for support.

'What does it look like to you?'

'Clive, I think it confirms once and for all that there is someone behind this. The gang in France were carrying out orders and with them under lock and key, this mastermind has turned to some other mates to get Molly in the UK. But why?'

'Dunno. I hope it's not another Tour de France. This caper was a bad novel and now it's worse. It's just sinking in that you can disappear in this country. We haven't got a clue, literally, where Molly and her kidnappers are. They could be anywhere.'

'OK, but not for long. The press are on to it. Whoever they are know that we have the two gang members arriving in the UK shortly; they know that the police have interviewed Molly and James; and they must know that we know who the owners of the French farmhouse and house are. Which brings me on to my researches. Are you ready?'

'It'll be a welcome change. Have you got anything real?'

'Yes, I have Watson. The property trail led to Mary Johnson and a clue that she was now a Brigg. It's not such a common name, unlike Briggs, so I followed up on many of them. When she is buying property she uses the Mary Johnson name and, from the Land Registry, I've been able to string together a list of properties bought and sold in her name, including the two French properties which she still owns. All of these are in her own name. So I had to go down the married route to get a Brigg connection. We women can get away with using our maiden names for virtually everything. So married ladies and even formerly married ladies can lead a double existence. Except for the marriage certificate, obviously.' She paused.

'Are you leading a double existence Mavis?'

'Don't be silly, not-so-young man. So that left searching for a Ms Johnson marrying a Mr Brigg at some time or other. They might not still be married but, if our informant is right, they must have been married once, and around the time of the Nuneaton sale and purchase.'

'So you searched on that, yes?'

'Yes. There are a lot of Johnsons but not so many Briggs. Eventually, and that's a euphemism, there were three in the last fifty years. I took the view that as Ms Johnson currently owns two properties in France, she probably got married to this Brigg fellow within the last fifty years. Anyway, there are three possibilities that coincide with an assumed marriage at the time of the Nuneaton transaction. There's Frederick Brigg, George Brigg or Harold Brigg. Take your pick. I'm compiling where each of these specimens is now. It's not done yet but I feel that one of these could be our Mr Big, given the lengths that Ms Johnson and hubby have gone to, to cover their tracks.'

'Good work, Holmes. Perhaps not long now to a discovery. Have you got any dates for linking up with Sue and Matt?'

'Oh, thanks for jogging me, yes, all fixed up for this Saturday. Badminton booked for five o'clock, then back to mine. Sue and I are doing food; you and Matt are doing beer, wine and cheese, OK?'

'You're a star.'

'I know.'

NINETY-SEVEN

James didn't know what to do or say. To anybody. He had found the girl of his dreams. He had, after a fashion, rescued her from criminal forces in France and brought her back to Britain. They had had extensive interviews and discussions with the police, including going to the nearest police station to their work. But, fool that he was, he had left her to find her own way back, all of ten minutes' walk, and she had been pinched again. He wasn't there at the time but he had to blame himself. Maybe this time it was for real and they would finish her off. He could visualise the tabloids, even the tabloid they were about to have an exclusive with, taking him and the police to task. Pictures of ashen-faced family and boyfriend; the gory details; didn't anyone realise the danger she was in? Yet another tragic tale of a family falling apart; he could write the stuff himself. He phoned Fraser.

'Hi, pal. You've heard.'

'Have, Jimbo, very sorry and all that. What next?'

'No idea. It's all my fault. What shall I do?'

'Look mate, you stay strong for Molly. She doesn't want a weeping willow. Wherever she is, she knows that you are out there doing your best and looking for her. If you're a lucky man to have her, she's a lucky woman to have you.'

'I owe you a drink for that dose of common sense.'

'Well said. Tonight any good? I'll pop round to yours.'

'Done.'

Next he phoned Ellie.

'Hi. Got any mad ideas on this one?'

'Nope. It's all crazy. What is it about my dear sister? It's like there's a sinister plot.'

'I'm starting to think it may be exactly that. But who, what, where and why?'

'I've absolutely no idea. But if there is something connecting all this madness together, then maybe, just maybe, there is a someone behind the scenes calling the shots. Keep in touch. Bye.'

'Bye.'

He went back to the flat, via the supermarket. He told his flatmates that Fraser was coming round and he'd got the booze in.

NINETY-EIGHT

The next few years went in a whirl. Barry decided to continue the scrap metal business and secured the rights to scrap from the sites that Frank's building company bought. With the land at the back he opened up first a lorry park, then some of his own vehicles for heavy-duty industrial deliveries and then, opportunistically from one of his clients, a demolition business. He could rent the heavy plant and found he had a knack for dealing with the workers. They were tough but one could say euphemistically that they were refreshingly blunt and straightforward. He could respond to that and earned a grudging respect from surprising quarters. There were a lot of cash payments but he had always kept good records. No-one had ever disputed his payments, in whatever form they were paid, and this bolstered his reputation for fairness. Even so, they were a rough lot and, apart from an inaugural visit by Sylvia, she never visited the site again.

The company did well. It kept to its chosen path with the 'controlled incrementalism' that Barry had set and liked. He felt you knew where you were. It grew slightly faster than the building industry generally and its perceived value crept up so that eventually it was noticed on City radar screens. Barry retained full ownership and kept debt firmly under control so that the financial recession of the late noughties left it unscathed as the company had kept itself well out of the banks' clutches. Eventually, with the change of government, things stirred in the City.

Barry had noticed that a former industrial building adjacent to his site was getting visits with men in suits taking photographs with their cameras. He made enquiries for the demolition contract for an assumed redevelopment next door. At every stage he was rebuffed. After a long winter of minimal activity, it all became clear and he received a cash bid for everything in his company from a merchant bank acting on behalf of a client.

He called Frank and asked him if he knew anything. He didn't but did say that if the money was right he should take it. Sylvia agreed. It was helped by the bidder saying they would take on the workers for at least six months and when payment terms were agreed together with a three-month handover consultancy, it was all over. With the money in the bank, Barry wouldn't need to work again.

'It's serious hobby time,' he said to Sylvia.

'You mean cruises and a villa in Marbella?'

'If you want. Let's go home for a quiet evening, love.' This was after the final signing.

'Yes. I'm up for that. Shall we be boring and have a takeaway? Singapore noodles do it for me.'

'Naughty old you.'

'Naughty was what I was thinking of.'

NINETY-NINE

Peter and Martin were finally escorted over to Britain a week after the hearing. Hortense and Henri had taken closing statements from them but nothing new emerged and they persisted in clinging on to their story that they were casual workers looking for work in rural France. And, naturally, they continued the line that Molly was similar and they had given her accommodation, despite all that the French magistrate had condemned them with.

They had been put in a van which drove to Calais where a Sussex Police van collected them and caught the ferry over the Channel to Dover and continued to police custody at the Sussex town some miles to the West. Clive and Colin Heath, a spare detective stationed there, were scheduled to interview them the day after delivery.

Clive got there early and was introduced to Albert Hall.

'Yes, I know, don't say anything. It's my parents' fault. I've been appointed to be the solicitor for Peter Ruff and Martin Round pending your investigations.'

'I'm Clive handling the original kidnapping and its consequences. Your name's brilliant; I hope we will all be in concert. Who appointed you?'

'I received a phone call to represent them yesterday morning.'

'Yes, OK, but from whom?'

'I'm not at liberty to disclose that as it is immaterial to their defence. They have the right to be represented.'

'Of course. This way, sir.'

They signed in and went to the interview room where Colin was waiting for them with some fresh coffee.

'I don't know how long this will take but it might go on a bit.'

'Hi, I'm Clive. Yes, I think it will.' Albert was silent.

After a few pleasantries, Colin said he would get them in. Pete and Martin were brought in with a constable also in attendance. Everyone introduced themselves. Clive noticed that Pete and Martin had clearly not met Albert before. Albert went out of his way to say he was on their side and he would advise them on whether to answer the police's questions or not, as their right.

Clive opened with the events near the South Downs over two months ago. He described the events in as much detail as he had got from James and Molly. The two guys were stony-faced.

'Do you admit that you gave a lift to James and Molly and after a short distance drew up and overcame them with force and drugs, left

James unconscious and abducted Molly to another place?'

Albert whispered to Pete.

'Sorry, no whispering. This is all on the record and being recorded.'

'We gave a lift to a young woman and dropped her off a few miles on her and our way.'

'That is contrary to the evidence we have.'

'It is my recollection.'

'And mine.' These were Martin's first words. He had a London accent as well.

Clive and Colin slogged over this time and again. They were two jobbing workers looking for work and they gave a lift to a young woman on a Saturday morning.

'The young woman, let's call her Molly, shall we, has identified you both on French police premises as the two who abducted her in Sussex and held her against her will in two locations in France. How do you explain that?'

'We meet a lot of girls and we help them out. We gave a lift to a young lady in Sussex and we gave accommodation to a young lady in our jobbing experience in France.'

'Did you recognise her as the same woman?'

'As I say, we meet a lot of girls and I do not recollect they were the same woman. She was a travelling worker just like us.'

'How do you know that?'

'That's what she told us.'

And so on ad nauseam. Albert hardly needed to butt in as Pete and Martin just kept on repeating the same old lines. Colin decided to be heavier.

'If you repeat this stuff in Court under oath and it proves to be lies, which we know they are, you will be severely taken apart for perjury and lying under oath. The penalties for that are very severe.'

'Thank you for that. We'll have to see, won't we?' This from Martin. Now it was Albert's turn.

'We appear to have reached a stalemate for any further progress today and I need to consult with my clients. Gentlemen, do you have any further questions for today?'

'Where is the 4x4 you were driving that Saturday morning when, as you said, you kindly gave a lift to a young lady?'

'I borrowed it from a friend for a weekend job.'

'And then you drove it to France?'

'We returned it back to him after we'd done the job.'

'And the name of this kind friend?'

'I just knew him as Bob, someone I'd worked with on a site a week or two before. He said we could borrow it that weekend.'

'Why don't I believe a word you've said?'

Pete just shrugged.

'Interview over. Messrs Ruff and Round are being returned to custody here for a further interview later.' Colin brought it to an end. Albert requested and was granted an immediate meeting with his clients.

'I hope Albert gets them to see sense. The evidence of identity and the antics in Sussex and France are well documented and recorded. A barrister will make mincemeat of them in court,' Clive said.

'They'll admit to it eventually. They'll have to. I read this interview as though they are under strict instructions to protect who or what is behind this adventure.'

'Agreed. Shall we try again tomorrow same time?'

'OK, and then we charge them.'

HUNDRED

Julian phoned Malcolm Knutsford. He had tracked him down as the Chief for the MNO investigation and had looked up his records. They had never met but they had had a case in common some years ago. One of Julian's bright young things had been caught up in a horse race betting group and Knutsford had been a stickler for following through to catching all of them.

'Good morning, Malcom, it's Julian Foxley here from the MoD.' He wasn't officially but it always got results.

'Good morning, sir. How can I help you?'

'I believe you are running the Molly Otsworth kidnapping case. Are you any nearer finding the perpetrators?'

'I have two officers on the case and the kidnappers are now back in the UK under further questioning. May I ask what is your involvement?'

'Well done on bringing them to justice. We are interested in whether there is someone or an organisation behind the kidnapping who may be directing operations. He or she or it may have their tentacles into wider matters that concern us.' Julian was pleased with his use of 'we' and 'us' and 'wider' as they had nothing to do with this seaside Mr Plod.

'You may well be right. My officers believe so too and are currently following up some rather tenuous leads, in my view.'

'Would you be good enough to keep me in the loop on their progress? I will not get in your way.'

'I understand. I'd rather keep it at official lines of reporting, if you don't mind, sir. If you are who you say you are, you will know who I report to and I would rather you linked in at that level. Thank you for your interest. Goodbye.'

Julian also replaced his phone, none too pleased.

'Percy! Here.'

HUNDRED AND ONE

Barry and Sylvia were enjoying their cruise in the Mediterranean. They had flown to Athens and joined this exclusive cruise company for two weeks dropping in at the major towns and cities and a few charming isolated ports able to accommodate a cruise liner. It was idyllic.

These last few years they had tried out and largely enjoyed the life of the seriously rich. Barry had joined the most prestigious golf course in the neighbourhood, taken a box with his premier league team, travelled business class to many parts of the world. When they went up to town, they stayed a few days in their favourite Mayfair hotel and took in the top shows. Barry had dabbled with some business colleagues in talking through some potential M&A deals. He kept in touch with Frank, now getting on a bit, and those he had enjoyed working with. Sylvia had given up her work. The boys were through their boarding schools and college and Barry had found them openings in London. The elder one was with a bright up-and-coming estate agency cum property company and the younger one in media and IT near the Silicon Roundabout, Old Street. Both took to London life with many friends from school and college starting afresh like them. Barry had also helped them with the rent on their flats so that they only had to share with one or two others. The boys were off their hands apart from the occasional phone and social media updates.

In truth, Barry and Sylvia were content, happy with each other and just a teeny bit stale and bored with life. They had no daily grind, no household chores, hardly any commitments and could do exactly as they pleased. In further unkind truth, Barry's work had roughened him at the edges, he was coarser now having had to deal with the coarser side of life. Neither he nor Sylvia had much intellectual interest in anything, they did not read much and found themselves mixing with people much like themselves – characterised by rich, aimless followers of trends and fashion, and doing endless rounds of predictable social get-togethers with shallow acquaintances. Apart from travelling on holidays or going to their villa or spending time at other people's villas or country houses, they would be hard-pressed to say what else they did with life.

On top of this, neither of them knew how to communicate their boredom to each other without it sounding like criticism or blaming their good fortune. They were lying on sun loungers on the top deck; not a cloud in the sky and a comforting pleasant heat with it. Barry tried.

'You know, love, I miss the challenge of business, solving problems, finding out how to motivate people and the sense of achievement.'

'I told you to get a few non-exec board appointments to keep your mind busy. But I know what you mean. I was sick of the sight of references and CVs by the end. I'd quite fancy assessing someone now. Funny isn't it?'

'Mmm, not sure a few non-execs are right. You're not in the real game and then it's your fault when it all goes belly up. I'll need to think of a few things to get up to; set myself some challenges; first up is getting my handicap much lower and win one of the competitions.' But in his mind he was working on something more difficult and actually more risky. He wanted to play a risky game and win it against all the odds. Like being two sets down at tennis; like needing a hundred runs to win and only two wickets left; like putting a few grand on the favourite and a no-hoper for the Derby; like challenging an established position and winning.

'OK darling but leave me out of it. I've always got the boys to worry about and my bits of business and my lovely groups of ladies for golf, wine and of course the ultimate – da di da – shopping!'

'No comment. It's a tasting menu tonight and Naples in the morning. Both OK with you?'

'See Naples and die. Go on with you.'

HUNDRED AND TWO

Clive got back in the afternoon to find Mavis looking excited. Her eyes shone and she was tripping over her own tongue to tell the world about it. It had to be to Clive first. But he got in first.

'Those two of the gang won't say a word and we reckon they've already perjured themselves several times over. The solicitor will have to get stroppy with them if they're to have a chance. We're meeting again same time tomorrow if that's alright with you. Mavis, is something bothering you?'

'Clive, shut up, sorry to be rude but listen. Mary Johnson, our Mary Johnson, you know the haphazard property woman?'

'Yes?'

'Well she's not Mary and not Johnson, well she is but she isn't.'

'Mavis have you had a triple expresso and brandy?'

'No. Listen. She is or at least was a married lady marrying a Mr Brigg and her full name on the marriage certificate is Katherine Mary Johnson, now Kate Brigg. What do you think of that?' She jumped up and down and did a twirl. Clive could have commented but didn't. She looked great.

'Right. Well done. And who exactly is Mr Brigg?'

'Quite. He's the Mr Harold Brigg, now a retired businessman. One of the three we had found previously.'

'And you and me are thinking that Mr Brigg is Mr Big using his wife's property for clandestine purposes?'

'Exactly. It's good isn't it?'

Clive was impressed and did his utmost not to show it. He had the Saturday social coming up in two days and wanted to keep whatever little gravitas he had till then.

'Very well done, Watson.'

'It's Holmes actually.'

'You're right, it is. Now next thing is – can we get something on Brigg before I meet Ruff and Round again tomorrow? If you're right, and I'm sure you are, they should be shocked when we show them we know something they don't expect us to know.'

'I'm on it. He's not on Google but that shouldn't be a problem. Appears to be still married to Katherine Mary. I'll see what more I can dig up.'

'All OK for Saturday? Meet at the leisure centre say 5?'

'Yep, court booked for 5.30, don't forget the booze.'

As if.

HUNDRED AND THREE

The days slipped by and the afternoons were getting darker now. Molly was so bored that she was starting to think about escaping again and being on the run. But that wouldn't work here. The house was totally secure and she could hear noises downstairs and in the next rooms most of the time. The talk was soft and she could not make out any of it. She tried to engage her captors in conversation without any success and when she asked for something to occupy her time, she was given more DVDs, newspapers dated from before her captures and a book of Sudoku puzzles. She organised her day into activity slots; there were meals three times a day, her physical workouts, maybe a DVD in the evening and then reading and Sudoku in between. She thought she might write a simple novel about a girl being captured three times and escaping twice but her request for pencil and paper was denied. She asked every day.

Then one afternoon, Doug came in and locked the door behind him.

'Hello Molly, how are you?'

'Could be better. Like out and about.'

'Yes, of course. But you are comfortable and being well looked after?'

'I suppose so. It's a very nice house and apart from my freedom, wanting current TV and newspapers, seeing my family and boyfriend, meeting my girlfriends, getting back to work to earn my living, it's OK.' She attempted a sarcastic smile.

'Yes, I know, it's hard on you but I just wanted to pop in to say it won't be long now. I can't actually say what "it" is or will be but just to reassure you, first you will not come to any harm and second you should be a free agent in not too long.'

'Well that's something to hold on to I suppose. Tomorrow, the day after?'

'Be patient, Molly.'

'I have to be. A thank you of sorts for letting me know.'

'We'll give you an hour's notice of whatever the something is.'

And Doug left as he had entered, silently and the door locked behind him.

Molly tried to work out whatever this something was all about. It was all so silly. She wondered what James and Ellie were up to.

HUNDRED AND FOUR

James and Ellie were not up to anything. They had both gone back to work. Clive had kept them up to date on his progress with the gang but on Molly there was nothing. CCTV had revealed nothing, nor car searches over the capital, and there were no reports of any strange activities that might be relevant to this getaway car. James stabbed on his phone calculator. If they had driven no more than fifty miles, that covered well over 7,500 square miles; and if they had driven exactly fifty miles, the circumference around London was over three hundred miles long. He pictured in his mind a needle being dropped into a haystack. So, what was positive? One, she was probably in the UK and even more probably in England. Two, she had not come to any harm before so was unlikely to be harmed now. Three, Pete and Martin were in police custody and were no doubt getting a grilling. Four, nothing else.

Ellie had gone back home to Henry and Annabel. They were in disbelief, unable to imagine that Molly could be swept up off the pavement in the middle of London and disappear without trace.

'How can these things happen? You read about things like this in the papers but you never imagine it could happen to us.'

'I know, Mum, it's just not fair. We have to pin our hopes on the two they have in Sussex. James gets reports from the police now and again. We have to keep our mobiles on and be patient. I'm pinning my hopes that Molly has not put herself in danger and her captors have never before put her in danger.'

The press had been in contact with James and the Otsworths and, under police and legal guidance, they had said nothing other than,

'We are awaiting developments and we hope our darling daughter is safe. The police are doing all they can.'

Henry did not approve of any public campaign bearing banners stating 'Free Molly Now' as he found them distasteful and counter-productive. It was much better for whoever was holding Molly to realise it was a fruitless, boring venture and she would be quietly released eventually. His and Annabel's unspoken fears were that her body would be dumped in a tip somewhere just off the M6 and be found decomposed several months later at a recycling plant. They never discussed this.

HUNDRED AND FIVE

Clive and Colin met at the latter's station the following morning. Albert had already arrived and had had a separate meeting with Pete and Martin.

Clive briefed Colin on Mavis's findings and her further findings on Mr Brigg. Colin weighed this up.

'That's very useful and could be a whole new route. Shall we find out how they have responded to yesterday's ultimatum and no doubt Hall's briefing first?'

'My thoughts exactly. Get them thinking they are happy with their new line of defence, have a coffee break and then take them into a new line of enquiry.' They went into the interview room where the four of them were waiting. Colin did the necessary preliminary statements and then started.

'No doubt you have reflected on how we finished yesterday and Mr Hall may have given you a dose of reality as well. We are going to go back over everything we discussed yesterday to evidence any revisions for the record. Everything today is recorded and counts as the official record. Mr Ruff, we'll start with you and the lift you gave to James and Molly on the South Downs road over two and a half months ago. Please tell us what happened.'

There was a change of content and tone as, in turn, Pete and Martin gave an account of all that had happened from giving a lift to James and Molly that Saturday morning right through to their being apprehended in France by Alphonse and Henri. It appeared that they had now recognised that the evidence and corroborations against them were overwhelming and that Albert Hall had drummed this into them. Even so, much of their story stayed the same. They meant no harm to James and Molly and dumping James so as to take Molly over to France was 'just a game' you know, 'high jinks' and so forth. They still claimed that they were jobbing workers looking for work and a holiday in rural France; they still claimed that Molly was doing the same and that they looked after her safely and fed and housed her.

'But you still kept her under lock and key and denied her her freedom. She was restrained by you both and by your French colleague?'

'That was for her safety; she didn't know where she was and she would not have been able to find her way back to Britain.'

'Because you had put her in that position and held her against her will. She escaped and you went looking for her.'

'For her protection. We obviously would be coming back to the UK for Christmas and we would have brought her back.'

'Then you captured her again in a town and imprisoned her again in the house.'

'We felt responsible for her. We liked her as a young woman and I know she has confirmed that she was not harassed either sexually or in any other way. She was good company.'

'She had no choice, did she? She would have worked out, especially after the initial abduction, that there was no point in squaring up to you, physically or verbally or merely being a pain in the bum. She had to go along with your flow until she found opportunities to escape.'

'That's what she did. She didn't have to escape; we were looking after her and would have brought her back.'

Colin signalled a coffee break and he and Clive went outside while Pete, Martin, Hall and the constable stayed in the interview room.

'So Hall has agreed to go down the silly-but-well-meaning kidnap route. No harm done etcetera. What's that going to be? A short sentence and community service and compensation they won't be able to pay?'

'Dunno. Might be a bit longer than that because there was violent abduction originally. Now, how do we play the Brigg card? I suggest right now with our opening sentence. They won't be expecting it and it'll tell them that we know something they didn't think we did, yes?'

'Agreed.'

They went back in and Colin let Clive start because he had discovered the Brigg connection. Well, Mavis had.

'Mr Ruff, tell me about your connection with Mr Harold Brigg.'

Pete faltered for a second or two, then pulled himself up. This pause was a giveaway, Clive thought.

'I don't think I know a Mr Harold Brigg.'

'Try again, Mr Ruff, before I ask Mr Round as well. May I remind you that this is all on the record and will be subject to cross-questioning at the trial.'

'Excuse me officers, but please might I have a few moments with my clients?' Albert intervened.

'We'll give you five minutes and we'll be back directly.'

They went back to the other room.

'They've got to decide whether to shop their boss or keep him out of it.' Clive agreed.

'If they decide to implicate him, they will blame absolutely everything on him. Acting under orders throughout. They might get a lighter sentence but they'll have to face him eventually. That could be what they call interesting.'

'And if they keep him out of it, this Brigg will probably get them the best defence money can buy. It's a no brainer, Clive.'

They went back in. Clive restarted.

'Mr Ruff, what is your connection with Mr Harold Brigg?' Pete did not pause before answering this time.

'I do not know a Mr Harold Brigg.'

'Mr Round, what is your connection with Mr Harold Brigg?'

'I do not know a Mr Harold Brigg.'

'When did he approach you for this assignment?'

'He didn't. I told you I don't know a Mr Harold Brigg.'

'Mr Ruff, when did Harold Brigg approach you for this assignment?'

'He didn't. It was just a silly game with this couple hitching one Saturday morning.'

'How did you pick out the farmhouse in France?'

'We wanted a few months' let for some autumn work.'

'How did you find it?'

'We wanted that area of France and it was on one of the websites for letting.'

'So you had arranged it before you left Britain?'

'Yes.'

'Please let us have copies of the tenancy agreement and your contacts with the landlord.'

'That would have all got burnt in Molly's fire.'

'How did you arrange the house at such short notice?'

'That was Alain. He said he knew this house was available through a mate.'

'How would he know that?'

'Dunno. You'd have to ask him.'

'We will. How would you explain the coincidence that both the farmhouse and the house are owned by Harold Brigg's wife?'

'Maybe they've got a lot of property to let in France at this time. It's not the holiday season.'

The speed and apparent slickness of this response meant that was an expected question which needed a prepared answer. Clive motioned to Colin for a brief word outside.

'If they've never heard of Harold Brigg, why did Ruff pause before answering? He took his time. The question was unexpected. It means something, Colin.'

'You're not wrong. I noticed it too.'

'I've got a thought, it's simple but more open. Give me another go.' They went back in.

'Mr Ruff, what is your connection with Mr Brigg?' Pete paused even longer this time.

'I used to work for his company many years ago.'

'What was his first name?'

'Barry. Everyone called him Barry.'

'Mr Round, what is your connection with Mr Brigg?'

'I used to work for his company many years ago.'

'What was his first name?'

'Barry.'

Colin and Clive repeated all the questions they had asked previously and got the same answers. They got nowhere. There were no papers or phones to chase up. Their stories were co-ordinated and led nowhere. They or Brigg had thought this one through carefully, Clive and Colin agreed. They ended the interview and said there would be a further interview before charging later.

'I'll get on to Alphonse and co. to plunge Alain into the deep end. He knows none of this. We just need some link with Brigg this year. We can try to find him and interview him as well.'

'I'll see my boss here for what charges we can make at this stage. We've got a violent abduction and holding Molly against her will, twice in fact. There's plenty there.'

Clive phoned Mavis and told her that Brigg may be Harold on his birth or marriage certificate but he's Barry now. Might help tracking him down.

'Pete and Martin claim to have worked for his company years ago.'

'They, that's the Briggs, are an elusive couple. They live in Hampshire and I've got the address. Phone numbers don't seem to be available. The local police have sent a car round and there's nobody there at the moment. Neighbours, or rather nearby houses, and the village say they are never there and they are always off somewhere. And no-one seems to know when they'll be back. I'll look for other properties and at other records but, sorry, nothing to go on so far. They don't appear to have even a UK bank account.' Clive wasn't surprised. Then he phoned Alphonse; Henri answered the phone.

'Have you got anything out of Alain, like a British contact?'

'Absolutely nothing, Monsieur Clive. How are you?'

They chatted on and Henri confirmed that Alain knew nothing. Pete and Martin had latched on to him as another itinerant worker and they adopted him because he could speak French and translate for them. They had met in a bar and Alain invited himself to their gang on the basis that three would do more and more quickly than two. Clive reported all this back to Colin.

'Well in that case we have to charge them with the basics of an attack on Molly and James, abduction of the former and subsequently holding her against her will for two months. My boss reckons they won't get bail and we'll have to hope that this Brigg reveals himself to help their defence. We have put out an alert to find Brigg and his missus.'

They went back into the interview room and did the necessary formalities. Ruff and Round stayed passive throughout. Hall said he would prepare their case and be back.

Clive drove back and reported the day's events to Knutsford.

'Well done. Looks like case closed. Obviously guilty.' Clive reminded him that Molly had disappeared again without involvement by those two and that Brigg was nowhere to be found.

'You've no leads on Molly; and Brigg can be checked up on via the local boys near their mansion. Wind down and complete the paperwork and then you and Smith can get on with that car scam. Well done by the way, to both of you.'

'Thank you, sir.'

Mavis was not impressed by the Knut's response. She was into Brigg and told Clive that she would continue trying to track him down in her own time, first thing in the morning and at the end of the day. Clive nodded.

HUNDRED AND SIX

Percy had got hold of the name of Brigg via Julian's contacts. He found the large house in Hampshire, called 'Ferrous', and had taken a room at an unpretentious hotel a mile away. There were signposted footpaths everywhere and he had no difficulty scouting all around Ferrous with high-resolution field glasses. There were no signs of life. He chatted to one or two in the pub and in the local shops, passing himself off as a minor academic on a sabbatical who found walking helped him to think about his next paper which would be on 'Hampshire before and after the Black Death and its consequences'. This usually helped his listeners move on or change the subject. He wanted to be ignored as a mild eccentric and dropped Ferrous into conversation whenever he could. He learnt that the Briggs were never there, always abroad, had a gardener and a housekeeper in the village, and were filthy rich. A housekeeper sounded promising; they would surely contact her before returning for milk and meals and such like. He needed to find her without creating any suspicion. Dogs. A dog was the answer. Back at the hotel, he found the manager.

'Whose is that gorgeous labradoodle in the kennel?'

'Thank you, sir, it's ours or more correctly my wife's. She loves him but we have to keep him in the outhouses because it's not good for Nelson to roam around the hotel.'

'He's lovely. You know I walk around here pondering my studies. It would help me if I could walk him for you, if that would help you? Any time to suit you.'

'That's the best idea I've heard for months. Of course, any time, and thank you.'

'No, thank you. We'll set off in the morning and I'll bring him, I mean Nelson, back for lunch.'

Job done. Dogs open doors.

Next morning, Percy in an old tweed jacket and even older country-style anorak set off with Nelson. Percy by now knew all the footpaths surrounding the Ferrous land and they zig-zagged an approximate circle. The first few dog-walkers he met were pleasant enough but knew nothing. They exchanged idle chatter.

A dog ran up to them and it was clear that Nelson was on friendly terms with this one. Its owner appeared lumbering along, a lady of uncertain years, an old overcoat and a wearing a cheery smile. Ideal.

'Mandy, stop that! I'm so sorry sir but Nelson and Mandy have always enjoyed a romp.'

'So I see. They make a lovely couple. You must know all the walks round here. I'm Cyril by the way.'

'And I'm Yvonne. Nice to meet you. Yes, Mandy and I know every blade of grass round here. There's been a few changes but the grass stays the same.'

'The big house, over there, I can see they've made a few changes with the conservatory and the pool.'

'Yes, they have. Strange couple, nice enough but keep themselves to themselves if you know what I mean. Never there much and Ena sometimes doesn't know what's happening next.'

'And Ena...' Percy left the sentence hanging, feeling sure it would be completed.

'It's Ena Venables, their housekeeper, lives on the Green. A real good old stick, she's done for them for years.'

They parted the best of friends and felt sure they would bump into each other again.

The Green had a few benches so Percy sat and read a book while keeping a lookout for Ena. Nelson sniffed around a bit then curled up.

It was easy to guess who Ena was and Percy saw she was making for the Village Stores. He took up Nelson on his lead and went into the shop. *Need to see what Ena is buying.* He lingered over the toothpaste and the tissues and was rewarded with a close-up view of Ena's purchases: bread, milk, coffee, cake, greens.

Percy effected a semi-circle walk outside so that he could bump into Ena.

'Good morning, just taking Nelson for a walk on this lovely morning. Could I help you with your bags if you're going far?'

They chatted but his offer was declined. They were supplies for the people she did for. Nice for them to have something fresh in the fridge. It only needed a little more idle chat to work out they were due back tomorrow 'sometime'. They also parted the best of friends.

HUNDRED AND SEVEN

'Hello you.'

'Hello you!'

'It was my idea to meet up again. You remember this pub?'

'Of course I do. I drop in sometimes to remember those times.'

'It used to be a not-so-trendy-campari. What is it now?'

'Dry white at this time of day. You?'

'I'll have what you're having.'

They smiled at the reference.

'You with anybody, if you get my drift?'

'Not now and not for some time. Work is full on and I'm happy to wind down with mates in the evening. Being a couple can be draining. What about you?'

'I'm exactly the same and I agree with you.'

'Would you like to do some stuff together now and again? Obviously no commitments and all that.'

'Yeah, that would be fun. I'd like that.'

'So how about lunch here now? They do all the pub classics and some lighter stuff.'

'Yes, OK.'

HUNDRED AND EIGHT

Barry was starting to feel the heat. In more than one way.

He and Sylvia had been in their villa in southern Spain for a few weeks and were enjoying the midday sun in early December. A spell this warm was unusual this time of the year. It was very welcome and pleasant.

A solicitor had phoned to say that Pete and Martin had been charged and were being held in custody. How did Barry intend to go about defending them since he had put them up to do the job? Barry said he would get back to him.

Doug had phoned to say that they were still holding her and she had withdrawn into herself since escape was not an option. How did Barry intend to execute the end game? Barry said he would get back to him.

Sylvia had knocked up a seafood salad with a Spanish white, preceded by their customary large gin-and-tonics, lime and ice.

'Look love, this game has gone on far too long and now it's bearing down on you. It's not a game anymore. It's a right bore and I'm fed up with it. And you need to move on and do something useful.'

'Yep, you're right. I think I can wind this up now and achieve all I wanted to. It will take a few days to sort out. You happy to get back to the ranch?'

'Definitely. I've got my friends and our house. What could be better.'

'I'll get the return flights fixed for the day after tomorrow. We can enjoy our last day here together.'

'Come and have lunch then you can do your phoning round. I'll plan something special for tomorrow.'

HUNDRED AND NINE

They met at the leisure centre, got changed and were on court before 5.30. It was semi-serious play and they tried the three combinations of pairings and the most fun was girls vs boys. The men were hard-hitting, lurching around, getting points by brute force; the ladies were more strategic and tactical, more delicate and, if one were truthful, far more skilful. Clive saw that Mavis was always one of the winning couples and said so.

'Oh am I? Thank you for noticing.'

And Mavis noticed that Clive was always one of the losing couples, apart from when she partnered him, and didn't say so. Keep that one for the office.

They finished, showered and sat round a table with four lagers.

Sue looked over at the bowling lanes.

'We could do bowling next time. Looks tempting.' All agreed. Clive was relieved he didn't have to think of something for next time. He had had more experience bowling than badminton, relatively speaking.

They got in one car driving back to Mavis's place. She went straight into the kitchen with Sue to put the oven on and shouted at the men to open some bottles. And from nowhere came the sunshine beat of the Caribbean. Mavis and Sue swayed and sashayed around while the men looked beached.

'Come on, boys, feel the rhythm, doesn't it make you want to bop around?' They tried, they did try and their efforts helped reduce all four of them to a fit of the giggles.

'Maybe more later, I'll turn it down a bit.'

The evening was a success. How could it not be? It was consecutive scenes of eating, drinking and bopping around. Sue and Mavis were unanimously declared the winners and, at a natural time, Sue and Matt said their 'byes and sloped off.

'Shall we clear up?'

'Stop it Clive. Come on, let's dance a bit more.' They did and on a couple of the slower numbers, they held each other closely. Clive kissed her head and Mavis nuzzled up to him. Then the beat got quick again and then the music stopped.

'Let's tidy up a bit so it's not a mess for you in the morning.'

'Thanks, I'll get a load in the dishwasher if you can collect the bottles and glasses, ta.'

Ten minutes later, Clive motioned to go without much enthusiasm.

'I suppose I better get a taxi with what I've had.'

'Clive, come here.' She held him in her arms. 'There's nothing I'd like better than for you to stop over and I think I know you well enough for you to want that too. But we work together, it would be complicated, there would be tensions. Trust me, you are a great guy, solid as a rock, and I want more than anything in the world for our friendship to carry on and even develop. We're a great team; I want it to be right with you on Monday morning and on every Monday morning; and all of that even if, a big if, each of us meets somebody else. Are you OK with that?'

He kissed her as passionately as he had ever kissed anybody.

'That's my way of saying yes.'

'You must say yes more often, Mr Smoothy.'

'Sadly, all the logic in me says yes I agree. Those beautiful words could have been mine, only expressed more clumsily. If I'm seriously honest with myself, that's what I want too. Working with you is the joy of my humdrum life and I couldn't do anything to spoil that. And of course I fancy the pants off you.' Said with a beam from ear to ear.

He reached for his mobile on the sideboard and called a local taxi firm.

One more big hug and he was gone. Mavis put the leftovers in the freezer and poured herself another glass of wine. They both had sense and sensibility.

HUNDRED AND TEN

Barry's phoning was intense. First up, he phoned Hall back and said he wanted the best possible defence for Pete and Martin. Hall should get on with it and if he needed help to prepare the case, he was to get it. Barry said he would be able to fill in some gaps when he was back in the UK and he would be in touch again. Next he phoned to change the flights, pay the extra, and then called the garage to get his other car to the airport. Barry and Sylvia had decided that they would attempt to avoid any reception committee on landing by going to a different airport, taking a different car and going on to their other house in the west country. He had to assume that over this length of time, some geeky policeman would have tracked down ownership of the French properties. He had always covered his tracks but that particular path back to him was exposed. Then he phoned Doug.

'Hi Dougie. We're coming back day after tomorrow and going to the west country house. The exit plan will be one or two days after that. How is she?'

'I think that's wise, Barry. She is quite withdrawn and despairing and it's not nice to see in a young woman. Can I let her know that the exit plan is near?'

'OK but no details or info or timings. I have to keep it fluid at the moment.'

'The other thing is, I've been following events in Sussex. They've been charged and they might have talked. I don't think they would but you personally cannot rely on that.'

'Understood, Dougie. I've been in touch with their solicitor and he says they have managed to keep the separation. Be in touch. Bye.'

Finally, to Ena for the change of plan and could she call the supermarket that was local to the west country house to deliver everything they might need for the week following.

'What have you arranged for our last day, tomorrow?'

Sylvia had filled the day with golf, a gallery, some flamenco, and a lunch and dinner at places sparkly with award stars.

HUNDRED AND ELEVEN

'Morning Clive.' She smiled.

'Morning Mavis.' He smiled.

They each offered to make coffee for the other and had a pretend row about it. He touched her shoulder. She moved away.

'Clive, remember our serious chat.'

'And after it.'

'Clive, I'm serious.'

'So am I. Thanks for the coffee and of course the lovely evening on Saturday.'

'I'm getting on to Brigg. What other records can I search on?'

They got to work and Clive recognised that they had developed a deeper relationship between them. He was happy about it. He wondered how he would feel if she got together with somebody. Sufficient to the day…

After another fought-over mid-morning coffee, Mavis came up with something.

'Mr and Mrs Brigg appear to be still married and they have multiple cars and property. They do not appear to be at any of them at the present. His football club says he has not been to a match this season.'

'They are abroad to avoid the potential fallout from the Ruff and Round case. If he has no UK bank accounts, they must arrange everything from abroad. Big place, abroad.'

'My guess would be Europe for the ease of getting back. A few hours takes care of the whole continent.'

'Agreed. Depending on the Molly situation he may not need to return here. It all hangs on his intentions. It's like he's keeping us dangling by a thread until he cuts it and it's all gone.'

Mavis alerted all the police stations nearest to the Brigg properties with the message to report any activity. This was more in hope as the properties were generally outlying and there would be no resources to keep a steady watch on each. Also, the case was not so hot news. Barely mentioned on TV and radio, it was a mere paragraph at the bottom of an inside page in a few of the papers. The tabloid with the exclusive attempted to do a little better.

HUNDRED AND TWELVE

Molly wearily did her exercises to keep herself active. Even they seemed hardly worthwhile. She was infinitely bored big time. She had revisited escape possibilities, given her elusive qualities, and had had to dismiss them. There was always activity in and around the house; the door, window, Velux window, bathroom and all the walls and ceilings were solid and secure. They had removed all her personal belongings for risk of fire or damage and the heating was a single metal radiator in the bedroom and a towel rail in the bathroom. There was no possibility of a fire or crashing through a wall or ceiling. She wrested her sole hope on the words of Doug that it would not be too long. Whatever 'it' was, it could hardly be violence or worse. Maybe a ransom was finally and desperately being arranged. Her mother and father must be desperate by now and she surmised that an offer of ransom now would be speedily agreed.

Doug knocked on the door, unlocked it and came in. He smiled at her. He was a kind man and not cut out for keeping her, or anyone, captive.

'I've some news, Molly. We shall shortly be leaving and your time with us will be over. I can't give more details or time schedule but I suggest you get yourself ready for a journey.' Molly, always sceptical of good news, did a mental jig with be leaving and believing and hoped both would be true.

'Thank you, Doug. I can be ready in five minutes as you can see. I look forward to seeing you again very soon. What has happened and why is it happening now?'

'Sorry, my dear, no details means no details. Be patient.'

He left as quietly as he had come and locked the door behind him.

HUNDRED AND THIRTEEN

The last day in Spain was a Sylvia special. Everything worked to plan and Barry's nine holes were among his best. Six drives went more or less as intended; the critical second and third shots were seventy-five percent OK; and the putting, well, mostly satisfied the line 'onto the green and down in two.' That put him in good spirits for the rest of the day. They took coffee in a gallery of local art, which had just opened showing off some of the local talent. He bought a couple of oils for their villa – striking and colourful as he liked. Then an extended lunch with an extensive choice of fresh fish, his preferred Spanish white to wash it down and then relax to watch a troupe of flamenco dancers get very vigorous on the floor outside the restaurant. They returned to the villa for an amorous siesta which put both of them to sleep for a few hours. More G&Ts on the patio and then they strode off to the other local starred restaurant for a sumptuous, carnivorous evening, finishing with brandies. They took a taxi back as Barry said that he didn't think they could stagger back that far.

The maid had packed during the day. They fell into bed, rather less amorously than in the afternoon, and both were soon snoring out of time with each other.

The routine the following morning was well-practised and they didn't feel the need to say much during their final preparations and some breakfast. The taxi took them to the airport and even here they were able to enjoy the labelled lounge and priority last boarding to the top-class cabin. This process was reversed on landing in the UK and they were met and shown to one of his cars, luggage already packed in the boot.

It was a long drive because he wanted there to be no obvious connection between that house and its neighbouring airport. It mattered little as the executive saloon swallowed the miles in a couple of hours without stopping. It was dark as they approached the house. He slowed to check there were no vehicles outside the house; then opening the gate and the garage door electronically, swept into the garage closing both behind him. The lights in the house were on timers which they did not change. Barry thought that if they could both keep a low profile in the house that evening, they would have bought at least a day from any enquiring busybodies.

Barry phoned Doug.

'Hi Dougie, we're back. I'll be at yours in the morning and then go on from there.'

'You've a bit of a drive. We'll knock up a light early lunch for you. The young lady is expecting something soon and said she can be ready to order. If you leave here at, say, one for your onward journey, I'll let her know about twelve. Is that OK with you?'

'Spot on as ever, Dougie, and thanks for the trouble and a quickie lunch would be great. I'll bring you something from Spain. See you.'

Barry and Sylvia went to bed and chatted for a while.

'Has it all been worth it, love?'

'I'm sorry you've had to live through it and I recognise the support from you and the cost to you. There will be a big cost to me and I hope it's controllable.'

'I think you should work on what we want to do with the rest of our lives. We've got plenty of activities, clearly, but perhaps to get more involved with society, whatever that means. You've got a brain for business and of course there's always helping the boys with their careers.'

'Mmmm. Not sure on that last one. The boys need to work out their lives. Yeah, you're right, I can put more back and I think I should – that is after tomorrow's out of the way. Nighty night, my darling, and well done on the Spanish break. One of the best. Just like my drive on the third hole.' They kissed messily in the dark and went to sleep.

Next morning was like the previous morning. The routine of morning stuff, then into the car from the utility room and followed the reverse procedure of the previous evening, this time in daylight.

Barry didn't see any cars in the road nor the one tucked up a farm track.

HUNDRED AND FOURTEEN

Percy had concluded that later today or tomorrow was the day so he was able to have a leisurely morning and take Nelson round the Green. He bumped into a clearly agitated Ena muttering to herself.

'My dear lady, whatever is the matter? Sit down here on the bench and tell Uncle Cyril all about it.'

'First it's one thing and then that's not right. Change everything; stop what you're doing and do something else. And after all those groceries we carried back yesterday. I might just as well not have bothered. They keep doing that.'

'Well how can I help? Is there anything I can do to assist your distress? Maybe a coffee at the pub?'

'Thank you, you're very kind, sir, but it's nothing like that. They've only gone and changed where they're coming back to. It's the west country house and I've got to phone up and get stuff delivered there today.'

Percy realised at once what the game was but felt that pressing Ena for the address would look far too intrusive. He offered further soothing words and made a quick exit back to the hotel, dumped Nelson and got straight on the phone to Julian.

'I need the address and location of their west country house pronto.'

'I'll have to get back to you on that.'

'West country could be Exeter, Bristol, Salisbury whatever. I suspect they are landing tonight or early tomorrow and if we don't spot them it's back to needles and haystacks.'

'Calm down, Percy my boy. You'll know within the hour, trust me.' Julian put the phone back in its cradle. *So they're playing games too, at least that's consistent. Now, where was that list of properties?*

By the middle of the afternoon, Percy was driving west at a good speed armed with the postcode on his satnav. He would be in the vicinity in the dark and in a deserted rural spot he would definitely need to avoid attention. He deduced from his reading of the local roads on his laptop that there was only one road up to the property and he intended to position himself just off that road to have good sightings of any comings and goings. He was rewarded with the sight of the Briggs returning mid-evening but far too dark for a photograph and flash was obviously out of the question. They would not be leaving that evening because it was late and Ena's arranged deliveries would have been made that afternoon. He would have to find a hotel or B&B for the night and start again early next morning. He phoned Julian.

'They're back from abroad and probably in for the night. I'll position myself so I can see their exit in the morning. Shall I follow them?'

'Best not, he'll spot you and then know that we or someone is on to him. Report them leaving and we'll try to track their car. Position yourself halfway between there and London and await developments. I'm guessing he'll want to meet up with his accomplice who took Molly.'

Percy had found a somewhat seedy hotel, which suited him exactly, and told the receptionist/night porter that he would be leaving early in the morning. Please could he settle up now and creep out in the morning? His alarm went off early and in less than half an hour was in position up a narrow farm track from where he could see the entrance gate to the house. It was light when a car emerged and Percy was able to video the car and a glimpse of the couple in it. He phoned Julian who let the police know, securing in return early interview rights 'as a matter of national security'.

HUNDRED AND FIFTEEN

'Clive, Brigg is on the move. West Country Police just phoned through to say an exec saloon just left his west country house and disappeared speedily up the M5 motorway. They got the registration but lost the car.'

'So he's back from abroad. If Molly is anywhere within driving distance of London after she was last picked up, then friend Brigg will be changing to the M4 motorway back in the direction of London. Can you contact the car-spotting people, please?'

Mavis phoned through and was not given much reason for optimism. Traffic was busy and they had a long list.

'What can we do?'

'We have to wait.'

HUNDRED AND SIXTEEN

Barry had to assume they would be looking for him so he did not take the M4 with all its cameras. He turned off the M5 and took A roads going east and then ultimately to Doug's isolated Berkshire place. He had taken a few right-angle turns and was satisfied nothing was tailing them. Just before twelve, they drove up Doug's drive and into his yard.

The two couples had not seen each other for some years as Barry did everything on the phone. They were old friends with lots to catch up but now was not the time for that.

Doug told Barry that Molly was now on standby ready for departure. Barry had previously asked Doug for two extras to sit either side of Molly in the back of his car. Doug volunteered for one of them and his gardener for the other. They had lunch with Celia and Sylvia doing all the talking.

'Shall I stay with Celia here because you'll be bringing Dougie back anyway?'

'Please do stay, Sylvia, you'll be stopping the night here when the boys are back. Don't argue, it's all arranged.'

So that was that. Doug went upstairs and brought Molly down. Celia had done Molly a little packed lunch and a bottle of water. She also did something to her hair and offered some perfume and lipstick, both declined. Molly thanked her before she was wedged into the middle of the back of the car. Barry waved to the two ladies and drove off at some speed. They drove west avoiding motorways and main junctions where cameras could be lurking.

Molly could not know what was going to happen. She did not know or recognise any of these three men but the occasion did seem to have the air of finality about it. If they stopped for bathroom break, she would not rule out escaping at the back of the ladies'. Nobody spoke because it was like being in a railway compartment with strangers. After an hour and a half, without a pit stop, Barry announced, 'We're here.'

Molly could scarcely believe her eyes.

HUNDRED AND SEVENTEEN

'We've lost them. Or rather, they have lost them.'

'I'm not surprised. Despite what I thought earlier, Brigg would have kept off the motorways because of the cameras. That'll slow him up but not by much in that car.'

'What can we do now?'

'We have to be patient – but do you know what? I've got a hunch. Most times Morse's hunches paid off. Let's see if this one works.'

Clive picked up a phone, referred to his notes, and punched out a number.

HUNDRED AND EIGHTEEN

Barry leant over to the intercom on the gatepost to the gate to the drive.

'Hello Jonny, it's Barry here. Can you let me in? I've got something for you.'

The gate swung open and Barry drove up the gravel drive to the front door of the house. They all got out of the car and waited a few seconds at the front door before it opened. Barry held out his hand.

'Hello Jonny. Long time, no see. Here's your daughter.'

Henry hesitated a moment before shaking Barry's hand and then moving straight to his daughter.

'Molly dearest!' and gave her a big hug. Molly was dazed and bemused as to what was actually happening. She returned his hug and was then engulfed by Annabel and Ellie who had rushed out of the house.

'My darling girl, how we've missed you!'

'You OK, Mols?'

Annabel shepherded the female group inside to the toast-warm kitchen, each of them falling over each other in gabbling out words with hugs and kisses.

The male group were marooned outside, none of them quite knowing what to say next.

'Well I suppose you better come in,' Henry said. They followed him into the drawing room and sat round the crackling log fire.

'Please sit down, won't you? Annabel will get some tea soon when they've all calmed down. I'm thrilled Molly is back of course and thank you so much but, for the life of me, I haven't a clue what is going on here. And why you're involved.'

'Look Jonny, I know we've come out of the blue and it's good Molly is now back with her family. There's obviously a lot more but not for now.'

'Can we drop this Jonny nonsense? I'm Henry Jonathan Otsworth, known universally at school, college and early business life as Jonny because I didn't like Henry; but since then I'm universally Henry because I didn't like Jonny.'

'And it suited your rich City friends and sounds better.' There was an unmistakable edge to Barry's reply.

'The past is the past. Someone wrote that it's a foreign country and I'm inclined to agree.'

'That's somewhat short of an apology old chap; but it's a start.'

Doug sensed it was getting personal and said he would go and see if Molly was settled. He motioned to gardener Will to follow him. Henry continued.

'You've done all right for yourself. I saw the sale and press comment on what you ran off with.'

'I earned every penny of that and would have done for you and me if you hadn't done what you did.'

'I was left with no choice. We were technically at the mercy of the banks.'

'And rushed to the money, brushing aside anything or anybody in your way.'

'As I said, the past is the past. I've often wondered if you've done better than me. Not that I'm envious naturally. But if it helps, I congratulate you on your success. I vaguely know Frank and bumped into him a few years ago. He spoke highly of you as an operator.'

'I thank you. And still somewhat short of an apology. I have to say I have not followed your success because I've been busy – first working and latterly playing. If you're solvent and everything I see around me, including daughters, is down to you, then I congratulate you.'

'Thanks. Can I be clear about how you came to find Molly? What is your part in her rescue? Let me be as straight as I possibly can – I'm overcome by her return, my two daughters are everything to me. You never know how much until you think you've lost them. Thank you so much, Barry, thank you so much.' Henry broke down, tears forming in his eyes. He blew his nose and attempted to get his composure back.

'I'll see how Annabel's doing with the tea.' He joined the five of them in the kitchen and hugged Molly harder than ever. 'I've missed you so much, my darling. Are you sure you're quite OK?'

'I'm fine, Dad, honestly. I've been well looked after; it's just been so bloody boring. James and Ellie were wonderful in France and back here. Oh, James! Must phone.' She went into the hall to phone James.

Back in the drawing room, Barry sat quietly. Meeting Jonny again had been OK. Typical of him to be a Henry now; absolutely bleeding typical. If and when the atmosphere was ever warmer, he would tease him massively over that. He didn't want to tell Jonny about his role in taking Molly away and he hoped the case would now be quietly closed. He had engineered taking Molly because he could. Jonny had taken something of worth from him and Jonny deserved something precious being taken from him. It had taken well over twenty years.

He glanced at his watch and made to leave. He did not want to be found here of all places. He joined them in the kitchen and interrupted the tea proceedings.

'Dougie, we've done our job. We best be getting away now. We need to get back while there's still some light in these parts and get back to our girls in Berkshire. Bye everyone.' Doug also recognised the situation and said his goodbyes. He and Will joined Barry in the car and drove towards the gate, which Henry was fobbing open.

Their exit, however, was blocked by the arrival of a car stopping just the other side of the gate. Two policemen got out and went up to the gate, blocking any idea of an exit.

'Good afternoon Mr Otsworth, we have reason to believe that a Mr Harold Brigg is here.' It was Neil Poole with a colleague from the local police.

'A Mr Brigg most certainly is here, he and his friends are in this car. It's very good news indeed; he's returned my daughter Molly.'

'I'm very pleased to hear that, sir.'

Poole turned towards Brigg's car, its engine running and its driver ready to launch the car forward, and went to the driver's side. The window was down.

'Mr Brigg?'

'Yes, that's me.'

'Please would you and your associate accompany us to the station for questioning over the kidnapping of Miss Otsworth and certain other matters? Step this way, both of you.' Henry was flabbergasted.

'Now come on, Officer, what is all this about? He brought my daughter back and deserves all our thanks. He's a hero. I'm sure we can sort this out over a cup of tea.'

'It's not quite that simple, sir.'

'It's OK, Jonny, I mean Henry. I'll go to the station and sort it out there. Will, would you take the car back to Dougie's place and tell them we'll be in touch? Nothing to worry about.'

Henry had been slow to grasp the situation. He didn't know what had happened but it was gradually sinking in that Barry must be some sort of perpetrator. And his equanimity was giving way to total fury.

'Barry, if you're behind this in some way, I'll take you apart.' He went up to the car, opened the driver's side door and grabbed hold of Barry by the throat ready to shake him.

'Let's all calm down, shall we? Mr Otsworth, please move away from the car. Mr Brigg and your associate, please step this way.' The two policemen manhandled Barry and Doug into the back of their police car and locked them in.

Poole spoke to Will.

'I'm going to make an assumption that you are merely a hired hand. That's a compliment if it didn't sound like one. Please give me the address where you came from and your own address and the local police will take a statement from you tomorrow.' Will willingly gave the information, plus phone numbers, and Neil took note of the car registration number before sending Will back where he came from.

'Officer, what exactly is happening? I think we deserve to know what's going on.'

'You do, sir, but that will have to wait. Please report to the station tomorrow morning and we'll give you as much as we can at this stage. Goodbye, sir, and enjoy the happy return of Miss Molly.' And they were gone.

Henry, whose life had been turned upside down with the kidnapping, was now totally confused by its resolution. Daughter back safely in one piece but with no explanation other than that a former friend and colleague of decades ago was involved. He went back into the house; seeing the three of them happily together put him into an altogether better place.

They talked all evening.

HUNDRED AND NINETEEN

'Clive, it's Neil.'

'And?'

'You'll never guess.'

'Try me.'

'Brigg's car was there, Brigg was there, Molly returned in good shape, family overjoyed etcetera. We apprehended him and an associate in the police cell overnight. He's organised his personal solicitor to come in the morning and we'll take a full statement from him. He's as tame as a lamb and already said he will fully cooperate. How did you guess or did you know? Well done, mate.'

'Just one of those things. We just ran out of alternatives and I did wonder whether there was something behind that old court case. Ran out of time to research it but it was a hunch that worked. The next ninety-nine won't. Thanks for going round; we'll talk tomorrow.'

They rang off.

'Clive, you're a genius!'

'Careful now. It might go to my head.'

'Well it's a kiss from me, whether Knutsford sees us or not.'

HUNDRED AND TWENTY

Henry went down to the station the following morning and asked to see the officer in charge of the Brigg/Molly case. Neil had taken charge and the two of them went into a separate interview room. Neil gave a very rough outline of the extent to which Brigg was involved, with the proviso that a lot of detail was still unclear but they thought they had now got all the parties behind bars.

'It's terrible what he did and absolutely unforgivable of course. I'm absolutely furious with him and even now would have a scrap with him. But it doesn't achieve anything does it? I'm calmer this morning and want the prosecution process to run its course. But we go back a very long way and, although it was very wrong and spiteful to take it out on Molly in order to get at me, I have a very weird sort of understanding why he did it. Don't ask me to explain now but give me a chance later. I now believe Molly was never in danger, however frightened she may have been. You never know what demons there are in people. I owe Barry for help early on but I never imagined he would take unintentional offence to these lengths. I had put corporate survival ahead of a friendship and trusted that he would get over it. He must have taken it as personal treachery. I could kill him for what he did. We all have people grudges, don't we? But normally we dump them or forget them, don't we? Brigg can afford his legal expenses, as can I.'

'That's handsome of you, sir; but crimes have been committed so it is not a civil case between you two. I'm sure you will be welcomed as a witness, probably by both sides if that is your way of looking at it.'

'May I see Mr Brigg?'

'He's with his solicitor now and then we'll be taking him through every step from the beginning of September right up to now for his statement. And his solicitor will keep on wanting to confer. It's going to be long and drawn out so I would suggest later tomorrow or even the day after would be better. Go back and enjoy your family. Brigg will definitely be here overnight.'

Neil showed Henry out and then went through to his superior officer.

'How do we play this, sir?'

'I wish I knew. I thought it would be simple but I've got Drewett coming up from Sussex-by-the-sea and some big shot from Whitehall claiming he has first interview rights. In fact this Foxley bod has pulled rank and I've been instructed to let him and his buddy interview Brigg on their own without us in attendance. You can interpret instructed as meaning ordered. They'll be here late morning so Brigg will have to wait.'

'OK, sir, I'll await your say-so. Perhaps Drewett and I can handle Brigg after the Whitehall people have gone.'

'Yes, whenever that is. Back to your other work for now.'

Neil phoned Clive and gave him a sit-rep. Knutsford had tipped Clive off about Foxley so it was not a surprise.

'I'm just past Swindon so not long now. Foxley would be coming from central London so well ahead – in fact he's probably approaching you now.'

He was. Julian and Percy strode into the station as though they owned it and went straight into the Chief's office.

'Greetings, Officer. I'm Foxley and this is Percy. Now where's this Brigg fellow?'

'Good morning sirs, can I arrange coffee after your journey? Brigg is in the interview room.'

'No thank you, we're fine. Had enough of that stuff en route. Just show us where he is.'

They were ushered into the interview room and waited till the policeman in attendance had left. Brigg was sitting nonchalantly at a table with Hall, his solicitor. Julian launched into his opening serve.

'This is not a police interview and there will be no official record of this, er, discussion so you can go.' He indicated this to Hall.

'With respect, Mr Brigg is entitled to legal representation at every stage of these formal proceedings.'

'You don't go to the lavatory with him, do you? Here's a piece of paper to satisfy you that this is neither formal nor a legal process. It's a discussion on behalf of a government department and you are not required to be in attendance.'

Albert read the neatly typed notice and mouthed to Brigg that he did not have to say anything and he, Albert, would be outside when required. He got up and left with his professional stiffness fully apparent.

'Now Brigg, what's this all about? We want to know who's behind this and who put you up to this.'

'Who the fuck are you?'

'Let's keep this formal, shall we? You don't need to know who we are, other than that we are attached to a government department with full authority to interview you. The Chief Constable here and the one down south where the original kidnapping took place are fully aware of this interview and are authorised to allow us to interview you first. The police will be prosecuting you for kidnapping and no doubt related charges. We want to know who's behind you and who put you up to this. I repeat my question and won't do again.'

'There's nobody, it was just me pursuing what could be called an old vendetta. Revenge.'

'I find it difficult that someone like you would bother with that. Who put you up to it?'

'No-one, squire. My wife was not part of this and when she found out was not best pleased.'

'What is your connection with Molly Otsworth.'

'None. She is the elder daughter of my former friend and colleague now apparently called Henry Otsworth.'

'What is your connection with James Longton?'

'I became aware during this, er, incident that he is Molly's boyfriend. Never heard of him before.'

'Why are you referred to as Barry Brigg when our records and the police's indicate Harold Brigg.'

Barry smiled, trying to look superior having the better of this one.

'That's pathetic. I was always Harry until some bright spark at junior school joined up the top and bottom of the 'H'. It was round the school in minutes and I've been Barry ever since. It's alliterative, you know.'

'Thank you for that.' Julian didn't care for the implied condescension in Barry's tone.

'And Sylvia's not her real name either. It's the name I gave her and it stuck.'

'We are suspicious that someone external was planning a similar escapade for young Molly. Did you or are you working with other parties and, if not, did you or have you come across any other party crossing your path or frustrating your worst endeavours with this young lady?'

'Far from it. She kept escaping our clutches. It did not cross my mind until now that you guys or someone else might have helped her along. Is that what you two have been up to?'

'That's our business, but no. If that were the case, we could have picked her up at a moment's notice whenever we wished to.'

'So why didn't you?'

'That's our business and is not part of our remit today. Getting back to the main matter, have you made contact with Molly's and James's employer, owned and run by Williams and Goodall?'

Barry hesitated. He knew he had phoned Paul once to track down Molly but guessed they did not know that.

'No.'

'We know you phoned them a few months before the kidnapping. Why did you do that?'

'I have no recollection of that. I have business interests and me or one of my team could easily have phoned their company.'

'Mr Williams seems to recall it was more like a head-hunter's call, fishing around for information on Molly.'

'You said I was going to be prosecuted by the police. I'm sure they will raise that.'

'Mr Brigg, I suggest to you that some external or foreign body or non-friendly organisation put you up to kidnapping Molly. If you deny this and it subsequently turns out to be the case, the law will come down on you very heavily. It will be in your best interests to acknowledge outside involvement and indeed it may help your defence.'

Barry felt he had finally got the edge on this pointless interview. Maybe even these spooks had seen too much television.

'I'm sorry, guys. I'm a simple fellow. I did it all on my own – and that's off the record from what you said earlier.'

Percy joined in the questioning and the two of them persisted for a further hour, pressing him on everyone he had ever worked for or companies he had worked with. Julian prided himself on finding any Achilles' heel but it all came to nothing other than a simple revenge kidnap. They left the room.

'Julian, I think he is what he says he is. He was in scrap metal and called his house Ferrous. He doesn't strike me as someone who does the Times crossword over breakfast and looks for intrigue in the personal columns.'

'Then why the same plot as we were planning? It's uncanny.'

'Maybe coincidences are just that – just a coincidence. Like you, I don't believe in coincidences either but maybe this is one. It's his own little conspiracy of revenge and no-one else's. It might actually be the personal spat between Otsworth and Brigg that he claims it is. We have to go. I'll drop in to the Chief to make sure we get a full report of their interview with him. Maybe that will throw up something that we can latch on to.'

'OK.' Julian did not like loose ends. Clive and Neil were outside the interview room chatting with Albert.

'He's all yours. Good day, gentlemen.' Julian and Percy left after a brief word with the local Chief.

Clive and Neil went in to the interview room after Hall had had ten minutes with him. All had fresh coffee. Clive started.

'Mr Brigg, this is formal and recorded and you have your solicitor with you. This is the start of the process of your making a full statement of your involvement in this case and we will persist with questioning at any attempt by you to lessen your part in this episode. Note also that Messrs Ruff and Round have been questioned and will be further questioned to cross-check any discrepancies between your various accounts. Although thankfully no-one has been physically harmed, be in no doubt about the stress and mental anguish caused to Miss Otsworth and the Otsworth family. You have been arrested for your part in the kidnap and kidnap is a serious crime, for which the consequences will be serious. Do you fully understand the situation you are in here and the full nature of this and no doubt further interviews?'

Brigg and Hall briefly conferred by whispering and then both nodded.

It was actually straightforward for Clive and Neil. Barry admitted his part as the instigator and the controller of events all the way through the autumn. Pete and Martin were accustomed to taking his instructions and they did what he, 'the Boss', ordered. He admitted they were on bonus for job done. This had not been paid and would not be paid but Barry requested that he took the blame for them and he would help them into future jobs 'at some point'. Barry had come to recognise that the three of them would do time and requested that Pete and Martin's role in all of this was understood to be functional rather than sinister. They should be treated leniently and he, Barry, should take the major impact. The two officers made no comment.

Clive felt he had to mention the Whitehall interest but it was pretty clear that Barry had no idea what they had been talking about and took them to be a comedy act from a Whitehall farce.

'We won't record that.'

Hall requested time alone with Barry after them. Clive and Neil said they would be back in the morning. They left the room.

'Will I get bail?' was Barry's first question.

'Well you've played the decent bloke so far, hands up and all that. I think you may do on surrender of passport, a large surety and effectively house arrest at your house with daily reporting. The escape risk is enormous given your, er, situation and properties. And don't think of ever coming back to the UK. The stricter conditions you can agree to the more likely you'll get bail.'

'OK, I'll leave that negotiation to you. Can you get back to Sylvia and set about putting all my affairs in her name? I'm happy to trust her judgment if she wants to liquidate some properties because that's the world she came from. I'm assuming I'll go down for a good few years but with good behaviour and doing my bit for the youngsters in there on running a business, reading a set of accounts and general business wisdom, might I be out in a few years?'

'They won't all be like you, Barry, but I'll give you credit for being the right sort to be able to handle them. Yes, it will be a good few years and your barrister – I've got an idea or two of who – should be able to bring out your good side and lessen the impact of your bad side, i.e. no harm to Molly etcetera. But don't be too optimistic. And yes, I'll brief Sylvia fully and perhaps you two might want to hand something over to the boys.'

'Let's see what age I'll be when I get out. I want to settle up with Henry or Jonny. He did me wrong and I did him wrong. Can you ask the coppers for him to come in?'

Albert left and did all of that. He drove back to Berkshire and had a difficult two hours with Sylvia. She was as down to earth and as practical as ever. She asked Albert to stop over and they would drive back to their house in the morning. She would be able to see Barry eventually and hope to agree bail and discuss how Sylvia could run their affairs while Barry was inside.

HUNDRED AND TWENTY-ONE

'Look Julian, sometimes nothing means nothing.'

'I don't believe it.'

'Just because something appears to be straightforward, doesn't mean it isn't.'

'Appearances can be deceptive.'

'Can be but not always. This is an exception.'

'Truth will out. We just need a tiny clue that all is not as it seems.'

'And if there isn't, doesn't that mean all is at it seems.'

'I really don't believe it.'

'Here's Paddington. Let's find that watering hole and share a bottle of burgundy.'

'Or two.'

HUNDRED AND TWENTY-TWO

Clive and Neil were both into real ale and had no difficulty settling into a corner bench at the 'Barrel of Monkeys' each with a glass of Three No Evils Ale, not quarter of a mile from the station. Clive had phoned Knutsford and Mavis on how the day had gone and that there was more to do tomorrow. Clive could hear Knutsford frown and Mavis smile.

Clive and Neil congratulated each other and shook their heads.

'Rum business. There's no understanding some folk. Why bother?'

'People harbour their thoughts. You can't work out what gets other people. Just think of them we work with.' Clive momentarily thought of Knutsford and Mavis. No, he couldn't work them out either.

'So the future's uncertain and full of surprises. Tell me something new.'

It had to be steak and chips followed by reconstructed Black Forest gateau. And Three No Evils.

HUNDRED AND TWENTY-THREE

Two days after Barry's capture, Henry was shown into the interview room. He had been allowed thirty minutes. A constable sat in a corner with Barry seated at the table.

'Morning Barry, sleep well?'

'Morning, I've had better.'

'Look, Barry, I'm absolutely furious with you; but in a very strange weird way I sort of understand what you got up to. Maybe ninety-nine people out of a hundred would put a reverse behind them and move on. But you and, I hope to a lesser degree, me, always had something of the outlier in us. No, I can never, never approve of what you did. It was outrageous your taking Molly, my dear first born and darling daughter. If you are the same person that I knew all those years ago, I thank you for not harming her. I would have expected nothing less. But I'm going to try to put that behind us and for you and I, and Annabel and Sylvia for that matter, to find a way forward and, I know it sounds corny and repetitive, to move on.'

'I hope so and pray that we can. I spent all night blaming myself for this crass stupidity but you know some things or ideas don't show up as stupid until after you've done them. This was always stupid and Doug and Sylvia said so right at the beginning. I took my resignation and dismissal from yours to solicitors and even had my day in court. The sharpness and finality with which that judge delivered his put-down made me look guilty as well as stupid. That set me on a course to take the law into my own hands. Natural justice, not justice from the police or lawyers or the courts. The plan was revenge, big time, but never to hurt Molly. None of the boys would ever have hurt her; it must have been terrible for her, especially at the beginning. To your credit, Molly thwarted me at every turn except at the end and by then Sylvia had finally got through to me that it was all stupid. Then I brought this stunt to an end as quickly as I could. Henry, and I've spent all last night coming to terms with calling you Henry, I'm sorry for the hurt I've caused every member of your family.'

'Accepted. And I'm sorry for what I did and caused to happen all those years ago. Are we quits?'

'Yes.'

'And though I will clearly be a witness supporting the prosecution, I will give fair account of the past should your defence wish.'

'I'm going to say that Pete and Martin were mere players carrying out orders for money from a person who they were accustomed to take orders from. I'll use my lawyers for them too.'

'Well said, Barry. Shall we shake hands?'

'You and I were always unbreakable mates in the past and I hope we might be in the future. It's a pity about the gap in the middle.'

They shook hands and did a man hug. Henry left with a wave over his shoulder.

HUNDRED AND TWENTY-FOUR

'Hello you.'

'Hello you!'

'We can't go on meeting like this.'

'I hope we can.'

'Dry white at this time of day?'

He went to the bar and got two drinks.

'Well that saga seems to be over, just the court case to come. I hear there's a chance it could be over quickly.'

'Yes, let's hope so but also let's not talk about that. Molly's fine; James is fine; Mum and Dad are fine. Are you fine?' Ellie picked up his hand and kissed it.

'My dad's fine too, actually. I mean fine in his composure and where he is. He did what he thought he had to do and I'm so sorry Molly was on the receiving end. He kept all of his plotting strictly to himself and Mum; his mates were merely brought in to do what he said. Mum was against it throughout though they might argue that she's an accessory. Believe me, I knew absolutely nothing of all this. He'll be found guilty obviously but it's what the sentence is that matters now. Ellie, sweetie, are you going to fill me in on those disks you say you found and handed over to the police?'

'I believe you and it seems it was deep between our two dads and none of us knew anything like that. Those disks – I wished I'd never clapped eyes on them. No, when Molly and I argued about you, it went on for several days. Dad got roped in and read the riot act about sisters not falling out over boyfriends. He said, "Make up your minds and give the rest of us some peace." Molly flounced off, she can flounce you know, and she must have found somebody at college or wherever we were to record all her innermost thoughts. Wow, they were strong; she didn't hold back and it was deeply embarrassing to her and to me when we had this brought back to us a few weeks ago. She came to my room last night and we lay on the bed together and went over a lot. She said she was fully guilty about that and she was very happy with James and she sincerely hopes that you and I can pick up the pieces.'

'And so do I. Why don't we go bowling this afternoon and then the Italian?'

'Ken, why do you say the things I'm thinking?'

'We're telepathic, you and me. Come here.'

HUNDRED AND TWENTY-FIVE

It was lunch-time at the office and fairly quiet. James and Molly were munching healthy wraps from the trendy healthy vegetarian place round the corner.

'It's good to be back to normal, n'est ce pas?'

'No French please James, ever. Anyway, what's normal?'

'I guess being able to do what you want to do and are able to do without external buggeration.'

'Not bad, Mr Philosopher. But not dull?'

'Life is not dull with you, Molly.'

'I think that's a compliment. Thank you.'

'There's more. Will you do me the honour of never being out of my sight ever again?'

'Might there be another way of putting that?'

'Will you marry me?' He had knelt down. He gripped her left-hand third finger tightly; she didn't resist.

'James! Not here! Wye Eee Ess!'

Suddenly from behind various office screens, Fraser led virtually the whole office out with a big round of applause. Even Paul and Geoff came out and joined in. Rosemary tottered in with a tray of glasses and a few bottles of champagne mysteriously appeared. Paul said the obvious and announced the office was closing for the rest of the day.

HUNDRED AND TWENTY-SIX

The court case was held several weeks later. The initial hearing had already set up confessions all round and the case became predominantly procedural, formally going through the motions. Barry pleaded guilty throughout and even the prosecution was somewhat at loss as to how to put foot on throat. The judge referred to 'this unfortunate matter' and that Mr Brigg was contrite and extremely unlikely ever to bother the authorities again. Pete and Martin were given short sentences with community service. Barry was given a shorter sentence than he feared because he pleaded guilty. He was instructed to help Pete and Martin get proper jobs, and he himself to do community service with particular reference to the homeless. Sylvia was severely ticked off as complicit but was regarded as instrumental in getting Barry back on track. She received a short suspended sentence.

The counter charges of Molly's wilful destruction of two French properties were dismissed because Henry had already stepped up to restore both of them.

The judge praised Molly. It had been clear from the questioning that the judge had a soft spot for her; he said she was a fine example of resourcefulness, energy and determination. He wished her and her fiancé the best for the future.

Barry's solicitor, Sylvia, Henry and Annabel met outside.

'With assumed good behaviour and volunteering for duties inside, he'll be out very soon, Mrs Brigg. There's always visiting hours. It'll pass quickly. Thank you all.'

Henry took the ladies to lunch. James and Molly sloped off somewhere else.

HUNDRED AND TWENTY-SEVEN

'Well done on the Otsworth/Brigg case, Drewett.'

'Thank you, sir. We got lucky.'

'You make your luck. You and Smith did well. We can now say case closed now, can't we?'

'Yes, sir. Brigg is inside. All damage repaired, both personal and structural.'

'Let me know how the Evans car scam is proceeding in the morning. Your sleuthing has form now, Drewett.'

Knutsford let a tiny smile flicker across his face.

'Thank you, sir. See you in the morning.'

In the outer office, Mavis had her head buried in a thick file.

'The Knut has complimented us both on the Molly case.'

'Thank you, Clive.'

'Badminton tonight?'

'Yes!'

'Good.'

'And Clive?'

'Yes?'

'What are you doing for Christmas?'

THE END

ABOUT THE AUTHOR

N N Wood had a professional career preceded by one maths degree and followed by a Master's maths degree some forty years later. He found over his working life that using numbers was gradually replaced by the use of words. He enjoys belonging to a good book club and has long aspired to write this debut novel. He lives in SW London, has two grown-up daughters and two young grandchildren. He enjoys playing golf and bridge badly and the piano very badly. He wants to write another book.

Printed in Great Britain
by Amazon